THE TARNISHED SON

ALSO BY ELIZABETH MCKENNA

The Great Jewel Robbery – A Front Page Mystery Book 1

Murder up to Bat – A Front Page Mystery Book 2

Killer Resolutions

First Crush, Last Love

Venice in the Moonlight

Cera's Place

THE TARNISHED SON

Elizabeth McKenna

Published in the United States of America

ISBN-13: 979-8-326-00156-6

First Edition

THE TARNISHED SON

Elizabeth McKenna

The Tarnished Son is a work of fiction. Names, characters, places, and incidents either are the product of the author's imagination or are used fictitiously. Any resemblance to actual persons, living or dead, events, or locales is entirely coincidental.

Published in the United States of America

ISBN-13: 979-8-326-00156-6

First Edition

To Jim and my guardian angel Rose Helena *Slattery*

Also, a shout-out to Steve P. You're finally in one of my books! It's a short scene, but remember: "There are no small parts, only small actors." - Konstantin Stanislavski

{1}

ROSE

Saturday, September 2

Entry from the Journal of Rose McCabe:

I can't sleep. ~~We saw a man drown today.~~ Liam killed a man today on Geneva Lake, and we didn't tell the whole truth.

***

Earlier

My phone buzzed for the tenth time in the past half hour. My stepbrother, who made it clear I was a waste of space and deserved to be ignored or tormented based on his mood, needed me.

I deleted his message without opening it.

It was the last Saturday before Liam, or William Henry Clark III, per his high school registration forms, began his senior year. But instead of being happy that he was a little more than nine months away from freedom, Liam and his best friend Sawyer were feeling the end-of-summer blues and dreading the start of teachers and sports monopolizing their lives. They decided the only cure for their misery would be an afternoon on Geneva Lake with girls in bikinis.

But none of their friends were home, and I had become my stepbrother's last resort, which baffled me. Had he spared my life more than a glance over the past five years, he would have noticed my minuscule social circle. So, even if I wanted to help him out, I couldn't.

I adjusted the pillows on my bed for a more comfortable reading position. Liam called me a nerd and a bookworm, thinking these were hurtful insults. But it was better than being a shallow jock like him and his friends.

A page later, someone knocked on my bedroom door. Would Liam plead his case in person? It went against our unwritten rule of exchanging no more than one to two sentences when forced to be in the same room. An unfamiliar sense of power over my stepbrother gave me the courage to continue ignoring him.

"Rose? Can I come in?" Mom's muffled voice came from behind the door.

I winced, realizing my rudeness toward the only person who mattered to me in the house. "Yes, sorry. I didn't hear you knock."

She opened the door, and I held up my book. "Guess I was lost in another world."

A frown marred the pixie-like features of her face. "Sometimes, you need to be in this world, honey."

I pressed a knuckle against my lips to keep from asking why. It was an old and tired argument, and I knew what Mom would reply. Though I loved her to the moon and back, our personalities were polar opposites, which left us at odds every so often. Where she blossomed in a room full of people, I shrank into the nearest dark corner, enduring a slow death.

"I hear Liam wants a favor from you," she said as she sat on my bed, her feet dangling above the floor.

More out of habit than anything else, she leaned over and twisted a lock of my unruly dirt-colored hair away from my face. It was another trait we didn't share, as her ash-blond hair framed her face in a bob that swung with every move of her head but then settled into place when she stilled. The only things I inherited from her were my brown eyes, slim build, and below-average height, which I would gladly return for a refund. Genetics was so temperamental.

She took my silence as a willingness to continue listening to her pitch. "It's obvious you kids don't get along. It distresses Hank and me, but we understand. Blended families can be hard. However, Liam is reaching out to you. Maybe this could be a turning point in your relationship."

My real dad was a US contractor working in Iraq when the enemy ambushed his convoy. I was six when he died. We were living in Chicago, but growing up, Mom spent her summers in Williams Bay, and that's how she knew Hank. They reconnected via social media several years after Dad's death and married when I was ten. Hank's first wife divorced him after deciding small-town life wasn't for her. I overheard Liam tell Sawyer she was a street artist in Paris.

"He wants me to pimp out some of my girlfriends." I glared at my phone, which had buzzed again. "Like I even have any."

"I think both of those statements are pretty harsh," Mom chided, but her voice was kind. "He wants to have fun on the last weekend of summer. Don't you?"

My fingers tightened around the book in my lap. "Actually, I was."

"OK, but you admitted you don't have any friends. If you call a few girls from your class and spend the afternoon with them, maybe the first day of your sophomore year won't be so lonely."

I resisted the urge to correct her. No one "called" anyone anymore. That alone would be my kiss of death. Instead, I flipped over my phone and read Liam's latest message. His begging had turned into bribery, swearing to do my chores for a week, a promise I knew he'd break by Tuesday.

"High school is supposed to be a fun time filled with parties, dances, and dates." Her enthusiasm grew with each word. "Don't you want to do all of that? Surely, there are some nice girls in your class with whom you could be friends."

The odds of finding a true friend weren't in my favor. Mom went to a large high school in suburban Chicago and had thousands of kids to pick from. On the other hand, Williams Bay was so small that the norm was around thirty students per grade. Occasionally, someone new came, as I did five years ago. But overall, it was the same group for twelve years. If you didn't connect with one of the thirty in your class, you were out of luck unless you transferred to a school in a neighboring town.

Mom's hopeful expression, tinged with worry over her daughter, the outcast, filled me with guilt. Giving in seemed my only option. "I guess I could ask Isabel and Zoe if they want to hang out."

We did an English project together before school ended in June, and I had their cell numbers. Even though they were best friends, they had been nice to me, and I never felt left out.

Mom nodded and patted my thigh. "That's my girl. I'm sure you'll have a great time with them and the boys."

It took me several minutes to carefully word the text, and my stomach burned with acid when I finally sent it. True to my bad luck, Isabel and Zoe immediately responded with excited smiley faces, jacked biceps, and flame emojis, so I assumed they wanted to go. After all, Liam and Sawyer were the most drool-worthy in our high school. I guess it didn't matter that I was on the opposite end of that spectrum. Having to put up with my social awkwardness was well worth the price for a few hours of ogling shirtless boys baked golden brown from three months of the summer sun.

***

The girls met us at the lakefront at one o'clock, and we walked a short distance to the pier where Liam's grandpa docked his boat. The vintage mahogany Chris Craft held five passengers, with two bucket seats in front and a bench seat in the rear. Thanks to his grandpa's loving care, it was in pristine condition with its gleaming varnish and shiny chrome trim.

"It's so pretty, Liam," Zoe exclaimed when we reached the slip. "It looks brand new."

"My grandpa acts like it's his baby. Sometimes, he spends hours down here just polishing it. Kinda crazy."

"I was surprised he agreed to let you take her out," Sawyer said with a wink in Isabel and Zoe's direction. "Doesn't he know how rough you are with women?"

"Ha. Ha," Liam deadpanned. "Make yourself useful and get the ropes."

Zoe, Isabel, and I sat with our hips touching on the bench seat while Liam started the engine and Sawyer untied the ropes. Then, we putt-putted away from the pier under a cloudless sky and a blazing sun. Before we left the no-wake zone that encircled the lake, everyone but me stripped down to their swimsuits.

As Zoe and Isabel stowed their tank tops and shorts in their beach totes, I envied their confidence in wearing such skimpy bikinis. Mom once suggested I work with my petite frame instead of hiding it in baggy clothes, but she didn't barely fit into an A-cup bra in a world that worshiped Ds.

"Aren't you hot?" Isabel asked me as she wound her long, loose curls into a messy bun. Her dark hair was inherited from her Puerto Rican mother, though her fair complexion came from her Irish father.

"No, I'm good." I ducked my head and wiped a drop of sweat before it could roll down my face. Yes, I was hot, but I didn't want to show my pale skin any sooner than necessary. The girls didn't need to know I'd spent most of the summer in my bedroom. I dipped my hand over the side of the boat and let the cold water course through my fingers. Droplets caught the sun's rays and sparkled like diamonds.

"Who wants a beer?" Sawyer dug into the cooler at his feet and held up two cans.

Isabel and Zoe consulted via best friend telepathy, then reached for the beers.

"Mouse?" he asked, using the nickname Liam had given me after our families merged and he realized I wasn't outgoing or popular.

The girls shot me identical questioning looks, which I ignored. Instead, I grabbed the unopened can and put it in a cup holder.

Sawyer cracked a beer for Liam and then opened his own.

"No one spill," Liam commanded before taking a long drink from his can. "My grandpa would kill me."

I didn't doubt it. The old grump made a Mafia Don look like a preschool teacher.

Liam expertly weaved around the anchored boats scattered across the bay our village butted up against, one hand on the wheel, the other holding his cold beer. Where he got his supply of alcohol was a mystery, one he gleefully kept from me. Not that I cared. I had never gone to a party, but I had overheard classmates bragging about how much they drank and laughing over who puked and who passed out. It wasn't my scene.

Geneva Lake was seven and a half miles long and two miles wide. Given its size, the wind, and the boat chop from tourists and locals, a smooth ride was rarely guaranteed. Today was no exception. Whitecaps dotted the deep blue water, bouncing us as if we were on a trampoline.

At the end of the bay, where the lake opened up, Liam gunned the engine and turned right, kicking up spray.

Zoe got the worst of the surprise shower and shrieked in dismay. "Liam, you brat! I didn't want to get my hair wet."

One side of her white-blond, flat-ironed hair dripped with water. She swept it up, pulled a scrunchie off her wrist, and secured a high ponytail. Her pretty mouth tightened into a pout, and she shot my stepbrother a harsh look from under full, dark lashes.

"Sorry, my bad." Liam grinned over his shoulder at her, enhancing his already irresistible face. Zoe melted into the red vinyl bench seat when he lowered his square jaw, a Clark family trademark, and cocked an eyebrow.

Flirting came as natural as breathing to him. While I waited for the rule book to arrive in the mail, he won the game blindfolded and with his hands tied behind his back.

Zoe leaned over Isabel and whispered in my ear, "Your brother's so delicious."

"Stepbrother," I reminded her.

Though we lived in Wisconsin, with his shaggy blond hair, cobalt blue eyes, and chill attitude that he shared with everyone but me, Liam could easily pass for a California surfer boy. He even had talked about attending college there before his mediocre grades ruled it out. Now, he'd be lucky to go to an in-state school, much to the angst of his father and grandfather.

"Does he like anyone?" Zoe watched Liam as he laughed at a story Sawyer was telling him.

I shrugged. More than one girl stopped by the house this summer, but it didn't mean anything. Girls had been chasing my stepbrother since the day I met him.

"Where are you going to head?" Sawyer asked Liam. He sat half-turned toward us, his legs spread apart and one elbow resting on the back of his chair. The boat jumped the waves and hit the water hard, but his body moved effortlessly in sync with the jarring rhythm.

"Fontana? We can anchor outside the swim area."

Having left their baby fat at the double doors of the school gym in sixth grade, the boys had similar tall and muscular builds from playing football, basketball, and baseball year-round. But while Liam was light, Sawyer was dark, his hair short and jet black, his eyes a creamy chocolate brown, and his skin several shades tanner than Liam's. They often competed for the top sports honors, but as far as I could tell, it had never affected their friendship, born in kindergarten.

A few minutes later, we arrived outside the swim area of Fontana's beach. Liam turned off the boat engine, and we drifted to a stop. Sawyer then set the anchor while Liam tossed life jackets from the cargo hold.

"Here, let me help." Sawyer reached for Isabel, who was struggling with her life jacket. His hands encircled her waist and touched her exposed skin, and she giggled uncertainly.

Smiling down at her, he scanned her body while his fingers untangled the straps and clicked the buckles closed.

The challenge in his eyes left me uneasy. I had heard enough conversations between Sawyer and Liam as they shot hoops or killed enemies in *Call of Duty* to know Sawyer was after only one thing—and it wasn't a meaningful, long-term relationship.

The boys knocked their beers together before chugging them, and then Liam threw a tennis ball into the water and yelled, "Last one in is in the middle."

Which, of course, was me. As everyone else jumped overboard, I finished buckling my jacket and inched down the ladder, wincing as the chilly water hit my sensitive lady parts.

After I swam to the center of where they floated in a large circle, Liam tossed the ball over my head to Sawyer, who caught it easily. He threw it to Isabel, who missed it. I lunged and paddled to grab the ball floating in front of her, but she got there first. This went on for several minutes until Zoe took pity on me. Her throw to Liam splashed down less than a yard away from me, and I snagged it before my stepbrother could. I smiled gratefully at her as we exchanged places.

When the boys got bored with the game, we dried off on the boat, and Sawyer offered another round of beers.

"Sure," the girls said in unison. I had yet to open my first one.

"Pop them over the water," Liam instructed. "They're probably shaken up."

Everyone did as told, but Zoe still got sprayed in the face, and Sawyer had to slurp up the mini eruption of foam from his can.

"My third shower of the day," she sighed, wiping off her face with her towel.

"Is your mom going to smell the beer?" Isabel asked.

"No, I do most of the laundry and housework now." Zoe's expression turned pensive. "Mom's been putting in a lot of overtime."

"Is everything OK?" Isabel whispered.

"Yeah, of course," Zoe replied in a bubbly voice, quickly switching moods. "Overtime is better than no time, right?"

While the choppy water rocked the small boat and everyone except me checked their phones, I wondered about Zoe's life. Before today, I assumed it was great. She was pretty and well-liked—and had a best friend. But her sadness a few minutes ago, no matter how fleeting, made me realize I knew nothing about my classmates.

"You gotta be kidding," Sawyer groaned, interrupting my thoughts. "I have to go."

Liam's head popped up. "What? Why?"

"Sammy didn't show up for his shift. I have to cover for him."

Liam snorted dismissively. "You aren't working there once school starts. Blow it off."

"I can't. I want to work there next summer."

"Dude…" Liam nodded toward Isabel and Zoe. "Don't bail on me."

"If I don't keep this job, I'll have to work for my uncle. And there's no way I'm roofing houses in ninety-degree weather." Sawyer rubbed a towel over his hair, creating random spikes, then put on his shirt. "Start the boat."

"Whatever. Get the anchor." My stepbrother slumped in the driver's seat and turned the key.

Sawyer did as he was told and was almost to his chair when Liam shoved the throttle lever forward. The boat jumped from the burst of speed, and Sawyer tumbled backward and landed on Zoe and Isabel. The girls squealed as he used his hands to push off their bare thighs to right himself.

With a devilish grin, he said, "Sorry about that, ladies."

He staggered to his seat and punched Liam in the arm. "Asshole."

Liam flipped him off as he drank from his beer before pointing the boat toward Williams Bay.

As we bounced across the lake at full speed, my body rose and fell on the bench as if I were riding a bucking bronco. I clenched my teeth to keep from biting my tongue and hung on to a metal bar beside me. Unaffected by the water rodeo,

Zoe and Isabel huddled in a deep conversation, probably deciding who would get Liam and who would get Sawyer.

Nearly to the bay, Liam swerved to avoid the wake of a much larger boat, but it caught us anyway, tossing ours as if it weighed nothing.

"Damn it!" Liam dropped the can he held into a cup holder. Grabbing his towel, he soaked up the spilled beer on his chest and the boat's carpet.

"Heads up," Sawyer said. "There's a paddleboarder."

My stepbrother took a few more swipes around his feet, and in those passing seconds, we closed the distance between the paddleboarder and our boat. Finally reacting, Liam turned sharply to the left, and our wake washed over the unsuspecting man. He wobbled for a breathless moment before pitching over the side and into the lake.

Liam laughed as he slowed the boat now that we were in the bay. "That'll teach him to stay near the shore. Stupid tourists should know better."

Zoe and Isabel paused their conversation and looked around, bewildered.

"What's going on?" Isabel asked.

I didn't answer, my attention on the man's bobbing board and the empty water around it. "Where is he?"

Liam reached for his beer and scowled at me impatiently. "Who?"

"The guy that fell off the board. I don't see him." My heart rate tripled as seconds passed, and the paddleboarder didn't break the water's surface. "I think he's in trouble."

Sawyer shielded his eyes. "I don't see him either. Turn around."

Liam made a wide arc and steered the boat to where the man had been.

"Did he swim to shore?" Isabel asked. "What was he wearing?"

"Blue shorts, I think," Sawyer replied. "I don't see him anywhere."

We reached the paddleboard, and Liam cut the boat's engine.

"We need to go in." I stood to flip down the ladder.

"Don't be stupid, Rose." Liam pointed to the depth gauge. "It's almost a hundred feet here."

Zoe's hands shook as she fumbled for her phone in her tote. "I'll call nine-one-one."

"Tell them to hurry," Isabel urged. "This is bad. Really bad."

Liam dumped the remains of his beer into the water and tossed the can into the cooler. "Give me all your cans."

Sawyer finished his beer and added it to the cooler, but the girls followed Liam's lead and poured their beers over the side of the boat. I handed in my still unopened can. We then scanned the lake and shoreline for what felt like an eternity until a police boat with two male officers arrived.

"Let me do the talking," Liam said to everyone, but his threatening look was only for me.

When the boats were close enough, he yelled, "We saw a man fall off that paddleboard." He gestured at the board several feet away. "We don't think he came up."

As the police officers conferred, it was all I could do to keep from screaming at them to hurry up and do something. Finally, one officer got on his radio.

"What was the man wearing?" the other officer asked.

Liam looked at Sawyer and answered, "Blue shorts, we think."

"And a long-sleeved shirt," I added. "Light-colored."

"Did you get that?" he asked his partner, who nodded and continued talking into the radio. "OK, do you have a slip nearby, or did you use the boat launch?"

"We have a slip," Liam replied, pointing toward the piers to the left of our village's public beach.

"Dock your boat and wait at the municipal pier until an officer takes your statement. Understood?"

"Yes, sir," Liam said in his ultra-polite voice reserved for adults.

A few minutes later, we drifted into the Clark's slip. Liam grabbed the cooler and jumped onto the dock before Sawyer could secure the first rope. A pair of seagulls perched on the canvas cover of a nearby boat took flight, squawking their annoyance at the interruption of their sunbathing.

"Where are you going?" I asked.

"Do you want to get caught drinking?" He looked at me as if I were stupid. "I'm taking the cooler to my Jeep. I'll meet you at the municipal pier. If anyone asks, tell them I went to the bathroom." He took a few steps and then stopped. "Also, when the police ask what happened, keep it simple. Say we were coming into the bay and saw the guy fall as we passed him."

Isabel and Zoe's faces crinkled in confusion, and my stomach braced for a tidal wave of anxiety at the half-truth. But Sawyer gave his friend a thumbs-up, and Liam nodded his satisfaction, assuming we all agreed.

No one talked as we finished securing the boat and then walked to the main pier, where we met up with Liam. As we waited for an officer to take our statements, two Water Safety boats joined the police boat, and an ambulance and three police SUVs came howling into the nearby boat launch parking lot.

Several minutes later, an officer approached us. Liam told our story first, and then Sawyer, Isabel, and Zoe repeated what he said word for word. When it was my turn, I found myself alone with the officer as the others had slipped into the crowd of gawkers that had formed.

Before I could give my statement, a black SUV pulled into the parking lot, diverting the officer's attention. A thick-bodied man with salt and pepper hair, wearing khaki shorts and a navy polo, hurried toward us, his flip-flops flapping against the pavement.

"Hey, Chief," the officer said. "Sorry to interrupt your day off."

The older man waved away the apology with his hand. "Update me on the situation."

"Approximately thirty minutes ago, a man fell off his paddleboard and went under between Conference Point and Cedar Point. He didn't surface. Divers are in the water, and we called for the drones."

"He was at the end of the bay?"

"Yes, sir. The water depth is around a hundred feet, so the divers are sweeping the bay, and the remotes will search outward as soon as they arrive."

Chief David Wick, head of the Williams Bay Police Department, studied the scene, which had changed from a rescue operation to one of recovery as more time passed. "I take it he wasn't wearing a life jacket?"

"No, sir. It was tied to his paddleboard."

"Of course, it was." The chief sighed deeply and massaged his forehead.

They continued to talk as if I weren't there, which often happened to me. Mom blamed it on my quietness, but I knew it was because I was easy to ignore. With my dull brown hair and childlike height, I blended into the background and became invisible.

"Who reported it?" the chief asked.

"Liam Clark."

"Hank's boy?"

The officer nodded.

"Has anyone told William Sr. yet?"

The officer pointed to my stepbrother, who was flanked by his dad and grandpa at the far end of the parking lot.

Dr. William Henry Clark Jr., aka Hank, seemed nervous. Though his feet never lifted from the pavement, his body moved in starts and stops, his hands finding his pants pockets, his face, and the back of his neck. He repeated the cycle as if it were a quirky dance.

In contrast, William Henry Clark Sr. stood stock-still facing the water, his wiry frame leaning on a cane as the tragedy unfolded.

The police chief asked about Liam's grandpa because, in 1837, Captain William Israel Clark settled next to the lake with his four sons. It didn't take long for the growing village to be called Williams Bay, with Captain Clark in charge. When he died, his eldest son took over, thus starting the tradition of the captain's descendants ruling over the residents. William Sr. was "elected" village president twenty years ago when his father became too frail. So even though six elected trustees were on the village board, everyone knew William Sr. had the final say in what happened in Williams Bay.

"Who else was onboard with Liam?" the chief asked.

The officer checked his notepad. "Zoe Smith, Isabel Murray, Sawyer Reed, and Rose McCabe."

Suddenly noticing me, the chief frowned as if trying to place who I was. He opened his mouth but abruptly shut it and headed toward the emergency personnel by the water's edge.

A shout came from the crowd, and several people pointed at a diver who had surfaced in the middle of the bay. His black neoprene-clad body swam slowly, one arm wrapped around an object. As the diver got closer, what he held became apparent, and two EMTs ran into the water to help him. The recovery operation was over.

Until this moment, I had harbored an illogical sequence of events where the man on the paddleboard had reached shore after falling in and would appear on the lake path any minute, wondering what all the fuss was. But now, I had to face reality and the part we had played in this stranger's death. I locked my knees to control my shaking legs and held both hands over my mouth to keep in my screams.

I stared at my stepbrother, but the distance between us made it impossible to see his expression. Was he sad? Distraught? Indifferent?

William Sr. turned to Hank and motioned with his cane. Then, my stepdad took Liam's arm and led him toward his Jeep. Realizing my ride was about to leave, I ran after them.

{2}

WILLIAM SR.

Sunday, September 3

My son paced the living room his current wife, Nora, had redccorated five times in the past three years. She called this version Shabby Chic, which meant filling the room with pillows, flowers, fake crystal lamps, and brand-new scuffed-up furniture. When she crowed about the great deal she got on a pair of bookcases that looked ready for the junkyard, I thought P.T. Barnum was right. There's a sucker born every minute.

Irritation spread through my body, growing into anger that threatened to choke me as I watched Hank from my recliner by the fireplace. Side by side, it was clear we were related. We were both six feet tall with the same blue eyes and strong jaw the previous generations of Clark men shared, but that was where the similarities ended. At seventy-five years old and despite a recent hip replacement, I had the physique and at least eighty percent of the strength I had at fifty-five. My son walked around in a "dad bod," whatever the hell that was. My brown hair had long ago turned gray, and I made weekly trips to the barbershop to keep it high and tight. At forty-seven years old, Hank pampered his brown curls with fancy products his wife bought at a beauty salon. He was a weak man and my biggest disappointment.

Hank paused before the mantel, picked up a family portrait, and studied it with weepy eyes. "I'm worried about Liam."

"Why?" I demanded. "The boy seems fine."

He shook his head. "Liam needs to talk about what happened and how he feels. If you suppress a trauma, you'll end up sick, both mentally and physically."

I sighed heavily and added an eye roll. "Did you read that medical advice on Facebook or Instagram?"

"I'm serious, Dad," he whined. "We need to do something for him."

The doorbell rang, and Hank looked bewildered as if he had never had a visitor.

I stomped my cane against the floor, but the thick carpet muffled my intended effect. "For goodness' sake, don't stand there like an imbecile. Answer the door."

He hurried from the room, obeying my command. A moment later, he returned with the village's police chief.

"Don't get up, William," the chief said as I scooted forward in my chair.

I nodded my thanks and shook the hand he offered me. "This hip replacement is more trouble than it's worth. The doctor says to give it time, but what the hell does he know? Anyway, have a seat, David. I assume you're not here to listen to me bellyache. Hank, pour the chief some coffee. He takes cream, no sugar."

Hank's eyes widened as if I had asked him to perform open-heart surgery. "I'll have to make some. There isn't any left from breakfast."

My single raised eyebrow at this earth-shattering news spurred him from the room.

The chief wedged himself into what remained of the couch after Nora had added two rows of unnecessary pillows. He leaned toward me, rested his forearms on his thighs, and clasped his hands. "I was wondering if I could talk to Liam again."

"Oh? Why?" I lifted my voice in surprise, though I had expected his visit. David wasn't the sharpest police chief, but he was thorough. "You have his statement, and the boy is so upset that I would hate to put him through any more pain. He's barely left his room since last night."

The chief's forehead creased as he studied his knuckles. "You see, William." He paused to clear his throat. "A witness to yesterday's drowning has come forward. His story differs from Liam's, so we need to confirm what actually happened before I can close the case."

"I don't understand. Didn't the other children on the boat give the same account of this tragic accident as Liam?"

"Yes," the chief agreed. "Almost verbatim."

"There you have it." I slapped my thigh. "Your witness must be mistaken. Perhaps they were too far away to see everything clearly? Or the afternoon sun blinded them?"

The chief squirmed on the couch. "The witness was on the lake path, which is a fair distance, but his version of the event seems plausible."

"In what way, David?" I kept my tone even with a touch of indifference to display we had nothing to hide or worry about.

He coughed into his fist, a stall tactic he often used when meeting with the village trustees. "The witness said a boat with two males and three females was coming at high speed into the bay and directly at the man on the paddleboard. When the driver swerved to avoid the man, he created a wake that caused the man to lose his balance and fall in. His description of the boat and the people on board matches your boat and the kids."

"I see." I let silence fill the room until the chief shifted his body again. "Now, we both know that Geneva Lake is rough on any given day due to excessive boat traffic and weather conditions, and yesterday was no exception. Most paddleboarders and kayakers stay by the shoreline for this very reason. The drowning victim was almost in the middle of the bay, correct?"

I waited for the chief to nod before continuing. "Then isn't it more plausible the man lost his balance because of less than optimal lake conditions rather than my grandson swamping him?"

He rubbed the back of his neck, and I took his troubled expression to mean he was unsure how far he could push me.

"Yes, that is a possibility," he conceded. But then he grew a spine and added, "I'll leave it for now, but when Liam feels better, I will need to ask him some more questions."

"Of course, of course. I'll call you as soon as the boy's ready." I pushed out of my chair, signaling it was time for the chief to be on his way. He followed me to the door, and I turned and clapped him on the shoulder. "Your annual budget proposal is due to the Finance and Personnel Committee at the end of the month. Maybe we can hire the extra officer you've always wanted."

The chief looked surprised and then pleased. "That would be great. We could use the help, especially during tourist season."

"Let's meet for breakfast tomorrow and discuss it further." I smiled slyly at him. "Off the record, of course."

We shook hands, and I guided him out the door before limping back to my recliner.

Hank appeared with a dish towel over one shoulder and a tray with three cups of coffee. Seeing David gone, he asked, "Did the chief leave?"

"Can't put one over on you." I planted my cane and eased into the chair, wincing as I lowered myself the last inch.

He set the tray on the coffee table, went to the window, and watched David drive away. "What did the chief want?"

"He asked to talk to Liam again."

He spun around. "Why?"

"Nevermind. I will handle this business from now on," I snapped. "You keep your mouth shut. And tell Liam to do the same."

"Why?" he repeated, reminding me of a three-year-old. "What's going on? I have a right to know, Dad. He's my son."

"Fine. Someone claiming to have seen the accident told the police Liam's reckless driving caused a wake that swamped the man on the paddleboard."

"So, they think Liam is lying?" he whispered unnecessarily since the boy would never hear him from his bedroom with those silly stick headphones in his ears.

"Yes," I grumbled.

The blood drained from his face, leaving him a deathly gray color and reminding me I had a funeral to attend later in the week.

"Do you think he's lying?" he asked me.

It was the million-dollar question. If pressed, my answer would be "yes," and I would probably die a rich man. "What do you think?"

His body wilted, and his eyes dropped to his bright, white tennis shoes. His inability to look me in the face was all the confirmation I needed.

I tapped the tablet I had been reading before Hank and David interrupted my day. "The *Lake Geneva Regional News* has already posted an article. They describe Liam as a witness and nothing more. That is what we need to say to anyone who asks."

He shook his head, not convinced. "What if…what if…they charge him with something? It could ruin his life. Should we hire a lawyer?"

"No. That would make Liam look guilty. I will handle David, and nothing will happen to Liam."

He walked the length of the room, one hand on his hip, the other on his forehead. He looked as if he might vomit. Finally, he asked in a shaky voice, "Are you sure?"

"The boy was not at fault," I said slowly, emphasizing each word. "End of story."

{3}

LIAM

Sunday, September 3

Dad had been hovering over me since we got home from the lake yesterday, and I was sick of it. Are you OK? Are you hungry? Can I get you anything? Do you want to talk about it? Do you want to see a therapist? I laughed in his face at the last one. Grandpa would never allow me to dump on a stranger, fearing I might stain the reputation of our perfect family.

That's why when someone knocked on my bedroom door, I shoved my AirPods into my ears and turned up the volume on my phone. The door opened, and there stood Rose, red-faced and geeky. Her head angled toward the stairs at the end of the hallway as if listening. Then, satisfied with whatever she heard or didn't hear, she came into the room and closed the door.

Staring at the bedpost to my left instead of me, she tapped at her ears.

I pulled out one AirPod. "What?"

"I wanted to see how you were doing."

"I'm fine, Mouse," I replied gruffly. "Why wouldn't I be?"

Her bottom lip trembled, and I thought she would scurry away, but she was determined to finish what she had started by coming here. "Because of what happened…because of us."

"What are you talking about? The dude fell off his board. He was eighty-two and probably senile." I pointed in the general direction of the lake. "He'd have to be crazy to paddle in the middle of the bay with all the boats zooming around."

She shook her head and whispered, "Our boat caused the wave that made him go under. We killed him."

I threw down my phone and jumped off the bed. With a frightened yelp, she backed into the door, one arm protecting her face and her free hand fumbling for the doorknob. Realizing she thought I would hit her, I quickly retreated, my face hot from shame.

"No. We didn't. It was an accident. And if you say it was our fault to anyone, my life turns to crap, and so does everyone else's in this family—including yours and Nora's. Dad would lose his job, and Grandpa would have to step down from being village president, ending the billion-year reign of the Clarks. Because who would want the father and grandfather of a killer running the school and village? And without Dad working, we would lose the house and have to move. So, the cushy life that you—and Nora—enjoy disappears. You don't want that, do you?"

Her forehead wrinkled as she puzzled over my question. Her brain must have been constipated because "No" was the only answer, but my stepsister was only smart when it came to schoolwork.

I waited another few seconds for her to say something and then tried again.

"Rose." Her body twitched at me using her given name. "It was an accident. A terrible accident."

She huffed at that, but at least she relaxed against the door. "What about the others? Are they OK with lying?"

"It's not a lie," I insisted. "But, yeah, they're cool."

She looked down and mumbled something I couldn't hear before slinking from the room.

I grabbed my pillow and screamed into it. Since it felt pretty good, I thought I'd do it again, but my phone pinged, interrupting my pity party.

Isabel is worried the police will find out we were drinking. She asked if you did anything wrong. Guess she and Zoe were busy yapping when you swerved.

I read Sawyer's message several times, cursing louder and more obscene with each repetition. Finally, I typed:

Tell her I'm taking care of everything. No one will have to talk to the police again.

You mean your grandpa is.

Whatever. Just keep your mouth shut.

What if Isabel still wants to talk about it?

Distract her.

How?

Just do something. You owe me. Remember?

He left me hanging for a few minutes, and then dots appeared.

```
OK, don't get
pissy.
```

```
                    Hard not to. This
                    is my life we're
                    talking about.
```

Without waiting for a reply, I swapped my phone for my pillow and screamed again.

{4}

ROSE

Sunday, September 3

My conversation with Liam didn't ease my worries. I had hoped he would agree to come clean with the police, but he was a Clark and a golden boy, and both put him above blame for any questionable actions.

I opened my phone and searched for any mention of the drowning. The top result was a brief post from the Facebook account of the *Lake Geneva Regional News*: "George Kankos, eighty-two, of Spring Grove, Illinois, accidentally drowned in Geneva Lake on Saturday. Funeral arrangements are pending."

Half a dozen comments were already displayed, and as I scrolled through them, I felt worse and worse. Though most were condolences like "So sad! RIP" and "The family is in my thoughts and prayers," the last comment stopped my heart.

Terry Black: A CARELESS BOATER MADE THE POOR GUY FALL. HE SHOULD BE CHARGED WITH MURDER.

Terry hadn't set any privacy settings on his profile. Based on the few pictures he shared, I determined that he was middle-aged, had lived in Williams Bay for ten years, and loved the water. He had also included his email address, which sparked an idea. Five minutes later, I had created an email address under a fake name.

I drafted and rejected several opening lines of a new message, my thumbs fumbling across the keyboard. Eventually, I settled on short and to the point.

HI TERRY

I READ YOUR COMMENT ABOUT THE POOR MAN WHO DROWNED YESTERDAY. I WAS WATCHING FROM THE BOAT LAUNCH PARKING LOT WHEN THEY BROUGHT HIM TO SHORE. IT WAS AWFUL. DID YOU KNOW THE BOATER WHO MADE HIM FALL? DID YOU TALK TO THE POLICE?

SUCH A TRAGEDY,

GINA

I squeezed my eyes shut as the email wooshed away. It would likely go straight to Terry's spam folder, but I had to try.

Half an hour later, my phone vibrated with Terry's reply.

HI GINA

NICE TO MEET YOU. DO YOU LIVE IN WILLIAMS BAY OR WERE YOU VISITING?

WE WERE TOO FAR AWAY TO SEE FACES, BUT TWO BOYS AND THREE GIRLS WERE ONBOARD. WE WERE HEADING OUT OF THE BAY TOWARD FONTANA WHEN I SAW THE BOAT ZIP BY. I SAID TO MY WIFE, THOSE KIDS ARE GOING TOO FAST. THEN, THE POLICE BOAT PASSED US. WHEN I READ ABOUT THE DROWNING, I KNEW IT HAD TO BE BECAUSE OF THAT BOAT. I BET THEY WERE DRINKING, TOO.

ANYWAY, I REPORTED IT, BUT WHO KNOWS IF IT WILL DO ANY GOOD.

TERRY

I frowned at his reply. Considering he accused a boater of murder, he hadn't seen the accident and wasn't a reliable witness. He was a social media troll and nothing more, but it made me wonder how many other boaters saw something worthy of reporting.

I went back to the news story and found things had escalated quickly into a witch hunt. Terry had added another comment similar to what he wrote in the email to me. Several people had already replied, the gist being the teenagers weren't responsible enough to be boating without an adult. A few even suggested they were a product of wealthy but absent parents.

Feeling sick, I wondered if Liam was aware of the public reaction to the drowning and if he would still stick to his half-truths. Either way, he wasn't in the clear yet.

{5}

WILLIAM SR.

Monday, September 4

I took my usual table at the Igloo, a kitschy, dome-shaped restaurant, and turned over a coffee cup. There were only two places in town to get a decent breakfast, and I preferred this one because I had gone to school with Jeanie, the owner. She bought the business some thirty years ago when it was called the Arctic Circle, and as far as I could tell, she hadn't changed the interior or the exterior since.

Strings of Christmas lights and faded gold tinsel lined the walls, along with photos of local historical buildings and artwork for sale. The booths and chairs were upholstered in lime green, red, and black vinyl, and if you were looking for company, you could sit on one of the stools at the front counter and converse with the wait staff and cooks.

Now that I thought about it, Jeanie had added some decorations. Various stuffed animals—snowmen, penguins, cats, and such—balanced on the curtain rods above the windows. My usual table sat in the middle of the room because of this. I didn't need a dusty toy landing in my eggs after a truck rumbled by.

Jeanie came over with a pot of coffee. "Good morning, William. How are you?"

"I'm good, but I'd be better if you'd finally run off with me."

"Oh, here we go again." She fisted her free hand on her hip. "You know I'm too much of a woman for you. It would never work."

"I'm willing to try if you are."

"You're an incorrigible dirty old man," she scolded, though the words lacked heat.

I patted her backside. "Which is why you like me."

We had a version of this conversation almost every time I came in. The women in my generation could take a joke without crying about sexual harassment whenever a man opened his mouth.

She laughed and swatted my shoulder. "Are you by yourself this morning?"

"No, the chief is meeting me." More out of habit than necessity, I reached for the menu.

"Today's special is a Jalapeno Popper Frittata if you're in a sassy mood—which you seem to be."

"Jalapenos?" I faked a blow to the chest. "I think you're trying to kill me."

"How else am I going to keep your hands off me?" A bell dinged in the kitchen. "My order's up. I'll come back in a few minutes."

I decided on French toast by the time David arrived. He settled into the chair opposite me and then shifted his utility belt and gun to a more comfortable position under his belly while Jeanie poured more coffee.

"Here's to Labor Day." I raised my cup and toasted him. "Summer's officially over in Williams Bay."

The chief slurped his hot coffee and winced. "That's fine with me," he admitted. "Things quiet down when the summer people and tourists leave. That's the way I like it."

After Jeanie took our breakfast orders, we sipped our coffee, relaxing until I decided to bring up what was on my mind. "Tell me, David. Are you going to turn this drowning into something more than it is?"

"That's what I like about you. Straight to the point."

"It's my grandson we're talking about here," I said defensively. "It could destroy his life if this gets blown out of proportion."

"And Liam might have taken a life," the chief whispered.

"We went over this yesterday, and I thought we agreed on what happened."

He held up a hand. "I'm not trying to jam the kid up. But the district attorney has to follow the law. And we can't ignore that a witness said Liam headed straight for the paddleboarder and swerved at the last minute."

"A witness who was far away on the lake path," I reminded him.

"And then there's the pressure from social media. In these types of accidents, the public often assumes the driver was intoxicated. Have you read the online comments on the man's obit? One says they saw the kids drinking beer earlier in the afternoon. We're still vetting the information, but…"

"And again, from *far away*, no one can tell the difference between soda and beer cans. Besides, you don't have any proof of intoxication, as the responding officer didn't test Liam."

Jeanie arrived with our breakfasts, and I held my tongue until David took a few mouthfuls of the morning special. Good thing I didn't have to go to Village Hall today. Once those peppers kicked in, he would be polluting the air.

"So, what's the worst-case scenario?" I reached for the warm syrup bottle, an extra touch Jeanie did for me.

"He's tried as an adult and charged with criminally negligent homicide." He ducked his head and shoveled a forkful of frittata into his mouth.

"A felony?" I leaned forward and shook my fork at him. "No. You have to make this go away, David."

He risked looking at me. "I don't know if I can. It's not like the old days. Now, everyone demands the government be transparent."

"Whatever the hell that means," I muttered.

"What it means is Liam may have to pay the price for his actions."

"If you and the DA can prove he acted negligently."

"Yes, that's correct. With the right lawyer, this could all go away. A few years ago, in the Wisconsin Dells, a jet skier ran into a fishing boat, killing one of the passengers who wasn't wearing a life jacket. He insisted the setting sun blinded him. Others said he was going too fast for the conditions. He was charged with criminally negligent homicide but pleaded no contest to three misdemeanors. After serving two years of probation, the charges were expunged from his record."

"And you think that is my best-case scenario?"

"Probably. Since Liam's a good kid from a good family, chances are they wouldn't try him as an adult. But it isn't up to me."

"But you could intervene with the district attorney or perhaps emphasize certain facts and not others." When he remained silent, I pushed him some more. "We've been friends for a long time and have helped each other out of tight spots in the past. This isn't any different. I'm sure you can find a way to protect my grandson from all this nonsense."

"William," he pleaded. "I still have a few more years to go before I can retire with my full pension. I don't want to lose my job."

"I would never let that happen, David," I assured him in a solemn voice. "Help me and my family, and you will be duly rewarded."

The wrinkles across his brow deepened as he considered my offer, and I fought to keep my expression composed despite my frustration over his doubt that I could do what I was promising.

Finally, he blew out a long breath. "OK. You're right, of course. I'll talk to the DA first thing tomorrow."

I nodded, satisfied. "Good. Your loyalty is certainly appreciated. Now, tell me what your adorable grandchildren have been up to."

{6}

HANK

Tuesday, September 5

Dad told me before I left this morning that he had solved Liam's "problem," and the news was icing on the day's cake. With that worry settled, I could concentrate on all the things I had been looking forward to for the past three months.

I loved the first day of the school year, even though some of the teachers and most of the students didn't. Every fall in the staff lounge and throughout the hallways, I heard, "Summer went so fast," and "I wasn't ready to come back." But I never agreed. When classes ended in early June, I counted down the days until September. I delighted in the energy of the grade schoolers and the snarkiness of the high schoolers. I relished the opportunity to change a child's life.

As superintendent of the Williams Bay School District, it was my world, and I ruled with a just and kind hand.

I passed the student-painted wall mural of our bulldog mascot near the front entrance and swept my fingers over his face. Our sprawling building housed kindergarten through fifth grade in the east wings and sixth through twelfth in the west wings. In the center, there were shared spaces, such as the cafeteria, two gyms, and an auditorium.

The bell for period one would ring in about twenty minutes, and I still had two hallways to go. As a tradition on the first day, I made it a point to say good morning to every teacher and check in with any new hires. I never wanted to be the aloof boss behind a closed door.

I stuck my head into what was now Ms. Taylor's science lab and classroom. She replaced an obnoxious, bitter woman who played favorites and pitted students against each other. I finally had enough of the drama and told the school board not to renew her contract. She could be someone else's misery this year.

I knocked on the open door, always respecting the teacher's domain. "Ms. Taylor? Sorry to interrupt."

The young lady sat at her desk, her teaching materials spread before her, and was as pretty as I remembered. Of course, she had been impeccably dressed for her interview, but once hired, people often leaned toward the bare minimum in meeting any written dress code. In fact, when I greeted the gym teacher earlier, I had to remind him the heavy metal band T-shirt he wore was inappropriate. After twenty years of employment, you'd think he could remember that.

But Ms. Taylor didn't disappoint me. Her blouse was a flattering green color that enhanced the red of her long auburn hair, and the floral scarf around her neck added a touch of dressiness without going overboard.

Her lips—painted a nonoffensive peach shade—curved into a friendly grin. "Good morning, Dr. Clark. And please call me Madison."

"Only if you call me Hank," I said with a smile.

On her tidy desk, the latest yearbook, open to students' photos, sat alongside a small stack of class lists.

"I like to match a face with a name before I meet them." She lowered her gaze, looking sheepish. "I feel at a disadvantage being new."

"What an excellent idea." Pride straightened my spine as she validated my recommendation to hire her straight out of college. "But never fear. By the end of the week, you'll feel like you've been here forever."

Her expression turned uncertain, and worry lines broke out across her smooth skin. After a beat of silence, she said, "I hope so."

I clapped my hands together. "I won't bother you any longer. I only wanted to say hello and ask if you needed anything."

She pushed away from her desk, swiveled slightly in her chair, and crossed her legs. Her black skirt slid up to reveal more of her toned thighs. Any man with a heartbeat would have appreciated the view, and I was no exception. I took a moment to savor the result of her workout routine before diverting my eyes to her face.

She pursed her full lips, tapped the pen she held against them, and then shook her head. "I can't think of anything right now."

"Awesome. But if something comes up, please don't hesitate to find me. If I'm not in my office, check the halls. I like to wander."

"Thank you...Hank."

"Have a fantastic first day, Madison." I left the room whistling.

Yep. It was great to be back.

{7}

LIAM

Tuesday, September 5

I tried to follow along as the new science teacher explained each section of the anatomy class syllabus in agonizing detail, but my mind kept replaying the diver carrying the old man out of the lake. I only got a break from binge-watching the accident when I took Nora's sleeping pills, stolen from her bathroom cabinet. I told myself it was an "accident" that had nothing to do with my driving because if the opposite were true, then I killed a man. And I didn't know how to live with that fact.

It was the first day of school, and Sawyer and I had the same class schedules. He had been glued to my side since the bell for period one rang. I couldn't tell if he was my protection or if I was his. No one had dared to give us any grief about the drowning, but the vibes from my classmates ranged from curious to accusing.

We sat on stools next to each other at a table with two nerds. Neither of us cared about science, so we purposely chose lab partners brainier than us—a brilliant plan I came up with back in ninth grade.

Sawyer nudged my knee with his. When I looked at him, he fanned himself with his syllabus and mouthed, "She's hot."

I scanned the room, seeing only the same heavily made-up faces from last year. "Who?"

"Are you blind as well as dumb?" he asked with a lift of his chin toward our teacher.

I shrugged and pretended to pay attention to what Ms. Taylor was writing on the board about lab schedules.

Since Dad was the superintendent of the Williams Bay schools, he had filled us in on the new teachers at dinner one night. Ms. Taylor had graduated from the University of Wisconsin, and this was her first official teaching job. With her long, wavy hair and porno-perfect body, she was better than any other teacher we had ever had. But I was in too bad of a mood to play along with Sawyer.

When the bell rang to signal the end of class, everyone zipped up their backpacks to head to the cafeteria for lunch, the only part of the day I enjoyed.

"Liam?" Ms. Taylor called out as my classmates filed out the door. "Can I speak to you for a minute?"

Sawyer gave me an envious look and a high five. "I'll save you a seat."

It wasn't necessary. Only the ninth graders wouldn't know where the jocks sat, and we quickly put them in their place if they picked the wrong table.

Ms. Taylor stood by her desk, and after the last student left, she said, "I don't bite, Liam."

I slung my backpack over my shoulder and shuffled my feet a few inches forward, hoping my bored expression made me look indifferent toward her summons. But then I inhaled, and her musky scent ambushed me. She didn't smell like the cheap floral perfumes the girls I dated bathed in, which burned my nose. Instead, whatever she wore hit me deep in the groin.

"I've been reviewing your transcript." She held it out, and I pretended to be interested in the piece of paper responsible for my future. "And while you've never failed a class, you haven't exactly exceeded expectations."

My jaw jutted out in a silent protest, and my eyes focused on the nearest corner of the worn metal desk. No one had to tell me my grades sucked. Long ago, I had put away my hope of getting into UCLA, my dream college.

She slid my transcript into a folder. "I heard you reported a drowning this past weekend." She slowly shook her head. "That must have been a terrible experience for you."

The change in subject left me confused and a bit in awe of the only person so far with the guts to bring up the paddleboard accident to my face.

She moved closer and placed a hand on my upper arm. "As your teacher, I'm here to help. Let me know if you need extra time with assignments as you work through the aftermath of such a tragedy. Good mental health is more important than meeting deadlines. Also, in regards to your transcript, I'm available for tutoring sessions if needed." She tightened her hold on my bicep, her colored lips forming what seemed like a genuine smile. "I want your senior year to be the best year you've ever had."

My brain felt thick, her powerful scent and caring words overwhelming me. I stepped back, breaking her grasp, and gulped fresh air.

"Thanks," I mumbled.

She nodded, seemingly satisfied with my lame response, and took a seat behind her desk. Her hands gathered her hair and draped it over one shoulder before becoming all business and organizing the papers scattered about. Then she turned and held my gaze with her cat-like green eyes. "That will be all. Enjoy your lunch."

***

Still dazed by my encounter with Ms. Taylor, I got a tray of food and joined the rest of the football team at our table on the far side of the lunchroom.

"What did our flaming hot new teacher want?" Sawyer asked, showing a semi-chewed bite of sandwich in his mouth as he talked.

"Nothing." I focused on opening my milk carton and unwrapping my spork and knife, hoping my one-word answer would be sufficient.

"Uh-huh."

So much for satisfying his curiosity. I'd known him forever, and his tone said he wouldn't let it go. "Fine. She wanted to discuss my grades."

Sawyer laughed, and I felt some satisfaction when he started to choke. When he could talk again, he said, "It's day one of the school year. How bad could they be already?"

"She was looking at my transcript."

His brow furrowed. "And?"

"If I need help, she'll tutor me," I snapped. "Now drop it."

"Sorry I asked." He shoved a handful of chips in his mouth, and one cheek bulged like a squirrel's. "But I wish she would say that to me. I'd be all over that offer."

A hand clamped my shoulder and pressed me deeper into my seat. "Run anyone over lately, Clark?"

I sprung up with fists ready and faced Chris, a six-foot-two lanky cornerback and the number three athlete in our school behind Sawyer and me. "What did you say?"

"Woah, someone sure is wound tight. What's the matter? Afraid that, for once, your last name won't get you out of trouble?"

Sawyer stood, shoving his chair into Chris's body. "Oh, sorry, Douchebag. Didn't see you there."

Anyone watching would think my best friend had my back, but I knew better. He hated Chris and took every opportunity to show it, whether a brutal hit on the football field or an elbow to the face on the basketball court.

"Boys, settle down," a deep voice boomed across the noisy lunchroom.

I slowly relaxed my fists and sat down. I may ignore Dad at home, but he ran the school and coached the football team. After being told a thousand times to respect both positions, I acted on autopilot.

He appeared by my side, and for the third time today, someone put their hand on me, which was ironic because we had been taught since pre-school to keep our hands to ourselves.

"First day of the term, and you guys are mixing it up already. What have I said about fighting?" Dad asked in his "I'm not only your coach but also your friend" voice.

"Save it for the other team," the jocks at the table said in unison.

He grinned broadly. "Exactly. See you at practice. Three-thirty sharp."

I picked at my lunch and thought about how Dad acted differently at school. Here, he walked the halls, cracking jokes and helping out whenever needed. Everyone loved him. But at home, he sneaked from room to room, avoiding Grandpa as much as possible.

Grandpa moved in at the beginning of the summer because of his hip replacement, and he seemed in no hurry to leave. When Nora asked Dad how long he was staying, he never gave her a straight answer. Maybe he was too scared to tell him to move out.

Sawyer gathered his backpack and tray. "I'll see you in class."

"Where are you going?" I asked.

"You told me to distract Isabel. She's in the library right now. Alone."

I had one minute to myself before the next challenge of the day arrived.

"Hi, Liam." Tara slid into the chair opposite me. One finger twirled a piece of her long brown hair while her eyes begged me to notice her.

"Hey." Given my current state of mind, it was the best I could do. We weren't dating, but occasionally we hooked up.

She was in Rose's class, so come this Saturday, when I turned eighteen, I would have to cut her loose. She definitely wasn't worth the risk.

She babbled on about her classes, who was in them, and an upcoming volleyball tournament that her team would probably lose. I nodded whenever she stopped to breathe but kept my head down, concentrating on my food.

Then, she whispered, "I heard about what happened."

I grunted and shoved a soggy tater tot in my mouth.

"It must have been awful to watch." When I didn't say anything, she put a hand over mine. "I've been defending you all day. And maybe you should ask your dad to make some kind of announcement about the rumors going around. People are saying some wild stuff about you."

"Like what?" I asked louder and harsher than I had intended. A table full of juniors turned toward us, and I held up my middle finger until they started eating again.

Tara stopped twirling her hair and scooted back in her chair, putting distance between us. "I don't know. Someone said you were swimming and pushed the guy off his board. Someone else said you swamped his board with your boat. Basically, they're saying it's your fault he died."

"That's bullshit," I hissed, and she flinched at the anger in my voice. "We saw a guy fall into the water as we passed him and reported it. I didn't *do* anything wrong."

The bell rang, signaling the end of the lunch period, and she seemed relieved. "I know you didn't. I believe you. Meet me at my locker after school?"

"Sure." I probably wouldn't, but lying was easier than the drama that usually followed the truth. She blew me a kiss before catching up with her pack of girlfriends on the other side of the cafeteria.

I scanned the faces of my classmates. Fricking losers couldn't mind their own business. I picked up my tray and dumped what I hadn't eaten into the nearest garbage can.

{8}

ROSE

Tuesday, September 5

My anxiety surged as I stood at my locker in the near-empty hallway, switching the books in my backpack with those I needed for the afternoon. I wouldn't have been in danger of being late if Hank hadn't cornered me. Mom probably told him to do it as if today were my first day of pre-school, not my sophomore year.

After triple-checking everything, I made it to English class as the fourth-period bell rang.

Mrs. Morales smiled at me as she closed the door. "Great to see you, Rose. How was your summer?"

"OK, thanks." I scanned the room, taking in the fifteen other students, all familiar faces.

From the far corner, Zoe waved and pointed to a desk next to her. I slid into it and took my time pulling out a notebook and pen so I wouldn't have to engage in small talk. But Zoe had gossip she wanted to share.

While our English teacher gave her first-day spiel and passed out syllabuses, Zoe leaned over and whispered breathlessly, "Isabel thinks Sawyer likes her."

Her gleeful expression made it obvious she thought this was good news, but I didn't.

"Why?" I asked, though I already knew I wouldn't like the answer. Sawyer practically lived at our house. I wouldn't wish him on my worst enemy.

"He sent her a dick pic." She covered her mouth to muffle her giggle.

Mrs. Morales stopped her prepared speech mid-sentence. "Do you have a question, Zoe?"

She picked up the syllabus on her desk and pretended to read it. "No. I'm good."

Mrs. Morales sighed, flicked her wrist to check her watch, and continued her lecture. When she turned to point at a list of books written on the whiteboard, Zoe mouthed to me, "I'll tell you more later."

I forced a smile and nodded.

For the rest of the period, time dragged, the forty-five minutes seeming like a hundred. I alternated between listening to Mrs. Morales and worrying about Isabel with Sawyer.

After class, Zoe waited in the hallway until no one was in earshot before resuming her gossip. "She showed me the pic this morning when I got to school, and I literally freaked out."

"I think it's a bizarre way to show you're interested in someone." A terrible thought occurred to me as we started walking, and I stopped abruptly in the middle of the hall. "Wait. Isabel didn't send a pic back, did she?"

"She might have." Zoe's tone was casual as she dug into the front pocket of her backpack and pulled out some gum.

"No," I wailed. "Why would she do that?"

"Because she wants him to like her. Duh." She offered me a piece of gum, then shoved two in her mouth and chewed like a cow. She'd have to spit them out before her next class, as most of our teachers outlawed anything enjoyable.

"What if he shows it to other guys? Everyone is going to be talking about her."

"It's just a body part," she said defensively. "It's not that big of a deal, Rose. Have you ever gone to an art museum? There are boobs all over the place—and dicks."

"If it's not a big deal, why did Liam spend a week begging my stepfather not to suspend Sawyer from baseball last spring? They didn't name the girl, but he got caught sending her pics from the team bus after a game."

Zoe made a face. "Eww. I always thought they took them in their bedroom. I wonder who the girl was. I bet it was Rachel."

"You're missing the point. Sawyer and Isabel could get into a lot of trouble if any adults find out."

"Who would tell?" She put a hand to her heart. "I'm not going to."

We reached the library where I planned to spend the free period I had next. "Please ask Isabel not to do it again. Sawyer's not as great as you both think he is."

"Are you serious? The guy's a hottie. Not quite on the same level as Liam, but no one in this school is."

"Please?" I tried to sound as if it was a life-or-death matter. "Promise me?"

Zoe rolled her eyes. "Fine, I'll talk to her."

I blew out a relieved breath. "Thanks."

"Hey, could I come over tonight for some help with our geometry homework? I didn't totally understand the example Bailey put on the board."

I hesitated, wondering if she wanted to see Liam and not me. Still, if I agreed, Mom might leave me alone for a while. "Of course, seven o'clock?"

"Perfect." The bell rang, and Zoe swore. "Late again! See you tonight."

Anxious thoughts controlled my head for the next hour. Instead of doing my reading assignment for English class, I debated whether to talk to Liam about Isabel and Sawyer. After all of Liam's pathetic pleading last spring, Hank agreed not to punish Sawyer if he swore never to send nude pics again. I was sure Liam would want to know that Sawyer hadn't learned the proper use of his phone. He might even agree his friend shouldn't be pursuing Isabel. But *conversing* with Liam was unpleasant at best. Even in a good mood, he was mean to me, and he'd been in a bad one since Saturday.

Then, my anxiety switched topics, and I agonized over a realization that had been festering in my mind since Saturday. If I hadn't given in to Mom by asking Zoe and Isabel to go boating, Liam and Sawyer might have found something else to do, and the old man would still be alive. From the comments left on his obituary page, some people thought Liam was at fault, but maybe I was also to blame. For once, I should have stood up for myself and done what I wanted to do instead of being a people-pleaser.

Tears wet my lashes, and a sob escaped my throat before I could clamp down on my emotions. The guy napping on his books a few tables away lifted his head with a questioning look in my direction. Realizing it was Chris—Liam and Sawyer's sworn archenemy but also a longtime crush of mine—my face turned volcanic red.

I swept up my stuff, fled into the hall, and smacked into Tara, my class's queen bee and Liam's friend with benefits. Reacting to my presence in her personal space, she shoved me into the nearest row of lockers. Books and papers flew from my arms and landed at my feet.

"Watch where you're going, freak." As she continued walking, she veered enough to land an expensive leather boot on my copy of *Lord of the Flies*.

Tara lived to make the girls in our school miserable. And because of my relationship with Hank, I was one of her favorite targets, especially in gym class. She knew I wouldn't blab to him, so it increased her power in the eyes of her followers.

For probably the hundredth time, I considered asking Mom about homeschooling, but it would be a waste of breath. She loved her time in high school and would never understand why I didn't belong in mine.

{9}

HANK

Tuesday, September 5

Dad's car was in the driveway, which was strange as he usually spent his day at Village Hall.

"Hello?" I called out, moving into the foyer.

A cough came from the living room, where I found him sprawled on the couch, one arm covering his face. Nora's designer pillows littered the floor, and the drawn curtains semi-darkened the normally bright room.

Having never seen him in a prone position unless it was nighttime and he was in bed, I hurried to his side. "Are you all right, sir?"

He lifted his hand and shooed me away.

I retreated a few feet, but concern made me press the matter. "Why are you home? Are you sick?"

"Damn it, Hank, can't a seventy-five-year-old man take a nap if he wants to?" He moved his arm enough so that one eye could glare at me. "I'm fine."

"I'm sorry. You scared me." Despite his assurance, his breathing seemed uneven. Until now, he'd never looked or acted his age, and I wondered whether I should believe him. "When did you last see a doctor? I mean, besides your hip operation."

He swung his feet off the couch and sat up. When his body swayed, his hands clutched the seat cushions. "I'm not discussing my health with you. I said I was fine. Now drop it." He patted his shirt pocket for his reading glasses that weren't there, then brought his watch up to his face and squinted at it. "What are you doing home?"

"I forgot some notes I made for football practice."

"Football," he sneered. "They should change the name to 'sissyball.' Is the team any good? Or will they stink up the place like every other year you've coached?"

"The kids try hard," I answered weakly.

"Ach." His lips twisted in disgust.

"They do," I insisted, though I risked more insults from him by defending my boys. "But we're a small school. The talent pool isn't big. It's not their fault."

"Yes, it is. There were even fewer students in my day, and we still won the Division IV state championship in my junior and senior years. We got up early and went to morning practice. Then, we went to class all day. Then, we went to afternoon practice. Then, we went home to do farm chores or part-time jobs. And after all that, we did our homework. We were lucky to get five hours of sleep a night. Unlike these "girlie-boys" who sit on their phones all day or play video games, we were tough. You're too soft on them."

I swallowed a sigh. This argument occurred every fall, and there was nothing I could say to win it.

He pushed himself off the couch, and I grabbed his arm when his knees buckled. "Are you sure you're OK?"

"Damn hip." He limped past me toward the foyer.

"See you at dinner?"

His answer, if he bothered with one, was lost in the noise of the front door slamming.

{ 10 }

LIAM

Tuesday, September 5

After classes, I walked into the football locker room and found several guys huddled around Sawyer. Nothing unusual about that except for the look of guilt on his face when he saw me.

"What's going on, ladies?" I asked. "Practice starts in five minutes, and no one is on the field." As team captain, I had every right to harass them.

A freshman who had been trying to prove himself as a tight end since the season started in August replied, "Sawyer's got pics from—"

Sawyer hit him on the arm. "Shut up." Then, he smiled at me. "Nothing, bro. We're all good to go."

Grabbing him by the collar, I hauled him into the shower room. His cell flew from his hand and skimmed across the tile floor as he tried to fight back.

"Dude. What's your problem?" He retrieved his phone and checked for damage before straightening his T-shirt.

"I can't believe you." I paced in front of the shower stalls, my vision blurring with white dots of rage. "After all I've done for you, you pull this crap again."

"You're going to have to be more specific," he said, playing dumb.

"What's on your phone?" I nodded at his right hand with my chin.

He shrugged. "Pretty much the same stuff that's on yours."

I shoved him against the wall and enjoyed his expression of astonishment mixed with fear. Then, keeping my shoulder pressed to his chest, I twisted the cell out of his hand. Sawyer didn't bother with a passcode, so a girl's naked breasts were displayed when I swiped up on the screen. A few more swipes revealed different angles.

"Is this Isabel?" I thrust the phone in his face.

Sawyer leered at the current picture before defending himself. "Don't blame me. You said to distract her."

"And you couldn't think of a better way to do it? What if my dad finds out again? You'll be off the team."

"Not going to happen. You're acting like an old lady."

"You showed that pic to half a dozen guys. You don't think one of them will tell someone else, and that person will tell someone else? It's like a virus that will eventually infect my dad. All you need is one person in this school who doesn't like you. And believe me, more than one person fits that description. Do you want me to make a list for you?"

"Wow, tell me how you really feel. I didn't know I was such a prick."

I deleted the pictures of Isabel and threw the phone at him. "Get your ass in gear. We're late."

As soon as we jogged onto the football field, Dad pointed to the track that encircled it. "Four laps, boys. Practice started already."

I glared at Sawyer before taking off at a run. If he wanted to keep pace with me, he'd have to work for it. But he never caught up, and I spent the alone time thinking about how to put out the dumpster fire my senior year was turning out to be.

{ 11 }

ROSE

Tuesday, September 5

Mom was making lasagna for dinner when I told her Zoe was coming over later. She was thrilled.

After finding nothing acceptable for the historic event on the pantry shelves, she grabbed a notepad and pen from her purse. "I'll run to the store for some snacks and soda. What do you want? Oreos? Doritos? There's time to bake some premade chocolate chip cookies. You like those, yeah?"

"Please don't make a big deal out of this," I begged. "Zoe just needs help with some homework."

"That doesn't mean you shouldn't be a gracious hostess, Rose." She opened the refrigerator, paused, and added something to her grocery list. "A little effort goes a long way when making friends."

She meant well and was probably right, but once again, her extroverted personality exasperated my introverted one. Mom didn't work outside our home. Instead, she spent most of her free time volunteering and chairing various committees. With her warm and easygoing manner, everyone in town liked her. It was a hard act to follow.

"Maybe some caramel corn, Fritos, and lemonade?" I suggested, trying to be a team player.

"Great. I should be back before the lasagna needs to go in the oven. Otherwise, I'll text you instructions."

"Sounds good." I ripped open a protein bar and settled on a stool at the breakfast counter. In addition to my geometry homework, I had to read the first two chapters of *Lord of the Flies* for English class tomorrow. I pulled out the book from my backpack and was quickly transported to a deserted island with a group of horrible boys.

***

Throughout dinner, Mom quizzed Liam and me about our first day of school. My stepbrother kept his answers to one-word sentences, which left me to pick up the slack. She and Hank exchanged worried looks as Liam picked at his lasagna, his head bent over his plate. It didn't take long for William Sr. to take control of the situation.

"Liam," he barked, making everyone jump. "Sit up straight and eat your meal properly. You're not a three-year-old."

"Yes, sir." He corrected his posture, but his gaze remained on his food.

"Dad," Hank said in a low voice. "Maybe take it easy on him right now."

William Sr. narrowed his eyes at his son and tightened his grip on his fork and knife until his knuckles whitened. "The boy's almost eighteen. How will he make it in life if he can't handle a little stress?"

Mom smiled brightly at William Sr. "I find it interesting that you called him a 'boy' in the same breath you implied he should act like an adult."

Her snarky comment sizzled over the dining room table like a firework on the Fourth of July. Liam lifted his head, his eyes darting from his stunned grandpa to his rebellious stepmother. In the silence, the floor clock in the corner chimed once, signaling the half-hour mark. William Sr. wiped his mouth with a napkin, then stood and shuffled from the room without uttering a final word.

Mom nodded at my plate. "Eat up. Your friend will be here soon."

For the rest of the meal, Mom and Hank talked about their day. Then, the topic inevitably turned to football and the dreaded, at least by me, Homecoming dance in early October.

"Do you two have dates yet?" Hank asked, with a stupid grin on his face.

Liam could ask any girl, and she'd say yes, even if it involved dumping her current boyfriend. Everyone at the table knew I wouldn't be going.

"When I was in high school, sometimes a group of us went together to dances," Mom said, the memory lighting up her face. "Usually, it would be all girls, but boys went with us a few times. It was so much fun. There wasn't any obligation to find a date. Just a bunch of friends having a good time."

I sighed louder than I intended to and immediately felt guilty when it shut down her reminiscing. But my mom was no quitter, and my lack of enthusiasm wouldn't stop her from trying to improve my teen years.

"We'll buy you a dress just in case," she said firmly before turning to Liam. "Does your suit still fit you?"

Liam blinked slowly at her. "I'm sure it does, Nora." A thump sounded from under the table, and he winced. Rubbing his shin, he scowled at his dad. "I'll try it on tonight," he added.

She nodded, satisfied. "Good. But at the very least, we should get you a new shirt and tie. We don't want the pictures to look exactly like last year's."

Fat chance, I thought. He'd never taken the same girl twice to a dance.

"So, birthday boy, got any big plans for Saturday night?" Hank asked Liam. "I can't believe you're going to be eighteen. Legally an adult. Old enough to vote."

"Old enough to be drafted," I mumbled, and Mom clicked her tongue at me.

"Hey, that's right," Hank said. "You'll have to register for selective service. I should go with you. Your grandpa went with me. It's a Clark tradition."

Liam didn't look thrilled at the suggestion. "I'm pretty sure I can do it online."

Hank's face fell. "Really?"

Mom drained her water glass and then gathered her dishes. "If you're going out Saturday night, remember we're having a family dinner at six. You're free to be with your friends after that."

"No drinking," Hank said sternly. "I can't have my starting quarterback suspended."

Hank was wasting his breath. Liam and Sawyer had planned a party and bonfire at Sawyer's house, and drinking would be the number one activity.

"I got homework." Liam pushed away from the table, ignoring his dad's warning and leaving his dirty dishes.

My stepfather seemed to deflate, his face and shoulders drooping. After the sound of Liam's feet pounding up the steps faded, I picked up his plate.

Hank forced a smile and shook his head. "That's OK. I'll bring everything in when I'm done."

"Mom will want the dishes now." I stacked as many as I could carry and headed for the kitchen as Hank reached for a second helping of lasagna.

***

Zoe and I were busy finding the area of various geometric shapes when Liam slipped past the dining room's archway.

"Hi, Liam!" she sang out.

I thought he would ignore her, but he reappeared in the doorway. "Hey, how's it going?"

"Good, but it would be better without geometry homework." She pushed away her math book. "Like I'm ever going to need to find the area of a trapezoid. It's just stupid."

He leaned a shoulder against the wall and crossed his arms. "You have Bailey for a teacher?"

Zoe ran her fingers through her long blonde hair and let it fall down her back in a shimmering wave. She wore a black crop top and low-riding gray sweats, though with the dining room table in the way, Liam could only see how the top showed off her "assets."

"Yeah, he seems nice," she said. "Did you have him?"

He nodded. "He let me do extra credit so that I'd pass."

"That's cool of him."

I drummed my pencil on my notebook, impatient to finish our assignment and get Zoe out of the house.

They locked eyes for a few more seconds before Liam flashed his "sexy" grin and continued to the kitchen. It was the nicest he'd been to anyone since the afternoon on the lake.

"He's so yummy," Zoe moaned, her body going limp in her chair.

I pretended to gag. "You don't know him."

"Sure I do."

"No, you don't. You only see what Liam wants you to see: the star athlete, the polite guy around grown-ups, the flirt. He *appears* to be a great catch, but that's not the real him."

"I don't expect you to like him," she said matter-of-factly. "He's your brother."

"Stepbrother."

"Same thing. I don't get along with my brother and sister. We fight all the time."

"I'm just saying you could do better."

"Like who? There aren't that many good-looking guys at our school."

Tired of the topic, I moved on to the next math problem. But Zoe still wanted to talk.

"Are you going to Sawyer's on Saturday for Liam's birthday?" she asked.

I snorted in disgust. "No."

"Why? Sawyer's parties are a blast."

"I don't like parties."

Her face clouded in confusion as if I were speaking an unknown language, once again proving that I had no business trying to be friends with my classmates.

"I think you should go with Isabel and me. Everyone will be there."

"That's another reason why I don't want to go."

"Please?" When I remained stubbornly silent, she suggested, "How about you go for an hour, and if you aren't having fun, you can leave."

I was about to refuse again, but then I realized it would give me a chance to talk to Isabel about all of Sawyer's bad points. I only saw her at lunchtime since we had no classes together.

"OK, sure," I said.

"Great!" Zoe wiggled a happy dance in the chair. "I can't wait."

"What can't you wait for, Zoe?" Hank asked as he entered the dining room.

She gave him an innocent smile. "Homecoming, Dr. Clark. It's always so much fun."

He walked to the china sideboard against the far wall, squeezing her shoulder as he passed us. After he rummaged in one of the cabinets and pulled out a bottle of Scotch whiskey, he said, "That's what I like to hear. School spirit is very important. Maybe you can talk this one into going to the dance."

"What? Why aren't you going to the dance?" Zoe asked wide-eyed.

I dropped my head onto my geometry textbook in defeat. It was as if she hadn't heard anything I said about not wanting to go to Sawyer's party.

"Because I don't want to," I whined into the book, leaving a spot of spit on page twenty-three.

"I bet if someone asked her, she'd go," Hank offered. "Do you know anyone without a date, Zoe?"

"For sure!" she replied. "Who do you like, Rose? I'll tell them to ask you."

"Oh. My. God. Enough." I lifted my head. "Hank, do you mind? We need to finish this assignment, and it's getting late."

He held up his hands defensively, the whiskey in the bottle sloshing with the motion. "So sorry. I didn't mean to interrupt." He winked at Zoe. "I'll take my nightcap into the living room."

She giggled and whispered, "I always liked your dad. He's so chill with everyone."

Stepdad, I thought to myself, not bothering to correct her out loud since nothing I said seemed to sink in.

{ 12 }

WILLIAM SR.

Wednesday, September 6

Much to my annoyance, the police chief failed to end the investigation into the paddleboarder's drowning, so Liam had to meet with the district attorney and jump through his hoops. David would pay for his incompetence, but I had yet to decide how.

As I waited for the boy outside the high school, I scrolled through the latest comments under a news story about the accident. Most were bloated condolences for a person they had never met, but that was how it was nowadays. Everyone farted their moronic thoughts into the air for the rest of us to smell.

My thumb froze above one addition from Sunday night. Fury surged through my body, hammering every muscle and nerve. I struggled to catch my breath as I reread it. Some bonehead had accused my grandson of murder, though he only said, "a careless boater." But matching Liam to the crime wouldn't take much brains. Was he the chief's witness, or did I have another person to discredit? Funny how David forgot to mention this comment, instead telling me about the beer-drinking ones.

Before I could read the twenty replies under the allegation, Liam opened the car door, and I shoved my phone into my pocket. "You're late. I've been waiting five minutes."

He didn't give me an excuse as he clicked his seatbelt. My jaw clenched at his insolence, but I left it for now and headed toward the DA's office.

"Remember, be respectful and keep your answers short and on point," I told the boy. "Don't offer any extra information."

He didn't respond, seemingly frozen in place, staring straight ahead.

"Do you understand?" My voice came out rough with impatience.

His mouth moved, but I didn't hear what he said—another irritating disadvantage of growing old. I didn't make him repeat himself. The only response he would dare give me was a "Yes, sir."

"Keep to your story, and everything will be fine."

That caught his attention. His head whipped around, his eyes twice their size. "My *story*? You don't believe me?"

I flipped on the car's turn signal and pulled into a public parking lot. "Doesn't matter what I think." I turned off the car and pointed at the entrance to the DA's office. "It matters what he thinks."

Liam pushed the up button at the elevators, and we waited, him with his hands shoved deep into his pockets and his shoulders hunched, and me grinding my teeth at the audacity of the DA to keep pursuing the incident.

I checked my watch. It was two minutes to two o'clock. "We'll take the stairs. The office is on the third floor."

He shrugged, and we found the door to the stairwell. Two flights into the climb, I doubled over, gasping. It felt like a heavy weight had been dropped on my chest.

Liam grabbed my elbow to steady me. "Sir, what's wrong?"

Shaking him off, I pulled out a handkerchief and mopped my brow.

"Should I call someone? Nine-one-one?"

"No, it's nothing. Just some heartburn." I dug half a roll of Tums from my pants pocket and popped two in my mouth. "Let's go. Being late is a sign of poor time management."

I ignored the concern on his face and continued up the stairs.

After checking in with District Attorney Jeff Fisher's secretary, she ushered us to a conference room where a middle-aged man and a younger woman sat in leather chairs at the end of a long wooden table. They stood as we entered the room.

"Jeff." I extended my hand. "Good to see you again. How are the kids and that pretty little wife of yours?"

"Great, thanks for asking. Becca got married this past May to a super guy." The DA was a fit man with faded red hair who spent too much time golfing. Sun freckles and age spots ran rampant across his face.

"Congrats to the newlyweds! Was it a big shindig?" I asked.

Jeff winced. "My new son-in-law is from a huge family. My wallet is still hurting."

I chuckled. "The price of having loved ones, am I right?"

"Yes, you are. And this must be your grandson. It's nice to meet you." Liam stepped forward, and the DA shook his hand. "I've known your grandfather for many years. Williams Bay is fortunate to have such a dedicated leader."

"Yes, sir," Liam said. "And I'm lucky to have him as a grandpa. He's been a great teacher and an inspiring example for as long as I can remember."

Jeff looked pleased, and I realized the boy might have potential as a politician after all. I would have to rethink the next ten years. If I could skip over Hank and give the village leadership to Liam, I would rest easier in my old age.

"William, I don't think you've met Carol Cox." He gestured at the woman to his right. "She's one of our newer assistant district attorneys and will take notes for me today."

I nodded, not bothering to offer my hand, and immediately dismissed her from my mind. The DA was the only one I needed to focus on.

Once we settled around the table, Jeff poured a glass of water from a pitcher and offered it to Liam and me. When we both refused, he took a drink and cleared his throat. Now that the social niceties were done, he seemed a bit uncomfortable, and I took it as a good sign for us.

He opened the folder in front of him. "I'm sorry for making you come in today, but I wanted to clarify a few things from the police report."

"Let me stop you right there, Jeff," I said to take control away from him. "It didn't occur to me before, but should we have brought a lawyer to this meeting?"

It was a lie, as it had occurred to me, but I decided the best thing we could do was play dumb and innocent.

He hesitated. "If you'd feel better with a lawyer present, we can set up a new appointment. It's well within your rights, but I was hoping for a casual discussion at this time."

I crossed my arms, pursed my lips, and pretended to consider my options. "We're here now, so let's see how it goes. We're both busy men, and I would hate to reschedule."

"Good." Jeff turned his attention to Liam. "If you would, Liam, please tell me in your own words what happened last Saturday on the lake."

The boy looked at me, and after I nodded my assent, he repeated the tale he'd been telling all week.

"Do you have any idea why a witness would say your boat's wake made the man fall off his board and contributed to his death?" he asked.

"No, sir. The bay was full of boats, making it super choppy. I was surprised he was where he was. It wasn't safe."

"So, you didn't come racing into the bay and swerve at the last minute?"

"No, sir. We did have to maneuver around several boats, but that's how it always is. I know better than to speed into the bay."

Jeff waited while the young woman scribbled on her pad. When her pen stopped, he said, "One final question, Liam. Were you drinking alcoholic beverages that day?"

I held my hand up to Liam's face to prevent him from answering. "That sounds like a question a lawyer should be present for."

"Off the record then," he conceded.

I dropped my hand and said, "Go ahead, Liam."

"No, sir, I wasn't," he said earnestly. "At my boater safety course, they warned us one alcoholic drink on a boat equals three on land, so it can be more dangerous than driving a car. Besides, I'm only seventeen."

Jeff nodded and reviewed a few more pieces of paper from the folder. Then he frowned. "This is odd. The police didn't take a statement from Rose McCabe. She was on the boat with you, correct, Liam?"

The boy looked at me, and I said, "Yes, she was. Rose is Liam's stepsister."

Jeff tapped a finger in front of his assistant. "Call Chief Wick. Ask if he wants us to get Miss McCabe's statement or if he'll do it."

"Is that necessary?" I asked. "The family and I were hoping to put this tragedy behind us. The kids have been through so much already, and I don't see the girl adding anything of importance."

Jeff's demeanor turned to practiced sympathy, almost apologetic, and I didn't buy it for a minute.

"I understand your concern. I really do. But it's good judicial form to dot the i's and cross the t's." He straightened the papers in the folder before closing it. "We'll leave it right there for now. I'll be in touch if we have any more questions for Liam."

"Great. Always happy to help a fellow government official." I pushed myself out of the chair and looked solemnly at the tabletop. "My heart goes out to the poor man's family. They must be devastated." I raised my head and sighed. "But his death could have been avoided had he bothered to wear a life jacket. Every year, a tragedy like this happens, and people don't learn."

"You're right, William. You are so right." He crossed the room and held the door for us. "Let me show you out."

In the elevator, Liam asked, "Is it over?"

The tremble in his voice stirred my anger; he sounded more like a mama's boy than the man I needed him to be. I turned to scold him but checked my temper when I saw his drawn and pale face in the fluorescent lighting.

"Yes, if your stepsister cooperates," I grunted, stabbing the button for the lobby.

{ 13 }

LIAM

Wednesday, September 6

We hadn't even tasted our pork chops at dinner before Grandpa wielded his fork at Rose.

"The DA wants your account of the paddleboarder accident. Apparently, you neglected to give a statement to the police. They won't close the case until you do."

She froze like a cornered animal, and I almost felt sorry for her. For the most part, she flew under Grandpa's radar, being too insignificant in his world to bother with. She turned a panicky face toward her mom, silently begging for rescue.

Nora patted her daughter's hand. "I'll take Rose to the station tomorrow after school. Will that be soon enough for you?"

Grandpa grunted. "Make sure her version matches Liam's. I want this investigation to end."

"What else would she say?" I asked, searching everyone's expressions. "Do you all think I'm lying?"

Dad and Nora made soothing sounds at me while Grandpa picked at his teeth. Rose shrank further into her chair.

"Truth or lie, it doesn't matter as long as we show a united front." Grandpa sawed off a piece of meat and inspected it, his lip curling with disgust. "I hope your wife learns to cook someday for your sake, Hank."

"Do something, or I will," Nora growled in a low voice to Dad, who was in mid-swallow and started coughing, making him unable or unwilling to stand up for his wife.

I slammed a fist on the table, and the silverware jumped, adding an exclamation point to my anger. "I want to know if you believe me."

Grandpa looked up from his plate with cold eyes. "Stop being so dramatic, Liam."

"This is bullshit." I bolted from the dining room, and Grandpa yelled for me to come back. I was rarely so disrespectful to him, and my feet slowed on the stairs as I considered the consequences. But then, the thought of falling into a drug-induced sleep, void of any nightmares featuring an old man drowning, had me moving again.

{ 14 }

ROSE

Thursday, September 7

I couldn't get out of the car. There was no physical impediment, but as I sat in front of the police station with Mom, my body refused to complete an everyday task: You arrive somewhere, open the door, and climb out. Maybe a tiny part of my brain matter was staging a revolt against the Clark men.

William Sr. told me to parrot Liam. But if he didn't cause the drowning, then why can't I tell what I saw? His account was only a partial truth. Shouldn't the police know he was driving too fast and not paying attention?

Mom turned off the car and reached for my hand. "Listen, honey. Hank and I were talking last night, and for Liam's sake, we want you to repeat what everyone else has said so we can move on."

"We? You mean Hank wants me to." I had to trust Mom wouldn't ask me to lie. Then, a thought struck me. She actually believed Liam—or was making herself believe. How could I tell the difference?

"Hank's worried about Liam, and so am I," she insisted. "We don't want our son's life ruined over an accident. Already, people are being so cruel on social media." She paused and shook her head. "My heart breaks for him."

"I bet the relatives of Mr. Kankos are also sad," I muttered darkly.

She looked confused until she placed the name. "Yes, I'm sure they're grieving. No one wants to lose a loved one."

"He had a wife and kids and a bunch of grandkids."

"It was a tragedy waiting to happen between the rough lake, risky location, and unsafe water practices. How many times have I told you to always wear your life jacket? This is why."

"But Liam was—"

She cut me off with a shake of her head. "Let's not make things worse by muddling the narrative, Rose. You have a tendency to overthink everything. You and Liam were witnesses to a terrible event and nothing more. I want our lives to get back to normal."

And that was the end of it.

{ 15 }

ROSE

Saturday, September 9

Sawyer lived on a defunct farm a short distance outside the village boundary. It was a perfect place for a party as the noise rarely reached his nearest neighbor. The only buildings that remained from the farm's glory days of growing acres of corn and soybeans were a rambling two-story house needing fresh paint and a neglected red barn.

When Zoe, Isabel, and I arrived on foot, the lit-up house resembled a beacon calling the faithful. Despite almost every teenager in the village having one, there were no other cars, only Sawyer's pickup truck parked near the barn. Most everyone walked to parties to avoid being pulled over for a

DUI by the village police, who seldom found any crime to occupy their time during a shift.

"Where are Sawyer's parents tonight?" Zoe asked Isabel as we turned into the long, dirt driveway.

"They had a wedding in Milwaukee. They won't be home until tomorrow," she replied.

Zoe snorted. "I wonder who'll have the bigger hangover, Sawyer or his mom and dad."

Isabel frowned. "My grandma and I drove past here a few weeks ago on garbage day. Their recycle bin was full of liquor bottles, the really big ones."

According to the rumor mill, Sawyer's love of alcohol was genetic, as most of the village considered his parents to be white trash drunks. It was the main reason Hank and Mom encouraged him to stay at our house as much as possible. They had a naïve belief that Liam's morals would rub off on Sawyer. It didn't occur to them that the opposite could also happen.

"I'm sorry," Zoe said. "I shouldn't have laughed. I heard his dad can be really mean when he's drinking. Does he ever say anything about his parents, Rose?"

I hesitated. It was true Sawyer had a grim home life, but I didn't want him to be the anti-hero in Isabel's love story. Instead, I needed the girls to believe he was a creep who would break Isabel's heart the second he got bored with her.

"Listen, I know you both think Sawyer is super hot and...whatever." My brain failed to come up with another positive description, probably to save my stomach a bout of nausea. "But if you heard how he and Liam talk about girls, you wouldn't like it. Neither one of them is worth your time."

I walked several feet, then realized they were no longer at my side.

When I turned, Isabel had her phone against her chest. "Sawyer's texted me some really sweet things this week. Maybe he hadn't found the right girl until now."

"Yeah," Zoe chimed in. "Like you've got to kiss a lot of frogs before you find your prince or princess."

I shook my head. "And what happens when they go to college next fall? Do you think they'll ignore all the new girls and come back here on the weekends to see you?"

Their unconcerned expressions told me I was wasting my time trying to convince them Liam and Sawyer were evil, so I inhaled a deep breath to curb my frustration and kept walking.

"Head for the barn, Rose," Isabel corrected me when I turned toward the house. "I want to dance."

Music poured from the barn's open double doors and every gap in the wooden boards that struggled to keep it upright. Two exterior spotlights on either side of the entrance erased some of the night's darkness. Inside, strings of white Christmas lights formed a pattern resembling a web spun by a sick, or maybe drunk, spider. The floor seemed to be a mixture of dirt and straw over a concrete slab.

Once our eyes adjusted, we found two kegs on ice ringed with classmates in varying stages of intoxication. After filling our red plastic cups with beer, Isabel and Zoe headed for the middle of the barn, where people were dancing. I begged off, saying I needed the bathroom and couldn't wait any longer. It was only a partial lie. The first part of my plan for the night was to find Liam and Sawyer so I could keep tabs on them. The second part was to pee before the bathroom was used for everything but peeing. The third part was to stay sober and head off anything Isabel and Zoe would later regret.

The house wasn't as crowded as the barn but was as loud due to the music blasting from the living room. I asked a few people in the kitchen if they had seen Liam or Sawyer. Liam's last known whereabouts ranged from an upstairs bedroom to the trampoline outside. No one knew where Sawyer was. After dumping my beer into the sink and filling my cup with water, I headed upstairs.

The bathroom was unoccupied, so I took care of business. When I opened the door, Liam was leaning against the wall with his eyes closed. In the unguarded moment, his misery was as tangible as the sharp stench of cheap alcohol currently overpowering his body spray.

"Hey," I said, and his eyelids rose to half-mast.

"What are you doing here, Mouse? You're too good for parties."

"I came with Zoe and Isabel, and I never said that."

"But you act like it." He lifted a bottle of whiskey to his lips and downed a good ounce of the amber liquid. "Are you guys the Three Musketeers now?"

"Hardly. They're—" I almost said they were only using me to get to him and Sawyer, but he didn't need to know that. He already thought I was the most pathetic thing on Earth.

He took another long drink and burped.

"Are you OK?" I asked as his eyes stumbled around my face, unable to focus.

"I'm great. It's my eighteenth birthday." His tongue tripped over "eighteenth," making him sound like a toddler.

When he started to take a third drink in less than two minutes, I reached out and pulled the bottle away from his mouth. "Maybe take it easy and pace yourself. It's still early."

"Now *you're* going to tell me what to do?" He choked out a laugh. "Shit."

"I just thought passing out on your birthday before ten o'clock wouldn't be fun. But, hey, go for it."

"That's the whole point of this." He waved the whiskey in a lopsided circle. "To get lit and black out." He pushed past me. "I gotta piss."

I called out his name as he closed the door. When he hesitated, I quickly said, "I get that you don't like me, but if you want to talk about...stuff, I'm here."

The door opened a few inches.

"What did you tell the police?" he asked, his face hidden behind the wood slab.

"What everyone else said." The words tasted terrible, like I imagined guilt and remorse would.

He slammed the door the rest of the way.

***

That went well. I waited in the hallway for a few minutes before giving up.

"Good talk," I muttered, wondering why I had even bothered to be nice to him.

I paused halfway down the stairs to scan the living room for Sawyer. Word must have spread to the other three high schools in the area, as I didn't see anyone from Williams Bay. The strong, musky smell of weed filled the air, and someone had turned up the bass on the music. The thump, thump, thump drilled into my head, making me wince with each beat.

I decided to check on Isabel and Zoe in the barn, so I headed for the kitchen and the door to the backyard. As I reached for the doorknob, someone tapped my shoulder.

"Hey, Rose. What's up?"

I stared blankly at Chris, the hottie from the library who I woke with my crying. Kill me now. Liam and Sawyer talked trash about him all of the time, but he sat two rows behind me in my Current Events class and seemed really nice. Also, his participation in discussions proved he read more than sports blogs—a big bonus in my world.

"I'm Chris," he enunciated as if I were simple.

"I know who you are." My eyes darted to the left and right. "Why are you talking to me?" I blurted out.

"Just being friendly?" he answered in a mystified tone.

I cringed, feeling like a complete idiot. "Sorry. Forget I said that."

He smiled, and I noticed his slightly crooked front tooth. The imperfection added to his attractiveness, somehow making him more approachable. He was taller than Liam by a few inches, and his warm blue eyes matched his T-shirt. His dark blond hair was buzzed short, and matching stubble covered his chin and cheeks. When he shoved his hands into his cargo shorts pockets, I wondered why he wasn't holding a red cup like everyone else.

"I've never seen you at a party before," he said.

I appreciated that his tone was curious rather than mocking. "Not really my scene."

He nodded. "Totally understandable."

"But it was Liam's birthday, so…"

"Eighteen. He must be stoked."

I thought of the misery on Liam's face in the upstairs hallway. "I guess."

"Are you heading to the barn?"

"I don't know. I mean, maybe. Yes, probably. Eventually." I pressed the heel of my hand to my forehead and breathed in and out deeply. "I'm looking for Sawyer. Do you know where he is?"

He let out a short, humorless laugh. "No, I avoid him as much as possible."

"Then why are you here?"

"Fear of missing out?"

"Ah, the bane of our generation."

"Exactly."

"I should probably keep looking for Sawyer." I gestured behind me with my thumb.

"Sure. Guess I'll see you in the barn when you run out of"—he looked into my cup—"water."

My insecurities hit me like a gut punch. I didn't belong at a party, and Chris now knew it. But then he leaned in and whispered, "Your secret is safe with me."

***

After taking a detour through the backyard, I found Zoe and Isabel playing beer pong with two varsity football players in the barn. The girls were losing with three cups on their side of the long table, while the boys had nine. When Zoe saw me, she squealed and hugged me until I risked suffocation.

"You can play next," she slurred.

"That's OK. I'd rather watch."

Isabel closed one eye to aim before tossing the ping-pong ball at the boys' cups. It flew to the right of the table and rolled into the darkness, not even close to the cup she was trying to hit.

"Oh, Izzy, you're so bad," Zoe moaned.

"I can't help it, and you're no better," Isabel pouted. "Let's go dance."

We pushed our way into the mob of sweaty bodies in the middle of the barn. Someone had put on a classics playlist, and the Go-Go's were singing *We Got the Beat.*

When Isabel sang, "Everybody get on your feet," at the top of her lungs, I was both impressed and optimistic that maybe I had found some friends with whom I had something in common. I loved the eighties, and when Zoe twirled me around, I forgot my awkwardness and let the music take over my body. We danced for several more songs until our thirst sent Zoe and Isabel to the nearest beer keg and me to the house for water.

***

Back in the barn, I spied Sawyer and Isabel pressed together as they climbed the ladder to the loft. When his mouth nuzzled her ear, she tossed her hair and laughed, and for a breath-stopping moment, they teetered backward before regaining their balance. I didn't need to be popular to know what would happen when they reached the top. Sawyer's loft was legendary.

My thumbs beat out an urgent text to Liam saying that Sawyer needed him at the ladder to the loft. I figured he was more likely to react to a plea for help from his friend than me. If he did, though, I didn't know how to convince him to help me. All I knew for sure was that I was going up that ladder, and, hopefully, Liam would be with me.

But first, I had to make it through the dancing crowd. I waded in and emerged on the other side with stomped-on toes and a damp shirt, looking like I had run through a beer sprinkler. After a quick prayer to the Universe, I grabbed a rung, but a male voice from behind held me in place before I could lift a foot.

"Where's Sawyer? I thought he needed me."

I turned to see my highly intoxicated yet still glum stepbrother had exceeded my expectations.

"Forget that. Come up to the loft with me," I replied.

"You aren't my type, Mouse."

A counter-insult popped into my head, but I shoved it away. I needed him more than my pride needed soothing. Instead, I went with, "You have to save Isabel."

His head wobbled as he squinted into the darkness above us, his body swaying unsteadily. His carefully unkempt hair was matted down on one side, and I wondered if he had been with Tara.

"If you go up there, you don't need saving. Just fifteen minutes of privacy."

"Sawyer took her up there, and she's totally drunk," I shot back. "Do you want that on your conscience? Because I don't."

Liam cursed loudly. "I'm so sick of that dude."

"Then help me." I resisted the urge to shove him at the ladder. "Please. We're wasting time."

"Whatever."

His feet slipped on the first few rungs before muscle memory took control of his drunken brain. I waited until he was halfway up, wondering what I would do if he fell, and then followed him.

At the top, I crawled forward and felt coarse pieces of straw under my palms. The illumination from the Christmas lights didn't reach this high, but the flashlight beam from Liam's phone revealed two bodies intertwined in a hay pile.

Sawyer's raised hand blocked his eyes, and I heard the last part of what was probably a long string of swear words from his mouth.

"Mouse thinks Isabel shouldn't be up here," Liam said, making me the chief fun killer.

Sawyer sat up, and Isabel rolled off his chest and settled deeper into the hay. Her hands searched the air around her. "Where'd you go?"

"Maybe Mouse should mind her own business." Sawyer patted Isabel's thigh, and she giggled. "She seems to be having a good time, and if she wanted to leave, she could."

"She can barely walk," I said. "And I'm not letting her stay up here with you."

"Reel your sister in, bro. Her holier-than-thou attitude is ruining my buzz."

"Stepsister," Liam and I said in unison.

Then he floored me by saying, "But she's right. Isabel is lit, and it isn't cool of you to take advantage of her."

Sawyer burst out laughing. His body rocked with each snort until he lost his balance and collapsed beside Isabel.

"There you are," she exclaimed in a sing-song voice. "Where have you been?"

He struggled to sit up. "Whew. Thanks for that." He wiped his cheeks with his sleeve. "I haven't laughed so hard since we got high at the beach and convinced that freshman there were alligators in the lake. Because, you see, *you* lecturing *me* is pretty damn funny."

Liam's neck and shoulders tensed under his T-shirt, and I worried he would bail on me if we didn't wrap up this crisis soon. So, I moved toward Isabel to see what Sawyer would do.

He pointed his finger at me. "Not so fast. Don't you want to know what kind of person Liam is?"

I shook my head. "I have ears and eyes. I doubt you could tell me anything new."

Sawyer kept going anyway. "I think he's secretly jealous of me. Now that he's eighteen and can't be a slut, he doesn't want me to have any fun either."

"You're being a dick," Liam said in a raspy voice.

Sawyer deflected the insult with a lift of his chin. "How many girls have you taken up here? Ten? Fifteen? Twenty? And they were all drunk. You're no better than me."

I tried to check Liam's reaction, but his face was in the shadows. Deciding I was on my own, I closed the distance to the hay pile and pulled Isabel to her feet.

"I don't feel good," she mumbled.

"Then let's go for a walk outside." I guided her to the ladder but had no idea how to get her to the floor below.

"Give her to me." Liam lifted Isabel into his arms as if she weighed nothing and shook her once.

Her head flopped against his chest, and she squinted at him. "You're not Sawyer."

"At least you got that right," he sighed. "Hold on to my neck, Isabel, and don't you dare puke on me."

He headed to the rear of the loft. Feeling triumphant, I gave Sawyer the evil eye, then hurried after my stepbrother toward a staircase hidden by the darkness.

Liam carried Isabel to the firepit, where a few people roasted marshmallows. After he set her on the ground butt first, she tipped over and curled up as if ready for bed.

"You're on your own now," he said, freeing himself from any more responsibility. "Good luck."

Before he could sulk away, I grabbed his arm. "Thanks. I appreciate your help."

The flickering firelight cast shadows on his face, making his scowl more intimidating than usual. "Whatever. Just don't bug me for the rest of the night. It's my birthday, you know."

"Yeah, happy birthday," I said to his back as he disappeared into the darkness.

{ 16 }

LIAM

Monday, September 11

Ms. Taylor walked between the lab tables, handing out the anatomy quizzes from last Friday. Occasionally, she smiled at a student and said, "Good job." I hunched over and rested my chin in my palm, sure I had failed.

When she got to me, she placed my quiz face down. "Please see me after class, Liam."

Sawyer snickered, and I twisted in my seat so I wouldn't have to look at him. He was full of attitude because of Saturday night in the loft, and spending all day together wasn't helping either of our moods.

The bell rang, and everyone else rushed to be first in the lunch line. Sawyer pretended to trip so that his backpack smacked my shoulder.

"Dick," I muttered under my breath.

He retaliated by coughing "Prick" into his hand. For the first time ever, I wished I was on defense instead of the quarterback so I could slam him to the ground during football practice.

Once the room was empty, Ms. Taylor took Sawyer's seat. She studied my face as the noise in the hallway drifted toward the cafeteria, and my stomach reminded me it was lunchtime.

Was I supposed to do or say something? I'd never had a teacher treat me this way before.

She let out a long sigh. "What's going on with you?"

"Sorry?" The question came out sarcastic, my go-to reaction when I was nervous.

"Come on, Liam." She turned over my quiz and tapped it with a fingernail painted cherry red. An image of her nails raking my back had me crossing my legs. "Your grades aren't great, but an F is beneath you."

"I…I didn't have time to study. It won't happen again," I assured her, suddenly worried she'd tell Dad, and he would suspend me from football.

"I'm sure it won't." She leaned in and rested an elbow on the table. "What are you and Sawyer fighting about?"

Her breath smelled like mint, and her musky perfume clouded my brain, which made a useless attempt to figure out why she cared about my social life. Trying to act both cool and surprised, I raised my eyebrows and asked, "What do you mean? We're solid."

She slowly shook her head, rejecting my words. "I grew up with three brothers. I know when someone's got their jockstrap all tangled up."

For a moment, I considered telling her about my miserable life: the fear of being arrested over what I may or may not have done, the pressure of keeping Sawyer in line, and my overall failure as a Clark. She'd probably get it since she wasn't much older than me, unlike if I told a real adult.

But instead, I said, "Just a misunderstanding. It'll blow over."

"Huh." The concern in her eyes changed to disappointment. "If you say so. But I'm here if you need someone to talk to or want some tutoring." She stood and smoothed the wrinkles from her skirt. "Can you help me retrieve a box from the storage room? I promise it won't take your whole lunch hour—unless you want it to."

Confused by what seemed to be happening between us, I froze in my seat. If she were one of the girls in my class, I would swear she was flirting. But she was a teacher, so I had to be mistaken, right?

On her way to the door, she stopped and asked over her shoulder, "Are you coming?"

Then she winked.

***

This past summer, Dad found me on the couch looking bored, so he made me organize the school's main storage room by grouping all the educational materials by the names on the labels. When I was done, each teacher had an island of stacked supplies they would use throughout the year. But when Ms. Taylor flipped on the overhead light, there wasn't even a clear path from one side of the room to the other. Teachers had rifled their piles and left unneeded supplies wherever they had landed during their search.

"It's a mess, isn't it?" Ms. Taylor said with her hands on her hips. "I think my stuff is still over here."

She headed to the far right corner of the room, and I obediently followed. After zigzagging and pushing a few things out of the way, we stopped at her island of boxes. She bent over to examine the labels, and her blouse shifted, flashing the lace edge of her red bra and a good amount of cleavage. I forced myself to look away, though the view was as good as expected.

"Here we go." She pointed to an oversized carton with ACCU-SCOPE printed in black letters on its sides. "Can you grab it? But be careful. It weighs a ton."

I moved a few things and then squatted to lift the box.

Her eyes appraised my body, igniting every nerve below my waist. "Wow, you're strong. I had to ask that nasty secretary to help me carry it when it was delivered." She started toward the door, picking her way left and right, her three-inch heels making her unsteady. "Tell me if you get tired and need to rest. Your dad wouldn't be happy if I broke the star quarterback—or my new microscopes, for that matter."

I sucked in a breath and let it out slowly before following her. As we walked through the halls, she talked nonstop about our next anatomy unit and what we'd examine under the microscopes I carried. None of it registered because even though I was legally an adult as of Saturday, I was still a teenage guy, and Ms. Taylor was quickly becoming my number one fantasy.

"I'll have to store the box in the back room for now," she said when we reached her classroom. She grabbed a ring of keys from a desk drawer and unlocked a door leading to a small room. A counter ran around its perimeter, and cabinets and drawers filled the spaces above and below it. "Hmm, I guess you'll have to put it on the floor for now."

As I carefully lowered the microscopes where she pointed, I heard the door shut behind us. When I turned, she said, "Oh, look. I got you all dirty."

She pulled a paper towel from the dispenser above a sink and wet the edge before rubbing at a spot on my cheek.

"There, that's better," she said in a soft voice that left me useless. The drumming of my heart muffled the click of her high heels on the tile floor as she shifted so that our noses almost touched. "Thanks so much for your help."

I tried to swallow, but my mouth was dry. Usually, if I was this close to a girl, I was in control and knew what to do, but Ms. Taylor made me feel like a virgin. Using one of her long fingernails, she nudged aside a piece of hair that had fallen over one of my eyes, and then, just like that, she stepped away and smiled knowingly.

"You'd better get to lunch before they stop serving." She held the door open for me, and I stumbled from the back room. "Liam," she sang out, stopping my retreat and raising my hopes for something I knew was wrong. "Don't forget your backpack."

{ 17 }

HANK

Friday, September 15

I hadn't checked in with the new teachers since the first day of classes, nearly two weeks ago. Even though it was Friday afternoon and all of the veterans were long gone, I figured some of the rookies would still be around, and I was right. When I peeked into Madison's science room, she was studying numerous papers scattered across her desk.

I rapped lightly on the door jam. "Hi, there. Do you have a minute?"

She smiled when she saw it was me. "Of course, Dr. Clark." Her hand flew to her lips. "Sorry. Hank."

I chuckled. "I thought I'd make the rounds. See how you're doing now that you have a few weeks under your belt, so to speak."

She blew out a long breath and motioned for me to come in. "Things were going great until I compared my lesson plans for next week with the ones your previous science teacher left behind for my biology class."

I couldn't stop myself. At the mention of that woman, I lost my civility and grimaced in disgust.

Madison arched an eyebrow at my reaction. "She was really that bad?"

"You have no idea. The havoc that woman tossed around like candy…" I closed my eyes and shuddered. "Anyway. What's the issue?"

"Well, I hate to admit it, but biology is my weakest subject of all the sciences. I thought her notes might help me, but they are hard to follow, and I don't understand the sequence of the material she presented. She taught genetics before the basics of cells, and even *I* know that would be incredibly confusing to a student." She motioned at the chair next to her desk. "Do you have time to take a look?"

"Of course. Anything to help." I took a seat, and our arms brushed as I leaned in. After reading what she pointed at with a pen, my hatred for the former teacher doubled. "I had no idea she wasn't following the prescribed curriculum."

"Are you any good at biology?" The corner of her mouth turned up in a hopeful, crooked smile.

My face grew hot. "I am more comfortable with English, history, and current events. Science was never my forte, sadly."

"Shoot. Then I guess I'll spend my nights memorizing the textbook."

"I'm sure your boyfriend will understand. It's for the good of the children, after all."

"No worries there. I don't have a boyfriend. It's just me and Daisy, my cat."

I made a "pfft" sound. "I can't believe that. Any young man would be lucky to date you."

"Maybe that's my problem. The guys my age are so immature." She shifted her bare leg, and I felt the warmth of her body through the cloth of my pants.

I tensed for a moment, unsure if I read her right. Deciding there was only one way to find out, I laid my arm on the back of her chair and leaned in farther. When she didn't move away—or slap me—I said, "Let's study the material together. Two heads are better than one."

She rested an elbow on her desk, and as her fingers played with a lock of hair, I imagined sinking my hands into her thick mane. She wet her lips and opened her mouth to speak, but a knock on the door interrupted her answer.

"Ms. Taylor?" a familiar voice said.

I quickly dropped my arm from Madison's chair and shifted my body away from her.

Madison seemed unperturbed at my motions or the interruption. "Yes, Rose?"

"I found my chemistry assignment for today. I guess I stuck it in the wrong folder." Rose offered her the paper in her hand.

"Great, but I still have to consider it late and deduct five points." Madison pointed with her pen at a wire basket on the corner of her desk. "You can put it in there."

Rose sniffed as she turned in the homework, and I suspected she was trying not to cry. As a straight-A student, being punished was foreign to her. She caught my eye but left without another word when I remained silent.

My shoulders slumped with guilt for not intervening. Liam and Rose knew not to expect special treatment from teachers because of their relationship with me, but Rose was a good kid and a bit of a social misfit. I didn't like seeing her sad.

"Now, where were we?" Madison asked, her voice full of all kinds of invitations. When she slipped off a heel and stroked my calf with her painted toes, thoughts of Rose flew from my mind, and my body perked up.

I slid closer to her. "I think we were talking about biology."

{ 18 }

ROSE

Thursday, September 21

I read through my English essay for a final time and then clicked Print. As I waited for the printer to spit out the pages, a car door slammed, and then another. My bedroom faced the street, and I saw Mom and William Sr. coming up the walkway from the window. Good. I had hoped she'd be home in time to correct my essay before dinner.

I left my room but stopped at the top of the stairs when I heard their loud voices.

"I don't care what you and your cronies think," Mom declared. "The village is growing, and the services must keep pace."

"And where will the money come from for a new fire station?" William Sr. demanded. "You want your taxes raised?"

"If it will guarantee my house won't burn to the ground, then yes."

"The village board won't support another referendum. I'll make sure of that."

"Then maybe the board needs some new blood. *Younger* blood."

"If you want a big city, go back to Chicago. Don't let the door hit you on your way out."

"Are you senile? That makes no sense. Building a station that can house the fire trucks and meet the firefighters' needs does not change the idyllic feel of Williams Bay."

"First a fire station, then a McDonald's, then a Walmart."

With Mom on so many committees, she and William Sr. often disagreed on the village's future. I started downstairs, hoping my sudden presence would end their argument, but in the next breath, the fight turned uglier.

"Oh, for heaven's sake. That would not happen, and you know it. And you would love for me to leave your son, wouldn't you?"

"I didn't like Hank's first wife. She was a flighty hippy who spent all day thinking she was some great artist, but at least Lily wasn't a home-wrecker."

Mom gasped at the insult. "You have no idea what you are talking about. Their marriage was over long before I came to town."

"You *would* think that," William Sr. said dryly. "Lily was blindsided when she found out Hank was having an affair with you."

I sank to the landing, unable to believe what I had heard.

"That's not true." Her voice shook as she added, "You're lying."

"Am I?" he challenged. "My son is weak. He can't pass a candy counter without taking a taste. In fact, I bet he has a sweet little thing on the side right now. Ask him. I dare you."

"I don't have to. I trust my husband—even if you don't. You're a hateful, bitter old man who loves interfering in people's lives. I swear I'll end your control over this family."

William Sr. laughed. "Good luck trying. My boy won't be able to stand up to me even when I'm dead."

Mom yanked open the front door and slammed it behind her. A minute later, her car started, the engine revving angrily before the sound faded as she drove away. William Sr. chuckled as he limped into the living room.

I wrapped my arms around my trembling body, unsure what to do. Part of me wanted to charge after William Sr. and demand he take back his lies about Mom and Hank, but I also wondered if they were true. I had seen how Hank acted with other women and had assumed he was unaware of his overly friendly creepiness. But if William Sr. was telling the truth about his son, then Hank's intentions were despicable.

My phone vibrated with an urgent message from Zoe asking for homework help, and I swore softly. The vile old man downstairs and Mom's marriage problems would have to wait.

{ 19 }

LIAM

Thursday, September 21

Tara's hand stroked my stomach as we lay on her bed. Her parents were at a play, so she had all but begged me to come over. We were breaking their rules by being alone and in her bedroom, but Tara loved to be a bad girl.

She snuggled deeper into the crook of my arm and sighed. "Do you want to fool around?"

I looked away from my phone and the displayed stats for our opponent tomorrow night. The Pirates' defensive line weighed almost twice as much as ours, which meant I would be on my backside most of the game. The Williams Bay Bulldogs flat-out stunk. Maybe I should have tried harder to convince Grandpa to let me go to a bigger high school. I might have gotten noticed and been offered a football scholarship. But the Clarks bled orange and black. Woof, woof. End of discussion.

"I'm good." It wasn't what she wanted to hear, but I didn't feel like doing anything else. Lately, I barely had the energy to get out of bed in the morning.

She ran a finger above the waistband of my shorts. "Are you sure I can't change your mind?"

"We've been over this," I said evenly, trying to control my temper. "I'm eighteen now, and you're only fifteen. If you want to hang out with me, we have to keep it legit."

She propped herself up on one elbow and faced me. "I've been with older guys before. They never cared about my age."

Her pouting lips made her look about twelve, the opposite of the effect she was going for. "Did any of them have a homicide charge hanging over their heads?"

The line between her eyebrows deepened. "You said your grandpa took care of things, and it was over."

I shrugged. "Probably, but the DA could still file charges if they wanted to. Either way, I don't need any more attention from the police."

"I think dating a convict would be cool. We could have conjugal visits, and you'd be so fired up to see me." She ran a hand up my thigh, attempting to do just that.

"Are you fricking kidding me?" Maybe she thought it was funny, but I wasn't amused.

"What?" she asked defensively.

"Do you think my life is a joke? Do you think I like having people call me a spoiled brat and a murderer behind my back?"

She flopped back on the bed and crossed her arms. "I was only trying to make you laugh. You're so crabby all of the time."

"Sorry my bad mood over my sucky life is interfering with your fun." My tone was mean, but I didn't care.

She threw her hands in the air. "All I'm saying is you used to want to do more than what we're doing right now, which is nothing. I miss the old Liam. Girls have needs, too, you know."

I sat up and swung my legs off the bed. "I gotta go."

She grabbed a handful of my shirt and pulled. "Don't. I'm sorry. We can do whatever you want to do."

I shook my head at her. "I want to go home."

"Please, Liam, stay." She batted her eyes at me. "I'm OK with only making out."

But I knew she wouldn't be satisfied. Kissing would lead to other things. Then her parents would catch us, and because they didn't want Tara dating an older guy, I'd end up talking to the police—again.

"I'm going. See you tomorrow."

{ 20 }

ROSE

Saturday, September 23

From inside the fitting room, I heard Mom's footsteps and the rattle of hangers. She stopped in front of my door. "Here, honey, I found more for you to try on."

I gathered my rejects and hoped this new batch would have a winner. So far, Mom and I had disagreed on everything from style to length to color.

We exchanged dresses, and I quickly discarded two, leaving four possibilities. After wiggling into the one I liked the best, I critiqued it in the three-way mirror. It was simple and not terrible. Maybe it would be good enough for Mom.

"Do you have one on? Can I see?" she asked.

I opened the door, and she nodded after having me slowly twirl.

Relieved, I considered the sleeveless sheath dress again in the mirror. Overall, the fit was good, and the burnt orange didn't wash me out like some of the other colors I had tried on. The classic neckline made me feel safe, and the above-the-knee length kept it from looking too old ladyish.

Mom pinched and tugged the material here and there. "I think this one was on sale. It's a little on the plain side, so let's jazz it up with some jewelry. Maybe gold tones would be best."

"Are you and Hank happy?" I blurted out, watching her reflection. Her body stiffened, and I swear there was panic in her eyes.

"Why…why would you ask that?" She lifted the dress's hem and inspected the stitching, though she knew nothing about sewing.

The fight I had overheard between William Sr. and her was the only thing I had thought about for the past two days. If Hank couldn't be faithful, Mom had to leave him. But how did I bring up something I shouldn't know? I checked the price tag under my armpit to stall.

The right words wouldn't come, so I backpedaled. "No reason. It's just a question."

After a few moments of awkward silence, she turned away and said to the corner of the dressing room, "Then, yes, we are happy."

If she hadn't hesitated, I might have moved on. But she had, so I countered with, "You don't do stuff together like you used to."

Her laugh sounded forced. "Once football season ends and some village business is settled, things will return to normal. You know that fall has always been a busy time for us."

"Do you want them to return to normal? Do you like being married to Hank?"

"Yes, of course." But her voice was too bright, and she was still talking to the corner instead of me.

"And he loves you?" It was the closest I could get to asking her about William Sr.'s insinuations about past and current affairs.

"We wouldn't be together if he didn't." She pushed aside the clothes I had thrown on a small bench and sank onto it. "Some day, you will understand that marriage is work. Anyone who tells you differently is lying. Hank and I are committed to each other."

It seemed Mom was also committed to overlooking Hank's flaws—ones I had witnessed over the years and now understood more clearly, thanks to William Sr.

"You don't love him, do you?" she asked in a resigned tone.

I stared at my toes, unable to truthfully answer without hurting her. Hank had always been nice to me, but I had no strong feelings toward him like I did for my real dad. Sometimes, when I thought about all the special moments Dad and I had missed and wouldn't share in the future, I wanted to scream until I was hoarse.

Mom absently rubbed her palms together slowly. "I had hoped you would one day consider him your father, but I know I can't force that. It has to come from you."

"I've tried," I whispered, hating that I'd disappointed her.

"And I appreciate the effort." She stood and wrapped her arms around me before loosening her hold and kissing my forehead. She swiped a thumb under one of my eyes. "Is this why you have dark circles? You're worrying about Hank and me?"

It was the perfect opportunity to tell her it was that and much more. Maybe if I confessed what I really saw the day of the paddleboarder's accident—that Liam's reckless driving did cause the wave that led to the man's death—then I could sleep. Every night, the guilt of lying to the police, combined with Hank's unforgivable behavior, kept my mind spinning until exhaustion finally took over. But again, the words weren't there.

I shook my head. "School's really hard this year. I'm worried about my GPA."

"Oh, honey. No one but me will care about your high school achievements a few years from now. And please don't worry about Hank and me. We're doing great." She smiled, but her eyes shined with tears. As she opened the dressing room door with one hand, she swiped at her cheeks with the other. "Let's get this dress and hit the shoe and jewelry departments. And maybe cosmetics to find something to hide those dark circles."

{ 21 }

WILLIAM SR.

Saturday, September 23

I was trying to find a snack, preferably something salty and against my doctor's orders, when Nora and her daughter came in the backdoor loaded with packages.

"More pillows and candles?" I asked with a hefty dose of sarcasm.

The woman's answering glare made me chuckle. I rummaged some more in the pantry and found some Oreos. Sugar would do. I wasn't supposed to have that, either.

The daughter had pressed herself into the far corner of the kitchen. What did Liam call her? Mouse? It was fitting.

"Please take this stuff upstairs," Nora said to the mouse. "If you don't have any homework, I could use some help with dinner."

The mouse added her mother's shopping bags to her own, and I resisted the urge to yell "Boo!" as she scurried past me.

I shoved a cookie into my mouth. "What's for dinner?"

Nora's back was to me as she pulled dishes from the cupboard, and her body tensed at my question. "Spaghetti and a salad."

"So, nothing good."

She pointed at the stove. "You are welcome to cook something else for yourself."

"Where's my son?" I asked between cookies.

"I don't know. Maybe he's with his mistress. You'd like that, wouldn't you?"

"You misunderstand me. I'm on your side."

She turned around, a look of sheer disbelief on her face. "How do you figure that?"

"My family has run this village from the start. When I die, it will be Hank's turn. But I can't have my legacy in the hands of a self-indulgent man who strays and a cowardly wife who lets him. Hank needs to shape up. And whoever his wife is when he takes over must agree to the future I have planned for Williams Bay."

"And that's not me?"

I let my shoulders rise and fall, feigning my lack of control over the situation. "Whether it is or not is entirely up to you. Back off on all your highfalutin proposals and allow those in charge, mainly me, to make the decisions."

"Wow. You know that you and your buddies are supposed to be doing the will of your constituents, right?"

"The majority of the people in this world are stupid. It's up to men like me to ensure the correct things are done. Otherwise, society will fail."

"Do you even hear what you are saying? You are such a narcissist. And also, did you ever consider if you hadn't belittled Hank his whole life, he would be more self-assured and meet your expectations?"

"My father, a war hero and the toughest man I ever met, treated me the same way, and I turned out fine. Hank's faults are his own doing. I advise you to spend your energy on your husband instead of the village. Then he won't step out on you."

Near tears, she shook a trembling finger at me. "I want you out of this house and back in your own. You can hire a nurse until your hip is healed."

"No. I think I'll stay for a while longer." I had unfinished business; the closer I was, the better. "And don't bother complaining to Hank. My boy will always side with me."

I left her red-faced and blubbering, banging pots and pans on the stovetop. As I slowly made my way to my recliner in the living room, I sensed movement on the stairs. I didn't pay any attention to it, though. I didn't care about a mouse with big ears.

{ 22 }

ROSE

Saturday, September 23

Entry from the Journal of Rose McCabe:

Today, Mom and I bought a dress for the stupid dance. I wanted to talk to her about everything that's been bothering me but chickened out. I think I was afraid of her reaction. I couldn't handle her disappointment in me for not telling the truth about the accident or, conversely, siding with the Clark men and agreeing that Liam's story was for the best.

She claimed her relationship with Hank was great, but I could tell she was upset. Then, when we got home, William Sr. said horrible things to her, and I heard her crying.

Mom's deadbeat boyfriends used to make her cry, and now her husband and his father were doing it as well. I'm so sick of men being jerks to her. She doesn't deserve it. And it has to stop.

{ 23 }

LIAM

Wednesday, September 27

My game was way off today. None of my passes hit their mark, and my legs felt like lead. Dad blew his whistle when I tripped over my feet for the second time in the last four plays.

"Take a five-minute break, everyone." He motioned me to his side. "Are you feeling OK?"

"Yes." I stole a water bottle from a passing freshman, took off my helmet, and doused my head.

"Then what's wrong? You haven't played like this since the beginning of middle school."

I shook my wet hair, sending droplets flying, then combed it with my fingers. "Just hot and tired."

"Do you want to go home? I can make up an excuse for you. Maybe a day off would do you good."

"I'm fine."

"No. I think you should go home."

This was typical Dad, never listening to me. Why couldn't he believe me and let it go?

"Hit the showers, and I'll see you for supper." He scanned the sidelines and then called out to my replacement, "Reynolds, you're in at QB."

Everyone stared as I walked toward the endzone and the path to the locker room. There was an unwritten rule: You didn't leave a practice unless you were dead or injured. I was neither, so Dad unintentionally made my life worse by cutting me some slack.

As I passed Sawyer, he said in baby talk, "Oh, does the big, bad QB need a break? Do you have a tummy ache? Maybe your mommy can make you feel better."

Though I curled my fists when he added a rude gesture that would get him punished by any decent mother, I managed to check my temper. At this point, all I wanted was to be alone. If I got into it with Sawyer, Dad would make a stink. So, I kept walking and ignored the laughter from my teammates.

***

Someone yelled my name as I dragged myself through the school parking lot. I picked up my head, and Ms. Taylor waved at me. She stood by her car, which had its hood open.

"Can you help me, Liam?" she called out. "The stupid thing won't start."

I dropped my backpack and gym bag next to the white sedan. Here was another expectation I couldn't meet. As a guy, I was supposed to be mechanically inclined, but I only knew a few basics, like how to change a tire or jumpstart a car.

"Does it make any noise at all?"

"Click, click, click," she mimicked. "What does that mean?"

I pretended to examine the engine. "Maybe a dead battery."

"I have jumper cables. Could you jump me?" I don't know what my face did, but she burst into laughter. "Sorry. Let me be more specific. Could you jump my car?"

"Hold on a sec. You may not need it. One of your battery cables is off." She peered around me as I reconnected it and checked the tightness of the other connection.

"Huh," she said with a cute tilt of her head. "Does that happen often?"

"Yeah," I mumbled with little conviction.

"I'll see if that fixed it." She slid into the driver's seat, pushed the start button, and the engine turned over. "Woo hoo! Thank you so much."

I closed the car's hood and picked up my bags. "Glad to help. See you tomorrow, Ms. Taylor."

"Wait. Are you doing anything right now?"

I shifted uncomfortably. "Heading home."

"Are you hungry? I was going to get takeout and sit by the lake. It would be nice to have some company. I haven't met anyone my age since I moved here." When I didn't immediately say yes, she added, "You're eighteen, Liam. It's totally legit. Just two friends sharing a meal."

What the hell, I thought. It wasn't like she was asking me to have sex. I nodded. "Sure. How about burgers? We can go to Skips."

Her face lit up. "Hop in."

I opened the door behind her to throw my bags in the back seat but stopped. "I'd better meet you there. My dad sent me home early from practice. If he sees my Jeep in the parking lot, he'll worry something happened to me."

"OK, but don't stand me up, Mr. Clark," she warned.

I wouldn't dream of it, I thought as I trotted to my car.

***

We found a bench under a willow tree near the shoreline of Geneva Lake. As it was the middle of the week and late September, only a few fishing boats were in the bay. The water was as smooth as glass, quite different from the last time I was here. Almost a month had passed since the paddleboarder died, and I had managed to avoid the place until now. Suddenly, I didn't feel like eating.

"Is something wrong with your burger?" Ms. Taylor asked when I put it down without tasting it.

"No, I'm sure it's fine." I sipped at my soda, hoping that would stop her questions.

Her forehead wrinkled as she studied me, and then she hit it with the palm of her hand. "I'm sorry, Liam. I forgot about the boating accident. I should have asked if the lakefront would upset you. Is there somewhere different we could go?"

I shook my head. "It's OK. I live here and have to get over it."

To prove I could, I took a large bite of my burger and shoved a few fries into my mouth.

"Growing up by the lake must have been fun. Did you come here often?" Ms. Taylor asked.

"Every day in the summer unless I was playing baseball. There's nothing else for a kid to do in this town."

She laughed at my grumbling. "You don't know how fortunate you were because this is beautiful." She sighed, then added in a serious tone, "And deadly. I never thought it fair that nature was both."

"My grandpa says people don't respect the lake, and that's why they get into trouble."

She nodded as she sipped her soda. "Your grandpa is a wise man."

I didn't agree with her because there were plenty of days I didn't think he was.

"So, I understand you're part of a dynasty. Descended from the great Captain William Israel Clark."

I swept my arm like an actor in a bad play. "Yup. This will all be mine someday."

"You don't sound happy about it."

"I'm not." Ignoring the posted sign warning it was illegal to feed the fowl, I threw a fry at some ducks nearby. A beak fight broke out before the winner waddled away with his prize. The others huddled up and advanced on me, hoping for another crack at the prohibited treats.

"What is the plan? Come back here after college and wait for your dad to turn senile or die?"

"That's what my dad did." A wave of misery stirred the greasy food in my belly, and I fought the urge to upchuck. When I felt in control again, I added, "It's OK. Williams Bay is a great place to raise a family. It's quiet and safe, and the schools are solid. There are worse places to live."

"That sounds like your dad and grandpa talking. What would you rather do?"

I stared at the lake and imagined a life I couldn't have. "First, I'd go to college in California."

"That's about as far away from here as possible."

"That's the idea."

"What would you study?"

"I don't know. I never thought about it because I don't have a choice."

"Your dad seems like a pretty nice guy. Is this what he wants for you?"

I shook my head. "He's not in charge. Grandpa runs the show."

"But it's not fair to you, Liam. You need to speak up, or, if you want, I could talk to your grandfather with you. I'm sure we could convince him to let you do what you want."

I imagined what Grandpa would say the second Ms. Taylor opened her mouth. It wouldn't be polite, and it wouldn't be clean.

"I'd better go." I crumpled up my garbage and stuck it in the food bag. "Someone assigned a load of anatomy homework due Friday."

Instead of laughing, she seemed worried. "My offer for tutoring is still open. If you need it."

"Thanks, Ms. Taylor, but I'm good."

"Liam? Would you call me 'Madison'? I mean, when we're not in class."

"Sure. I can do that," I said with a shrug. "See you tomorrow."

As I walked away, I thought she looked sad sitting alone on the bench. But how could she be? She was out of school and on her own. I'd trade places with her any day.

{ 24 }

ROSE

Monday, October 2

Entry from the Journal of Rose McCabe:

I have to talk to Steve today. I wasted several days getting the guts up to talk to Jenna, and now I'm running out of time. Hank has to be exposed for the loser that he is, and the pep rally this Friday is the perfect opportunity. No more chickening out.

***

The boy, wearing low-slung jeans and a gray hoody, came out of detention and drifted aimlessly down the hall.

Swallowing my fear, I called out, "Steve?"

He ignored me, so I tried again."Steve, please, can I talk to you?"

Maybe it was the "please," but he stopped and turned around. I pulled out a twenty-dollar bill. "I heard you can get me what I need."

His head snapped back and forth, looking for anyone else in the hallway. "Jesus, are you crazy?" he hissed. "Put that away."

Confused, I shoved the money back into my pocket.

Swearing under his breath, he grabbed my arm and hustled me into a unisex bathroom. "Who told you that?" he demanded.

I shrank against the wall, putting as much distance as possible between us. "Jenna. She's in my gym class."

Jenna was uncoordinated like me but made up for it by being artsy. Since seventh grade, she had been in all the school plays, often as the lead. Her sense of style changed daily, frequently mashing genres, and her backpack sported the Grateful Dead's Steal Your Face skull patch. I had been sure she'd have the connections I needed.

His eyes narrowed as they took in my preppy clothes. Shaking his head, he said, "No. Raid your parents' medicine cabinet or ask them to take you to a doctor."

"It's not like that. This is a one-off. Sell me what I need, and I'll never bother you again."

He pinched the bridge of his nose and growled. Then, after a moment, he gave in with a shake of his head. "Fine.

But I'd better not regret this. Depending on what you want, it may take a few days. I'm only the middleman. Is that cool?"

"I think so. I was hoping to have it by Thursday night."

Steve ticked off the days on his fingers. "That should work. What do you need?"

I hesitated, suddenly worried about what I was doing. "No offense, but is your dealer or whatever reliable? What I get won't be laced with anything bad, will it?"

"Bad? You understand you're buying illegal drugs, right?"

"Yes, but I mean like Fentynal. Isn't that the stuff that everyone overdoses on without realizing it?"

"My product is good. My source makes sure of it."

"How?"

"Let's just say she has a background in science."

"She?" I asked, surprised. The entertainment industry led me to believe all drug dealers were male.

"Look, do you want to buy something or not? Cuz you're wasting my time."

I took a deep breath and nodded. "Yes. I definitely do."

{ 25 }

ROSE

Friday, October 6

I hesitated by Hank's office door as he was in the middle of a wet, sneezing fit. When finished, he blew his nose vigorously and wiped the tissue across his upper lip to sop up any remnants.

"Hey, kiddo. Hang on a sec. Darn allergies are acting up today. I can barely breathe." He pulled open a drawer, took out a packet of pills, and swallowed three without water. His eyes went to the industrial clock on the wall. "What's up? Shouldn't you be headed to seventh period? You have to check in before going to the pep rally."

"I wanted to give you one of the brownies I made for the Homecoming dance. I felt bad for telling you no last night when you asked."

He laughed. "I'd love one, thanks. I'll save it for after the assembly."

I bit my lip and looked at the plate I held. "OK, but to be honest, I don't know how good they are. Brownies aren't my favorite dessert, so I was hoping you'd try one before I drop them off."

"I'm sure they're delicious, Rose. You worry too much."

"Please? I would feel better with a second opinion."

"I guess I can force myself to eat one now," he said with an exaggerated eye roll.

Using a napkin, I selected a frosted brown square from the top of the stack. After Hank bit into it, I asked, "Well?"

He put on a show, puckering his lips and savoring the gooey morsels as if he were at a fine wine tasting. Finally, he smiled. "They're great. Everyone will love them."

"I can spare another if you are interested," I said, confident he wouldn't refuse.

"Of course I am, but don't tell your mother. I'm supposed to be on a diet." He popped the rest of the treat in his mouth and licked his fingers.

I handed him a second brownie. "You'd better save this one for later. You don't want to have a sugar crash."

He carefully wrapped it in the napkin I gave him and tucked it in his top drawer.

"That's so Mrs. Parker doesn't get tempted," he said with a wink.

The old woman could use some sweetness. She had run the school's main office since Dad was a freshman. Yet, for someone who worked with kids, she had never shown any signs of liking them.

"Good idea," I said. "Well, thanks for being my taste tester."

"Happy to oblige. You can leave them in the conference room with the other refreshments for the dance."

"Will do."

"Go, Bulldogs!" he said with a fist pump.

"Yep. Go, Bulldogs," I echoed indifferently before heading to the nearby conference room.

***

"Hurry up, Rose. The pep rally's starting," Zoe yelled down the hall at me.

I disliked assemblies, as they were never about anything important. But this one replaced Science, so I was all in. Though I didn't mind the subject and always got good grades, I enjoyed English and Social Studies more. And then there was Ms. Taylor. So far, I was not impressed. It was hard to respect someone in their early twenties who still acted like a teenager. She seemed to understand her power over the boys as they sat at their lab tables, drooling over her sexiness, and she indulged them. The only benefit was that she ignored the girls, myself included.

The lights dimmed as we entered the auditorium, which was three-quarters filled, as Hank made any event that promoted school spirit mandatory. From the orchestra pit, the pep band cranked out an unrecognizable song, and on the lighted stage, the football players waited in a loose line with the cheerleading squad in front of them. To fire up the crowd, the cheerleaders took turns shaking an orange pom-pom into the air and yelling, "Bulldogs!"

Isabel had been watching for us and waved us over to her row, where she had saved seats. We chatted about nothing until Principal Walker walked up to the podium.

Walker introduced the football players and the cheerleaders for several minutes, even though everyone already knew them. To end his part of the program, he praised the team's excellent athleticism, ignoring the current season's losing record.

Then, the cheerleaders performed cheers and stunts to "pump up the volume." Considering only half the audience participated, they did a good job. Next, our school's bulldog mascot strutted onto the stage. From the opposite direction, a football player wheeled a cart with a paper mache likeness of tonight's opposing team's mascot. It was supposed to be a panther but looked more like a lumpy black cow.

Our mascot circled the cart, feigning punches and kicks. The students egged him on, some yelling for bloodshed. A baseball bat appeared in Sawyer's hand, and he tossed it to the mascot, who held the bat aloft and pointed to the "panther." When the football players clapped and hooted their approval, the mascot swung the bat at the panther's head. It connected with a loud "thwap," leaving the head hanging limply, attached only by a thin strip of dried pulp.

Next to me, Zoe gasped. Our bulldog continued to pummel the panther until it was beaten flat.

"So, that was violent," I said.

"Who's in the mascot costume?" Isabel asked.

Both Zoe and I shook our heads. "Maybe a student?" I suggested. "I can't imagine a teacher acting that way."

As a football player wheeled away the decimated panther, Hank grabbed the microphone from the podium and walked to the edge of the stage.

"How's everyone doing?" he yelled, striking a rock star pose and causing a burst of piercing feedback from the sound system.

Across the auditorium, hands flew up to cover ears, and I cursed under my breath. A few whistles and "woo woos" answered Hank's question.

Not liking the lame response, Hank tried again. "I can't *hear* you. How's everyone doing?"

This time, about a quarter of the crowd let him know their current status, and mercifully, he was satisfied.

"I hope you all enjoyed Homecoming Week. It's been a lot of fun watching the classes compete against each other and seeing the costumes every day. In a couple of minutes, Principal Walker will announce which class has the most points and will win the coveted pizza party."

This finally excited the students, and Hank held up his hands to quiet them. "I know. I know. Who wouldn't want a pizza party? In fact, I'm starving and could go for a slice right now."

He paced the stage, trailing his fingers through his hair until he looked like he'd just gotten out of bed. "I love my boys."

He pointed the microphone at the football team and patted his chest.

"We love you, too, coach," one of the players called out.

"And can you guess who I love the most on our team?"

The players exchanged uneasy looks.

"My son," Hank whispered into the microphone. Then, louder, he asked, "Where are you, Liam? Come to Papa. Come on, now."

My stepbrother didn't move a muscle, so the players to his left and right shoved him forward.

"There you are. Gosh, I love you. From the moment you were born, you stole my heart." Hank threw an arm around

Liam's shoulders in a smothering half-hug. "You're the best thing that ever happened to me."

Liam's face turned red and furious. His mouth moved, but his words weren't loud enough to hear. I guessed they weren't a tender reply to his father. And, unfortunately for my stepbrother, Hank had more to say.

"This kid." Hank chuckled. "This kid was a terror when he was young. No matter what we did, he would escape the house, strip off all his clothes, and run through the neighborhood."

"He hasn't changed much," I joked, and Zoe giggled.

"Picture it," Hank continued. "His cute little naked butt running down the street."

When his father crouched, his body shaking with laughter, Liam walked off the stage. Gasping for air, Hank stood and wiped his eyes.

"Whew, sorry about that." He looked around for his son. "Where'd he go?"

A loud cough sounded from the wings, drawing Hank's attention. "Right. Moving on, I'd like to be serious for a moment." He looked at the football players. "These young men try so hard, but sometimes it's not enough." He stared at the scuffed floorboards beneath him for a beat before scanning the rows of students. "It's kind of how life is, you know? You try and try and try, but you still end up losing."

The auditorium was deadly quiet now.

Zoe leaned into me and whispered, "What the heck?"

"But not tonight," Hank yelled, and the sound system screeched again. "Tonight, the Bulldogs will not be denied!"

He tossed the microphone and dropped to all fours. Then, barking like a dog, he chased the cheerleaders around the stage. The girls retaliated by swatting at his back with their pom-poms. When one shaker got too close to his mouth, he chomped down on a hunk of the foil ribbons and ripped it away before using his hands and teeth to shred it. The cheerleaders shrieked when he next went after their ankles, nipping and snapping as they hopped about to avoid him.

Nobody did anything at first, unsure if this was a planned skit. But when it became apparent Hank wouldn't stop until he caught his prey, Walker ran out from behind the curtain and tackled him. With the help of Sawyer and another football player, they dragged a howling Hank away.

Principal Walker appeared again, adjusting his mussed-up shirt and blazer. "You're dismissed. Please go to your eighth period if you have one."

"That was weird," Zoe said wide-eyed as we joined the rest of the stunned students slowly filing toward the exits. "I mean really, really weird. I've never seen Dr. Clark act that way."

"It was like he was drunk or something," Isabel added, her voice full of concern. "Which he wasn't, right?"

They looked at me for a plausible explanation for why my stepdad went all rabid dog on the cheerleaders. But I had no intention of defending him.

I ducked my head, pretending to be embarrassed. "We'd better get to class."

{ 26 }

HANK

Friday, October 6

"What the hell was that, Hank?" Ray stood behind his desk and pointed at the wall.

I shifted in the chair reserved for disobedient students sent to the principal's office, and my gaze traveled his outstretched arm to the tip of his accusatory finger. His rigid posture and tight jaw made it apparent he was angry, but I wasn't sure why. My eyes narrowed at the wall filled with his credentials, and I wondered what it had done to offend him.

I ran my tongue across my teeth and realized all my spit was gone. Was there a disease that robbed you of making saliva? And could it come on suddenly? It better not be some kind of cancer. I wouldn't look good bald.

Paranoid, I raised my hand to check if I still had my full head of hair and hit myself with a water bottle. Thank God, but where and when did I get it? I drank half of the bottle without pausing, but it did nothing to wash away the dry, cotton ball taste in my mouth.

I gingerly touched a painful spot on my forehead and found a lump the size of a small stone. Adding to my confusion, bits and pieces of the pep rally circled in my mind like a kaleidoscope, coming together and then splitting apart. Ray seemed to be waiting for my explanation, but I had no idea what to say.

Realizing I couldn't answer his first question, he tried another one. "Are you OK? Do you need to go to urgent care?"

I fingered the lump again and shook my head, wincing as the pain spiked with the movement.

"Hank, do you remember what happened? With the cheerleaders? Your fainting?"

I fainted? That explained my head wound. Cheerleaders? I didn't want to know.

I drank more water, cleared my throat, and croaked out the first thing that came to mind. "Antihistamine."

"What?"

"I think I took too much allergy medicine. I feel really out of it." I never had a bad reaction before, but I needed to offer him something.

He crossed his arms and studied me.

"I also skipped lunch," I added in a moment of inspiration. "Maybe that's what did it."

"OK." He sat heavily in his chair and beat out a nervous rhythm with one finger on the desktop. "I guess that's as good of an explanation as any. Hopefully, the school board won't get wind of this incident, and we can put it behind us, but you know how gossip travels in the village."

Ray Walker was a townie like me, though he had been in sixth grade when I was a freshman. Technically, I outranked him as the school superintendent, but we always discussed issues and considered each other good friends.

"I appreciate your discretion, Ray." I stood to leave, but as I turned, the room dipped. I grabbed the back of the chair for support.

"Are you sure you don't want to see a doctor?"

I started to shake my head but remembered it would result in self-inflicted torture. "I'll go put some ice on it. That should be enough."

He studied me some more, his finger continuing the woodpecker impersonation on his desktop. I assumed he was weighing the school's liability and his role in my mess against our friendship.

His hand stilled, and he gave me a resigned smile. "If you change your mind, I can drive you."

I let out the breath I was holding. "Thanks. I appreciate it."

***

The staff lounge was empty, except for our newest addition, Ms. Taylor. Sorry, Madison.

She leaped from her seat on a worn couch that had seen better times. "Oh wow, did you hurt yourself?"

"You weren't at the pep rally?" I asked hopefully.

"No, I was grading papers." She moved toward the communal refrigerator. "I'll get you some ice. That bump looks nasty."

I plopped into the nearest chair and rested my head in my hands. "I have no idea what happened. I feel so out of it. Like I'm all tingly, but my body also feels so relaxed. I could go to sleep right here. Maybe I didn't eat enough today? Or I caught a virus?"

After cracking ice into a dish towel, she pulled a chair opposite me. When she sat, our knees touched, and neither of us moved to break the contact.

"Here, let me see." She leaned in and held the makeshift ice pack on my lump.

My eyelids sagged in relief as the cold deadened the pain. When I opened them a moment later, her face was inches from mine.

"Huh," she said.

"What? What's wrong?"

She pursed her lips as she stared for a few more moments. "Nothing. I'm surprised, that's all."

"About what?"

She took the ice pack away, and I immediately regretted it. I guided her hand back to my forehead. "About what?" I repeated.

She smiled as if we were conspirators. "That you would get—"

"Ooh la la, look at how cozy you two are," the school's French teacher said as she entered the lounge, startling us.

She was a fussy, birdlike woman in her early sixties who made a musical language like French sound like an untuned piano missing half its keys. Every June, I hoped she would turn in her retirement papers.

"Don't stop what you're doing on my account." Her shrill voice scraped against my eardrums.

"Madison was helping me with my injury," I said sternly to recapture my authority.

She snickered and patted Madison on the shoulder as she passed on her way to the coffee pot. "Don't worry. As the current flavor of the month, you'll only have to put up with his extra attention for a short time. Our superintendent is easily bored."

Madison made a rude face behind the teacher's back before offering me the ice pack. A giggle worked its way up my throat, threatening to worsen the situation. I quickly swallowed it and concentrated on holding the ice against my wound.

As we silently waited for the French teacher to leave, my gaze fell to Madison's full chest, but then the soft blues, greens, and purples of her silk blouse caught my attention. The blended colors didn't form a strict pattern, reminding me of an Impressionist painting. I got lost in their beauty until her voice broke my trance.

"Hank? Hank? Did I get you into trouble?" Madison rested a hand on my thigh.

I rubbed my eyes and sighed. "Don't worry. She's a busybody. Nobody listens to her."

"How are you feeling?"

"Like the world's turned upside down. Maybe I should go home and take a nap before the game tonight. I want to be my best for the boys."

"Good idea. Try to drink lots of fluids as well."

"Yeah, and I'm starving. I hope Nora has something planned for dinner. I don't think a concession hot dog will cut it."

"Nora?" Madison raised a thick eyebrow.

I hesitated, realizing my shaky allegiance to my spouse was now exposed. "My wife."

"Yes, of course," she said with a tight smile. "I assumed you were divorced—since you don't wear a ring."

Several soft raps on the lounge's door saved me from further discussion on that awkward topic—but only momentarily.

"Come in," I called out.

Rose opened the door, and her face hardened as her clever eyes took in the two of us sitting knee-to-knee.

Madison slowly removed her hand from my leg and shifted back in her chair.

"Hey, kiddo. Hi. Um." My brain sputtered and twirled as it searched for a coherent gear. "What's up?"

"Sorry to bother you," she said in a tone that didn't sound regretful. "But Mom didn't answer her phone, and I wanted to go shopping with Zoe and her mom. I need a few things for the Homecoming dance."

"Mom?" Madison repeated. Her eyes flicked between Rose and me as they tried to discern any family resemblance.

"Rose is my stepdaughter. You probably didn't realize that with the different last names and all. I've been married to Nora for what, five years now? Almost six? Though we knew each other when we were young. She used to summer in Williams Bay." Realizing I was rambling, I clamped my mouth shut.

Madison nodded slowly. "Guess I'll have to brush up on the history of this town. There seem to be a lot of families related by marriage or blood. Reminds me of the mafia."

"That's a good one," I laughed until I started to choke. Madison reached forward and thumped my back several times. When I could talk again, I quickly said, "Back to your question, Rose. Yes, you can go. Do you need any money?"

"No, I got it covered."

"Who's your date?" Madison asked, and I cringed, knowing how sensitive of a subject it was for Rose.

"I'm going with Zoe Smith," she answered in a flat voice, her annoyed expression making it clear it was none of Madison's business.

Perhaps Madison didn't pick up on Rose's irritation because she continued the conversation. "You know, I thought you two were together. You make a cute couple."

Rose's pale skin turned the color of a cooked lobster, reminding me of my hunger. "We're not dating. Zoe's a friend."

Madison placed a hand over her heart. "Oh, my bad, but good for you. So many kids buckle under the pressure of dating and trying to be popular."

"See you at dinner, Hank." My stepdaughter spun on her heel, copying one of her mother's often-used mannerisms, and disappeared.

I blinked a few times, staring at where my stepdaughter had been. When she didn't reappear, I switched my gaze to Madison, who looked as pretty as ever.

"I should drive you home," she said firmly.

This time, I accepted the offer. "That would be great."

She took hold of my elbow and helped me to my feet.

"Wait. Do you hear that?" I asked.

She cocked her head and concentrated on the quiet room. "Hear what?"

"Someone's calling my name," I whispered.

She listened again. "I don't hear anything."

I held up a finger. "There it is again. Yep, just what I thought. It's the brownie Rose gave me earlier. I left it in my desk drawer, and it's calling, 'Hank…Hank…'"

"Argh," she groaned with a laugh. "You are horrible."

"I have to retrieve it. Otherwise, Mrs. Parker will eat it. I've never been able to prove it, but I think she searches my office when I'm not there."

"That's awful! She certainly doesn't deserve a sweet treat."

"I'll split it with you. I had one before the pep rally, and it was delicious."

"Thanks anyway, but I'm limiting the sugar in my life."

"I could never do that. I'm pretty much addicted to chocolate. You must have a ton of willpower."

"Not really. I find other things to give me pleasure," she explained with a playful twitch of her lips that revved my imagination.

After stopping at my office, we continued to the parking lot. Madison cracked terrible dad jokes on the way, and by the time we got to her car, tears ran down my cheeks. I dried them with my sleeve and realized that, despite whatever I had done at the pep rally, it had been a long time since I had laughed so much.

{ 27 }

WILLIAM SR.

Friday, October 6

Nora was visibly irritated when I told her I needed to ride with her and her daughter to Liam's football game. Usually, I would take my own car, but I hadn't slept well last night, and fatigue was catching up with me. It wouldn't do for the village president to fall asleep at the wheel and have an accident.

We rode in hostile silence on the way to the high school, which was fine by me. After Nora said she wanted me to pack my bags, I overheard Hank and her fighting. I was still sleeping in the guest room, so as I predicted, my son chose me over his wife.

The parking lot was almost full when we pulled in. With the Bulldogs' losing record, only the players' parents and the mandatory pep band usually endured the frigid hours in the stands. But since it was homecoming, and there would be a half-time show, everyone and his brother had shown up.

"Drop me off as close as possible." I pointed at a secondary road that ran to the equipment shed behind the concessions stand.

Nora mumbled something under her breath as she passed the remaining free parking spaces. After crawling through several groups of fans also using the road, she pushed too hard on the brakes, and the car lurched to a stop. My seatbelt pinned me to the leather seat, and I instinctively fought against it.

With a satisfied smile, she asked, "Will this do?"

"Typical woman driver," I snarled before opening the door and pushing myself out. I stuck my head back in and added, "Don't leave without me unless I say you can."

When she stared dully at me, I slammed the car door.

I started for the home team bleachers but detoured to the concession stand, where the police chief and the high school principal huddled. They were dressed in warm coats, knitted hats, and gloves for the October night temperatures and held steaming drinks in styrofoam cups.

"Hello, Principal Walker. David," I said energetically, grinning and shaking hands. I wrapped my scarf tighter around my neck. "It's going to be a nippy one tonight."

Despite my pleasantness, David looked uncomfortable, though he offered me a cautious smile. He had avoided me since Liam's and my visit with the DA, and his instinct served him well. I had finally cooled down to the point where I could be civil to him, but the police chief soon would find out the penalty for his incompetence. The village board had finalized the budget for next year, and he was in for a surprise.

"Can we beat the Panthers?" I pretended to study the players warming up on the field.

"I hope so," Walker said. "It's been a tough season, and it sure would boost the team's morale. Is Liam fired up?"

I wagged my head. "He most certainly is. That boy loves to compete. It doesn't matter what ball is in his hand; he's ready to play."

"Just like his grandfather, huh?" Walker looked wistful. "Except for the basketball team ten years ago, our student-athletes haven't had much success since your day. I guess kids have other priorities now."

"TV and computers," I grunted.

Both men nodded, their solemn expressions more appropriate for a funeral than a sporting event.

"Well, I want to give the boy a few tips before the game starts." I mimicked throwing a football, and they laughed.

"Get yourself some hot chocolate first. They might run out," Walker advised as I limped away.

"Will do," I answered with a wave. "Talk to you after we win!"

I didn't say goodbye to David.

***

Liam was taking snaps from his center, so I stood in his line of sight and waited until he joined me on the sideline.

"I'm glad you came, sir." His warm breath released clouds into the October night air.

I poked him in the chest with one finger. "You'll have to be a leader to beat this team. Can you do that?"

"I'll try." He said it with conviction but didn't look me in the eyes.

"Don't try." Frustration hardened my voice. "Just do it. You have to have the right attitude. Show those farm boys what a Clark can do. They may be big, but they're also slow. Use that to your advantage."

A whistle blew, and the dread that flashed across his face told me I had wasted my time. I pushed him toward his team, which was lining up for the national anthem. "Tear out their throats, Bulldog."

On my way to a seat on the fifty-yard line, I greeted several families and even held a baby. My presidential term ran for another year and a half, but it was never too early to campaign.

***

The halftime score had the Panthers up by four touchdowns. When the Bulldogs exited their locker room, they walked to the field with their heads hanging.

"Come on, men. Hustle!" shouted an assistant coach at the rear of the group, but only Liam picked up the pace, and I could hardly call it running.

Disgusted, I climbed down from the bleachers and caught my son by the arm, ignoring the two assistant coaches flanking him. "Hank, you haven't taught these boys a thing. It's an embarrassment. We're getting slaughtered."

"Everyone is doing their best," Hank said, sounding exhausted. His bloodshot eyes drooped as if he might fall asleep where he stood. "I'm proud of them for not giving up under adverse conditions."

"Are you seeing the same team I am? Because what I see is a bunch of babies who need their diapers changed."

"Please, sir, lower your voice. Their parents will—"

"Ach." I cut off his begging with a wave of my hand. "Tell Liam to keep the ball and run every time. Your wide receivers are too scared of being hit to be of any use to you."

Hank sighed. "Thank you for the advice."

"It's not advice," I snapped. Before I could lay into him some more, his face blurred, and my body broke into a sweat despite the forty-degree temperature.

"Sir, are you OK?" he asked, sounding farther away than the few feet separating us.

I rubbed a gloved hand across the sudden tightness in my chest and took several painful breaths to relieve it. "I'm fine. Go lose your football game."

{ 28 }

LIAM

Friday, October 6

Sawyer crossed his arms, leaned forward, and spat in the middle of the huddle. "What's the plan, QB?"

I glared at him and his cocky attitude. He had dropped eight out of the ten passes I had thrown to him in the first half. He was either having the worst game of his high school career or hated me so much that he didn't care about losing in front of the whole school.

"I don't know." I scanned the sidelines and found Dad sitting on the athletic trainer's table with his head down. He wasn't even holding his clipboard anymore. A few feet away, the assistant coaches, whom we all called glorified waterboys, stood arguing. "I think we're on our own."

"What's wrong with your dad?" a freshman guard dared to ask me. "He was a total nutjob at the pep rally. I had an uncle who—"

I scowled at him, and he shut his mouth.

"So? What's the play?" Sawyer taunted. "We're almost out of time."

"I can see the scoreboard." I took a deep breath and randomly picked something from memory. "We'll do that Hammer Counter Run that we practiced last week. On three."

My former best friend snickered. "Awesome. Are you going to be the hero now?"

I dug my fingernails into my palms. The play required me to keep the ball and run through a hole created by the offensive line. "Maybe if you could catch a pass, it wouldn't be all up to me."

Sawyer's face hardened, and his hands curled into fists. Knowing what would come next, I squared up my body, but then the idiot freshman guard moved to the middle of the huddle, his bulk filling the space between us.

"Wait, Liam, I don't remember that play," he whispered.

"Just fricking line up and block your man." I clapped my hands. "On three."

Five seconds later, I was on my back behind the line of scrimmage. The freshman who was supposed to protect me offered me his hand, but I knocked it away.

Sawyer laughed as we huddled up again. "Perfect execution. Way to go, QB. What's next?"

Enough was enough. I punched him in the stomach with everything I had. He doubled over, and when he found his breath, he lunged for my throat. Whistles blew, and everyone—except Dad—came running from our sideline, but I didn't care. I got in several more shots before we were pulled apart.

The head referee pointed at us. "You two, you're out. Hit the showers."

"Hey, ref, come on," one of our assistant coaches begged. "Our team is getting crushed. The boys needed to let off some steam."

The referee set his jaw. "They're gone. Now."

I picked up my helmet, which Sawyer had ripped off at some point, pushed through my teammates, and trudged to our locker room. Inside, I dropped onto the bench in front of my locker and rested my head in my hands.

A few moments later, Sawyer came slamming in, cleats clicking loudly on the concrete floor. His locker was near mine, so I slid to the end of the bench, giving him plenty of room. He started to strip off his uniform and pads, so I did the same.

Finally, I couldn't take it anymore.

"How can you still be mad at me?" I demanded. "You're with Isabel. What happened in your loft on my birthday didn't stop you from eventually getting what you wanted from her."

Sawyer huffed. "Maybe after all these years, I'm tired of the Liam Clark show."

"What are you talking about?"

"Everything either falls your way or off you like Teflon. You don't get good grades, so the hot new teacher offers to tutor you. You kill a guy on a paddleboard, and your grandpa smoothes it over with the police. You turn eighteen, and suddenly, I'm a predator for doing what you've been doing to girls for years. Everyone thinks you walk on water. You *never* get into trouble. You do the same stuff I do, but I'm labeled trash and a bad influence. I'm sick of it."

I jumped to my feet. "I didn't kill that old man!"

He looked me straight in the eye and nodded. "Yes, you did. Not on purpose, but you weren't paying attention because you spilled beer in your grandpa's precious boat. You were mad at me for having to go to work and ruining your fun. You took your anger out on the boat and were going too fast. Tell yourself whatever you want so you can sleep at night, but it was your fault."

My body started to shake, and I landed hard on the bench when my legs gave out. "What are you going to do?"

Sawyer grunted. "I'm going to take a shower."

{ 29 }

ROSE

Saturday, October 7

"Pizza's here," Hank called out before opening my bedroom door without permission.

A half-dressed Zoe shrieked and dived behind my bed.

"Hank! What the heck?" I grabbed the pizza box and pushed him into the hall. "We could be naked in here."

"Aach! Stupid me. I wasn't thinking." He stuck his head over my shoulder and leaned into my room. "Sorry, Zoe. You OK?"

"Yes, Dr. Clark. Thanks for dinner," she answered from her hiding place.

"Do you girls need anything else?" he asked.

"We're good." I closed the door before he could embarrass me more and set the pizza on my bed. "He's gone."

Zoe stood up and adjusted her strapless bra. "He's so goofy."

I frowned at the door and then locked it. "That's one word for him."

Zoe had come over so we could get ready for the homecoming dance, which I had no interest in attending and was having a hard time not feeling grumpy about. Despite what happened at Liam's birthday party, Isabel was still dating Sawyer. They were going out for dinner and meeting us afterward at school, where the dance was being held. Liam was going stag, and my insecurities told me that was why Zoe was in my bedroom in her bra and underwear and not because she was my friend.

She helped herself to a slice of pizza, settled against my bed pillows, and assessed my room. "Hey, when did you move here? It was before middle school, right?"

"I was ten, so fourth grade. We moved from Chicago after my mom married Hank. My real dad died, but maybe you already knew that."

"Yeah, the village loves to gossip." She pointed at a picture on my nightstand of a younger me in the arms of a smiling man. "Is this your real dad?"

I nodded. "I was six. My mom took it the day he left for Iraq."

I turned away and fiddled with a glass paperweight on my desk.

"I'm sorry," Zoe apologized. "I didn't mean to upset you."

"It's OK," I lied. "It was a long time ago."

"Was he a soldier?"

"No, a contractor that worked with the military. He was super smart, but I don't know exactly what he did."

"*That's* where you got your brains from." Zoe took another bite of pizza and then asked between chews, "Do you get along with Dr. Clark, like when he's being your stepdad?"

I reached for a slice, though the conversation was killing my appetite. "I don't know," I said cautiously. "My mom doesn't seem to have the best taste in men. She dated some real losers after my dad died, and I'm not sure Hank is much better."

"What were the other guys like?"

I blew out a breath and settled cross-legged on the foot of my bed. "The first guy I remember didn't have a job, so he slept on the couch all day and drank all night. The next one also drank a lot and fought with my mom all of the time. The last one cheated on her several times. She kept taking him back until the day she noticed him staring at me."

"Wow." Zoe's eyes bugged out. "Like he was a perv?"

"I guess." I picked off a tiny piece of mushroom that had made it to my half of the pizza and wiped it on the inside cover of the box.

"What was your real dad like?"

"He was big, like tall and muscular. We played a game where he pretended to be a giant. He'd throw me over his shoulder and fake-bite my legs. But he traveled a lot. My mom would be sad, and then he'd come home, and she'd be smiling and in a good mood. We'd go on picnics at this nearby park and then to an old-fashioned candy store, where they'd buy me whatever I wanted. I remember laughing all the time when we were together."

"That sounds nice." Zoe finished her slice and picked up another one. She was quiet as she chewed the first few bites. Then she said matter-of-factly, "I hate my stepmom, but I don't have to see the witch much since my dad moved to Florida with her."

"Did your mom want the divorce?" I asked.

Zoe used to live in a similar two-story house in our subdivision. After her parents split up, her mom rented a run-down cottage next to the highway that led into town. I never thought about how hard it must be for a single-parent family to afford our affluent village until I overheard Zoe tell Isabel on the boat about her mom working overtime.

"I think so. My dad was having an affair with the witch. She's not even thirty years old. My mom says she's only after his money."

My admiration for Zoe's mom skyrocketed. She chose a harder life over putting up with a horrible partner. "I can't stand it when men cheat."

"Yeah, you've made that clear."

My head shot up, but Zoe smiled, defusing my reaction.

"I don't understand," I said, trying to explain my anger. "If a guy wants someone else, he should break up with his partner and move on. Why does he have to make things worse by cheating?"

"My mom says it's all about sex."

"What? Like he's not getting enough from his partner and needs more?"

"No. She says sex is like a menu to them. They get tired of ordering chicken every night, so they go out and find some steak or pasta."

"But that hurts the person they supposedly love."

She shrugged. "They don't think it's a big deal because it doesn't mean anything to them."

"Well, it meant something to your mom because now you don't live with your father, and he's married to a steak instead of a chicken."

"I guess. My mom told me not to let a man treat me like that when I got older."

"Then, why do you like Liam? Because that sounds exactly like him."

Zoe slowly shook her head and gave me a sympathetic look, indulging my inexperience with guys. "He's hot, and I'm not looking for my soul mate. Besides, it would totally wreck Tara—and someone needs to bring that girl down a few notches."

"If Liam and Tara were serious, they'd be going together tonight. My mom pressured him pretty hard to take a date since it's his last Homecoming dance."

Zoe's face lit up. "So, I still have a chance?"

I laughed. "I guess. If Liam's who you want, go for it."

"Does he ever talk about it?" she asked softly.

"About what?" But I knew what she meant.

"You know. The accident with the paddleboarder."

I stood and circled the bedroom, finally picking up a Rubik's cube that had belonged to my real dad. Mom had given it to me on a rainy Saturday when we still lived in our apartment in Chicago. She had pulled several boxes of his stuff from the storage room and cried as she went through them. A few months later, she married Hank. Liam and I both sulked through the ceremony, neither wanting our families to officially unite.

My fingers worked the cube, turning the rows round and round, pretending to concentrate on the puzzle. "Nobody talks about it, especially Liam. It's like it never happened. He and William Sr. met with the district attorney, and I gave a statement to the police, and that was it. But he's been a total ass to me since that day—I mean more than he was before."

I stopped short of telling her about the family dinner where William Sr. ordered me to tell Liam's account of the accident to the police. The guilt ate at my insides and robbed me of sleep. I should have told Mom what really happened, but I feared Liam would be right and all of our lives would change for the worse, not just his. I should have been stronger, like Zoe's mom.

"Sometimes people lash out when they're hurting," Zoe said, breaking into my thoughts. "I didn't even see the man fall, and I've had bad dreams about the whole thing. Maybe Liam needs counseling."

"If he does, he won't get it. William Sr. would never allow it," I said bitterly, not bothering to hide my resentment toward the old man.

"That's so sad."

"Yeah. Anyway, can we talk about something else?"

"OK. How about this? You really don't have a crush on anyone?" she asked with a sly smile.

Chris popped into my mind, but then I collapsed onto the bed with a loud groan. "No. No. No."

***

The dance started at eight o'clock, so at seven-thirty, Zoe and I descended the stairs to squeals from Mom and wolf whistles from Hank. Mom and I had picked out a chunky gold necklace and matching earrings for my new dress, and Zoe wore a mid-thigh strapless black dress in a stretchy material that hugged her body. Large silver hoops hung from her ear lobes, and she tottered on stiletto heels. She had done an intricate braid in her hair, winding the tail into a bun, and then used a hot iron to add loose waves to mine.

"Pictures, we need pictures. Where's my phone?" Mom patted the back pockets of her jeans and then ran into the kitchen. "Found it! Do not leave this house until I get proof of how beautiful you both are."

"Where's Liam? Isn't he ready yet?" Hank asked. When I didn't answer, he yelled, "Let's go, Liam. Picture time."

My stepbrother clomped down the stairs, wearing sharply pressed khakis, a sportscoat in the colors of a fall forest, a starched white shirt, and a dark green tie, all bought after Mom rejected his clothes from the last dance he had attended. His hair had just the right amount of messiness so no one could accuse him of conceit, and his trademark scowl told everyone he thought the night would be lame.

Next to me, a starry-eyed Zoe seemed blown away by Liam's appearance. He did look good, but he was still a jerk.

"Are you sure you don't want to wear dress shoes?" Hank asked.

The only thing Mom hadn't approved was the high-top sneakers Liam wore.

"Never mind," Hank said when Liam gave him a dirty look.

Leaving his self-appointed throne in the living room, William Sr. joined us in the crowded foyer. "Well, look at that, Nora. Your daughter can look halfway decent. I'm surprised."

Mom let out a hiss, and Hank grabbed her hand, his face pleading with her to keep the peace.

"Liam, why don't you have a date?" William Sr. growled. He pointed his cane at Zoe. "This girl was free. Why didn't you ask her?"

Zoe tried to melt into the wall, her hair bun pushing a picture askew. To Liam's credit, he looked embarrassed at his grandpa's rude question.

"Sir, we trust the kids to make their own decisions regarding situations like this." Hank immediately moved out of arm's reach of his dad as if William Sr. might swat him for his insolence.

William Sr. pulled himself up to his full height and puffed out his chest. "When I was in high school, a girl wouldn't dare attend a dance without a proper escort."

"Thank God times have changed," Mom said, keeping her tone light even though her face showed her true feelings of irritation. "People shouldn't be defined by how often they date or if they get married. Some live their whole lives single and are happy."

"Those are the ugly ones," he smirked, pleased with his quick comeback.

"Would it kill you to be nice for once?" she asked, now in full fury mode. "No one deserves your insults."

"It's not an insult if it's the truth."

"It's not the truth. It's your opinion, and you should keep it to yourself."

"Aach. This one's no better than your last wife, Hank." William Sr. hooked a thumb at Mom. "You have terrible taste in women."

Hank, fearing his dad finally had pushed Mom over the line, stepped between them. "Sir, maybe you could go back to the living room so we have more room to take pictures?"

William Sr. took a final look at Liam, Zoe, and me. "Get a haircut, Liam."

"Yes, sir," Liam answered automatically as his grandpa retreated to his recliner, pounding his cane against the floor with every step.

"Let's take the pictures in the garden," Mom suggested. "Hank, do you need to leave now? Shouldn't the chaperone be there before the kids arrive?"

Hank checked his watch. "Oh, shoot. You're right. OK, kids, I'll see you at the dance. I hope you're ready for a great night!"

Liam and I mumbled goodbye, but with William Sr. gone, Zoe had recovered her perky personality.

"I can't wait, Dr. Clark," she said enthusiastically. "See you in a few minutes."

{ 30 }

LIAM

Saturday, October 7

Driving to the dance—a dance I never wanted to go to—all I thought about was how much I hated my life. My parents were the definition of stupid. Smile for the camera so social media knew we were one big happy family! Why would I want pictures to remind me of my senior year, which so far sucked? And what was with Grandpa? Maybe he was going senile. He had always been blunt, but lately, everything that came out of his mouth was cruel.

In the backseat, Zoe talked nonstop, slicing papercuts across my brain. Luckily, it was less than five minutes to the high school, so I didn't have to listen for long. She was sweet and definitely good-looking but too young. And for once, I wasn't interested in another conquest. If I allowed myself to think about it, I hadn't cared about anything since the day on the boat. But analyzing how I felt was useless. It didn't change a thing.

I parked in the school's lot and turned to the girls. "Let me know when you want to leave. And the sooner, the better."

Zoe looked wounded as if I had said I hated kittens and puppies. Rose seemed relieved and slid awkwardly out of the car. After adjusting her dress, she wobbled over to Zoe's side. She deserved some credit for going tonight since she dreaded the dance as much as I did.

I took a deep breath, got out of the car, and stalked toward the building, leaving the girls to fend for themselves in their ridiculous heels.

{ 31 }

ROSE

Saturday, October 7

Looking down at the decorated stage from the back of the auditorium, I gave kudos to the Homecoming Committee for transforming the bare space into a festive dance venue. In the official school colors of orange, black, and white, twisted streamers looped from the outer corners of the lighting gridwork above the stage and met in the middle, where a mirror ball hung. Loose balloons drifted across the wooden floor, changing direction whenever a pair of feet passed by. Balloon bouquets anchored the food and drink tables below the stage, and in the control room, a hired DJ played music and managed the lights. Though the dance had officially started, most of my classmates huddled in small groups, talking.

Sawyer and Isabel had already arrived, and she bounced up our aisle with a sullen Sawyer trailing behind. After giving Zoe and me hugs, she said, "We had the best dinner. I am so stuffed. I wish you guys would have come with us."

"We didn't need to crash your romantic meal," Zoe's fingers formed air quotes on "romantic." "You look great, by the way. And you were right. That dress looks better on you than the other one I liked."

Isabel struck a pose and then laughed. "You all look fantastic. Rose, I love your hair!"

I fingered a stray curl and blushed. "Thanks. Zoe did it."

Off to the side of us, Liam and Sawyer glared at each other. Isabel leaned in and whispered, "Liam is looking *gorgeous*." She elbowed Zoe in the ribs. "You need to do something about that."

"Girl, I'm trying my hardest." Zoe shook her head, exasperated. "Maybe if my wingman would help me out."

The girls looked at me with their eyebrows raised.

Before I heard anything else about Liam and Zoe hooking up, I said, "I'm going to get something to drink."

I made my way down the aisle, skirting around small groups blocking the way. More people had arrived, and some were finally dancing. As I poured a ladleful of punch into a paper cup, the DJ killed the flashing colored lights and turned on the spinning mirror ball, signaling a slow dance. This moment was high on the list of reasons I didn't want to go tonight since standing alone while everyone else coupled up advertised my lack of popularity.

I considered hiding in the nearest bathroom until the song ended, but Zoe and Liam were climbing the steps to the stage. I felt obligated to monitor his behavior for her sake, so I was stuck being a dork on the sidelines. Sawyer and Isabel were already glued together on the dance floor, but I ignored them. Isabel had made it clear she could take care of herself, so I had given up on trying to break them apart.

I moved away from the refreshment table and watched Liam and Zoe for a few minutes, but then I noticed Hank and Ms. Taylor as they chaperoned from the edge of the stage.

My stomach churned, and not from the sickly sweet punch I had drunk. A boss shouldn't touch an employee as often as my stepfather was. One minute, Hank's shoulder brushed Ms. Taylor's; the next, his hand landed on her lower back—and my science teacher appeared to welcome it.

Mom could pretend everything was fine between Hank and her, but the evidence was stacking up against him.

{ 32 }

LIAM

Saturday, October 7

Inside the auditorium, Isabel spotted us immediately. She dragged Sawyer over, and as the girls talked, he gave me the silent treatment. Screw him. I couldn't change the benefits of being a Clark or what everyone thought of him. The pint of vodka hidden in my glove box seemed like a good idea right about now. I'd wait in the car for the girls.

"Would you like to dance, Liam?"

Zoe stood before me, biting her bottom lip and looking fragile.

I hesitated, not wanting to hurt her feelings but also remembering my self-imposed ban on underage girls. Screw it. It was only a dance. I couldn't get into any trouble with a room full of witnesses.

"Sure," I said indifferently, playing it cool.

When she lowered her heavily painted eyes and smiled victoriously, I suspected I had been played. We linked hands, and she led me to the center of the stage. Above us, the mirror ball rotated, reflecting spots of light across the walls and floor.

With the help of her heels, we were almost the same height, and her hips felt firm under my hands. I shifted to bring her body closer to mine, and for a moment, my old self, the Liam who some called a manwhore, took over.

"I'm glad you didn't get in trouble."

Her warm breath on my ear snapped me out of the argument my head and groin were having. "For what? You'll have to be more specific."

She laughed lightly, and I liked how good it made me feel. "That day on the boat."

"Oh." My mood turned black again. "Yeah. My grandpa said it was over, so I guess it is."

"That's great, but, you know, we all would have stood up for you. Like in court, I mean."

I stopped swaying to the music and took a step back. Startled, Zoe teetered on her heels before moving forward to fill the gap between us. Her body took up the slow rhythm of the song, and mine automatically followed. After a few beats, I felt her relax in my arms, but my heart hammered away.

"Do you think I killed that old guy?" I finally asked, fighting the tremble in my voice.

She raised a bare shoulder and let it fall. "It was an accident. Right?"

I shifted so I could see her face. "But do you think I was to blame? Because I did something stupid?"

"I was talking with Izzy and didn't see what happened," she said, not answering my questions.

"He should have been near the shore, not out in the middle of the bay," I insisted. "It's not my fault he was an idiot."

Suddenly, her lips were on mine, silencing my self-defense. We kissed for the rest of the slow dance, and then the DJ put on a head-banging song, and the gyrating crowd pushed us apart.

{ 33 }

ROSE

Saturday, October 7

After the depressing love song ended, the DJ urged the students to tell him their requests. "Remember, this is your night. Make it special."

"Freebird!" Hank shouted as he handed Ms. Taylor a cup of punch. They had drifted from the stage to the food table during the slow dance.

"Sorry, I don't have that one," the DJ replied into his mike.

The confused looks of my classmates showed their lack of knowledge when it came to classic rock songs, but I understood Hank's worn-out joke that only he giggled at.

Zoe appeared at my side. "Oh. My. God." She squeezed my forearm, her body trembling with excitement. "That was awesome. I can't believe he said yes. Argh! Did you see us kissing at the end? And he smelled so good." Her head tipped back, and she inhaled deeply as if still in the moment. "Maybe he'll ask me out now."

"I'm glad you had fun." And I meant it. There was a lot more to Zoe than I had initially thought, and she deserved some happiness. I wished my stepbrother wasn't involved, but so far, he was behaving himself.

"Come dance with me," Zoe begged.

On the way to an open spot, we swung by Isabel and Sawyer, who had ignored the change in music. Isabel squealed when her friend grabbed her hand and ripped her from Sawyer's arms.

The three of us danced until the DJ shifted the mood to slow and romantic. Sawyer retrieved Isabel, and Zoe searched for Liam without making it too obvious that she wanted to dance with him again.

As for me, I was horrified to be standing alone in the middle of the stage. I quickly threaded my way through the groping couples. Freedom from embarrassment was within my reach when a tall body suddenly blocked my path.

"Hey, there," the body said.

I looked up into Chris's smiling face. "Hi. Sorry, I was just…" I waved vaguely in the direction of the bathrooms.

"Would you like to dance?"

Shocked by his request, I lost all communication skills and stared dumbly at him.

"Come on, before it's over."

He took my hand and led me to an open space. His arms circled my waist, and mine, having nowhere else to go, wound around his neck. When he pulled me close enough to feel his heartbeat, I understood why Zoe and Isabel chased the boys. The mixture of excitement, terror, and lust had me swooning like the lead in a historical romance novel. For the first time, I didn't want a slow song to end.

{ 34 }

HANK

Saturday, October 7

"Would it be OK if we took a break?" Madison lifted a high-heeled foot and rotated it at the ankle. "These shoes are torturing my feet."

"Of course. Let's sit down." I turned toward the auditorium's first row of seats behind us.

She grasped my arm and shook her head. "I have something else in mind. Come with me."

The reckless glint in her eyes got my blood pumping. I looked back at the students I was supposed to supervise and hesitated. But then, Madison smiled mischievously. "Mrs. Parker is here. We won't be gone long enough for anyone to notice. Come on."

On the stage above us, the school secretary circled the dance floor. There was a student conduct rule prohibiting "grinding" at dances; however, Mrs. Parker had decided to punish other moves she thought inappropriate. Any student moving suggestively or in poor taste got tapped on the shoulder and had to sit out for ten minutes.

I followed Madison out of the auditorium and was surprised when she headed for the building's main doors. She giggled at my expression, and I felt like I was sixteen again and playing hooky.

"It's Saturday night, and we deserve to have some fun, too," she said as she unlocked her car and got in the driver's seat.

I scanned the parking lot and opened the passenger door when I didn't see anyone. Her sensible sedan was spotless inside, which impressed me. So often, young adults bought flashy, high-end items with their initial paychecks but soon couldn't handle the debt. Once again, I was reassured that my decision to hire her was correct.

Madison started the car and flipped through the radio stations, settling on a classic rock song. Then she leaned over me, her ample chest nearly touching my thighs, and popped the glove box. "I put something fun in here just in case."

"Found it!" She righted herself and triumphantly presented a vape pen.

My good mood evaporated. If Madison had read the district's employee handbook, she would know vaping and smoking were banned on school property. Also, both habits were unhealthy, and I tried to keep as fit as my schedule allowed.

"You smoke?" I asked, making sure the disapproval was evident in my voice.

Her hand that held the offensive object dropped into her lap, and her brow furrowed. "This is weed."

"That's worse. Marijuana is against federal and Wisconsin state law."

She looked uncertainly at the vape pen and then back to me. "But I don't understand. You were high yesterday."

"What?" I said indignantly. "I was not."

"Yes, you were. When I saw you in the teacher's lounge after the pep rally."

"No. I had a bad reaction to allergy medicine," I said, repeating the "official" story for anyone who asked. I squared my shoulders and lifted my chin. "I don't do drugs."

She stared intently at me, weighing my explanation. Then, still skeptical, she said, "You sure looked high. Your eyes were bloodshot, and your description of how you felt was spot-on."

For a split second, she made me doubt myself and reality, but it wasn't possible. "I can assure you I did not use marijuana yesterday."

"Wow. OK. I'm sorry for the misunderstanding." She held up the pen again, but this time, her hand shook. "Are you going to fire me over this?"

If she were any other teacher, they would be packing up their desk, but I hated to endanger the career of someone so young over one mistake. She needed the guidance of a skilled mentor, not condemnation, and I was happy to fill that role. "No, I don't think that's necessary."

"Thank you. I need this job, so I appreciate it." She met my solemn gaze and blinked rapidly to stop the tears in her eyes.

The opening chorus of *Slow Ride* by Foghat interrupted the moment, and I lunged for the radio volume to silence the song.

"You know," she said, looking away from me. "I'm embarrassed to admit this, but I was in total awe of you during my first interview."

"Really? Why?"

"Well," she said slowly. "When I saw you interact with the students, I could immediately tell the kids liked and respected you."

A glowing warmth swept over me and settled in my belly. "I try my best to foster an enriched learning environment."

"And you do, but…"

I waited for her to finish her thought, and when she didn't, I prompted her. "But what?"

"I assumed everyone else did as well, but after the first week here, I realized some of the staff didn't appreciate you." She shifted in her seat so that she faced me. "And I don't understand why. You're so kind and supportive. You're a great boss."

I sighed. "There are a lot of politics in any school system, which leads to hurt feelings and resentment. I try to consider everyone's opinions on how things should be run, but ultimately, I must make the tough decisions. And sometimes, a teacher doesn't agree with me."

"Well, whether they realize it or not, they are lucky to have you."

"Thank you. That's nice of you to say."

Her eyes dropped, and her demeanor turned shy. "There was another reason I was in awe of you when we first met."

"Oh?"

"No. I can't tell you." She buried her face in her palms. "You'll think I'm silly."

I placed a hand over my heart. "I promise I won't."

"And you won't laugh?"

"Not even a snicker."

"I was in awe because you were so handsome."

I couldn't help it. I laughed. I knew I wasn't ugly, but for this gorgeous creature to think I was good-looking tickled me.

She pushed me on the shoulder and then pouted. "You broke your promise."

"I'm sorry." I muffled another chuckle with my fist. "Really, I am."

"What did you think of me? When you first met me?"

I cleared my throat, mindful I couldn't tell the whole truth. "I thought you'd be a wonderful addition to our staff, and I looked forward to watching you grow as an educator."

Her face fell. "Oh."

"Did I say something wrong?"

"No. Only, I had hoped…" Her voice faded, and she looked away.

"What did you hope?" When she shook her head, I said, "You can tell me anything. Scout's honor that it will stay between us."

"Of course, you were a boy scout. You are so perfect." She tucked her chin and said quietly, "I had hoped you found me attractive."

The cozy warmth in my stomach erupted into a blazing inferno, leaving me speechless. Finally, I managed to say, "You are a beautiful woman, Madison, but I am a married man."

She cocked a hopeful eyebrow. "Happily?"

Nora's smiling face filled my mind. I loved her, but… "Like all couples, we have good and bad days. Let's leave it at that."

She nodded. I turned the radio up, and we listened to the music, each lost in our thoughts. Mine involved moving from the front seat to the back, and I was on my fourth fantasy when her voice broke in.

"Did you ever smoke weed in college?"

"No. Back then, you needed connections to buy drugs. You couldn't just cross a state line and find a store. And you were never sure what you were paying for, so that was a big problem."

"Yesterday, when I thought you were high, I thought it was pretty progressive of you. It's becoming more and more acceptable as people realize its benefits beyond relief from chronic pain and seizures. I use it to curb my panic attacks. Or sometimes, if I'm exhausted, I vape a strain that peps me up."

"Really? In college, people smoked it just to have fun."

"I think natural drugs can be quite useful. For example, I read an article on using psychedelics to treat PTSD and depression. Several studies have shown promising results. A little bit of a magic mushroom could make you feel better for months. Who wouldn't want that instead of taking a daily pill with side effects? But, of course, Big Pharma would disagree with me. They don't want their profits taken away."

I nodded. "It's always about the money. But even if all of society accepted natural drugs, I'm pretty sure the school district would remain against them." I stifled a yawn.

"Speaking of being exhausted. It's almost my bedtime. Late nights are for the young."

She held out the vape pen. "This one peps you up."

I had to admit I was intrigued.

"Do you want to try it? I won't tell anyone, and it might make the night more interesting."

In her bewitching green eyes, there was a challenge. I followed the rules all my life because I was William Henry Clark Sr.'s son. Our family reputation and legacy came above all else, and there was hell to pay if I stepped even an inch out of line. In those first few days of college away from Dad's iron fist, I tasted freedom, but it didn't last. His constant long-distance reminders kept me in check. After graduation, he called me home, and I hadn't been allowed to leave since.

I reached for the pen. "How do I use it?"

{ 35 }

LIAM

Saturday, October 7

The slow dance with Zoe left me edgy, so I went outside to let the night air calm me down. I paced the front walk, but when it didn't help, I headed for my car and the vodka in the glove box.

After three huge gulps, I sighed, closed my eyes, and ignored my burning throat. Upon further review, the pain felt good, so I took another swig.

I was so tired. Tired of the dead paddleboarder in my head, of all the pressure and expectations from school and my family—tired of being me and living this crappy life. I wanted to scream or run away or scream while running away. But I couldn't. I was too drained to do anything.

I rested my throbbing head against the steering wheel and fought the urge to cry. I wasn't a baby, and acting like one wouldn't solve my problems. It was a favorite saying of Grandpa's that had been drilled into me since the time I *was* a baby, which was pretty dumb.

If only I could stop my thoughts, then maybe I could breathe.

The vodka finally did its job, and I started to drift away. But then, the slam of a car door jolted me awake.

Across the parking lot, a man and a woman walked toward the school entrance. I strained to see in the dark whose parents were stupid enough to show up at the Homecoming dance. For a split second, I felt sorry for the kid. They would definitely catch crap for this offense on Monday.

The man must have said something funny because the woman stopped and threw her head back, laughing. She bumped him with her hip, and he caught himself before falling over.

They passed under a light pole, and my brain exploded.

Why would Dad and Madison be in a car in the parking lot?

{ 36 }

ROSE

Saturday, October 7

"I can't believe it." Zoe pounced on me the second the bathroom door swung shut. "You danced with Chris. You're so awesome!"

I was relieved we were alone and no one else heard her gushing, but I was rather proud of myself. "It was no big deal."

"Are you kidding me? Hang on. I have to pee." She disappeared into the nearest stall. "After Liam and Sawyer, Chris is the most wanted guy in school."

"He's nice."

"Arggh." Zoe flushed the toilet and popped out of the stall. "He's more than that."

I was hesitant to share what I felt in Chris's arms, so I stayed silent while she washed her hands and reapplied lip gloss.

"What did you talk about? Is he a good dancer, or did you have to lead?"

I frowned. "I guess he did. I don't think I know how. And we didn't talk at all."

"Do you like him? He's in my first period. Should I ask him on Monday if he likes you? He must, or he wouldn't have asked you to dance."

"No! Don't do that." I wouldn't sleep the rest of the weekend if I had to worry about that conversation.

Her eyes widened at my frantic tone. "OK, I won't. Just trying to help things along."

"And I appreciate the offer, but please, don't say anything to him."

She shrugged and zipped her purse shut. "Ready? I hope there'll be at least one more slow song. Maybe I can corral Liam for it."

I growled my displeasure as she pushed me toward the bathroom door.

Back in the auditorium, not much had changed since we left. Sawyer and Isabel clung to each other, Mrs. Parker circled the stage like a hungry shark, and the DJ begged for requests again. I didn't see Liam, but considering his anti-social mood, that wasn't strange. He probably found a place to sulk for a while. Then, I noticed Hank and Ms. Taylor were missing. I could see one of them being AWOL, but both at the same time? My suspicions were immediately raised.

The music switched to a golden oldie by the B-52s, and I squealed in delight. Forgetting about my stepfather, I followed Zoe up the steps to the stage, and we joined some of Zoe's friends who were already dancing.

Halfway through the song, a commotion broke out near the middle of the dance floor.

"Yeah, Dr. Clark, go for it!" someone yelled.

Zoe and I shouldered through the crowd to see what was happening. It wasn't pretty.

Hank was wildly flinging his arms and legs while singing at full volume. My classmates watched with uneasy amusement, mesmerized by the spectacle before them.

When he fell to his knees and strummed an air guitar, Zoe said, "I think you should do something. He's acting weird again."

I didn't care one bit. The more Hank acted like an idiot, the sooner Mom would wise up. But for appearances, I pulled out my phone and called Liam. As I waited for him to answer, my eyes swept the auditorium for his brooding form.

"Yeah?" he finally said.

"Where the hell are you?" My fake, serious tone must have gotten his attention because he answered straight away instead of giving me his usual attitude.

"I'm in the back row of the auditorium."

I turned that way and squinted at a dark blob. "Your dad is making a fool of himself on the dance floor."

"I can see that from here."

"So, after the stunt he pulled at the pep rally, don't you think he should be acting—I don't know—more official?"

"He's an adult. He can do whatever he wants. Meet me at the car. Now."

I stared at my phone in disbelief and then looked at Zoe apologetically. "Liam wants to go. I'm so sorry."

"It's fine." Her face scrunched with concern as Hank raced around, high-fiving everyone. "Do you still want me to sleep over?"

I gave her a reassuring smile. "Yeah, unless you don't want to."

"I do. Can we tell Isabel we're leaving?"

"Of course," I agreed, happy to make my stepbrother wait.

{ 37 }

HANK

Monday, October 9

I felt sheepish. Maybe even stupid, but I needed to see Madison. Saturday night ran like a five-star movie on a loop in my head. She made me feel so young and alive. If I could bottle her bright spirit, I'd make a fortune.

It was lunch period for the high school students, and I found her rearranging the small room in the back of her classroom. Her curves were on full display as she stood on the tips of her pumps and stretched to reach a box on top of the cabinets. Her fingers had the edge of it, but she couldn't get a good grip.

"Let me help you with that." My body tingled in delight—and relief—when her head turned, and her generous mouth smiled at me.

"Hey, you." Her face was flushed, and she blotted her forehead with the back of her hand. "You're a lifesaver."

"I aim to please," I said with a laugh.

"Really." She drew the word out, coyly raising an eyebrow. "We'll have to see about that."

When she wet her upper lip with her tongue, I forgot to breathe. Worried I was making a fool of myself, I quickly brought down the box she was after.

"Just set it on the counter." She pointed at an open space in the far corner. "I'll deal with it later."

As I did what she asked, her breath on the back of my neck sent a shiver down my spine. I slowly turned.

"Would you like a reward?" she asked, her eyes glowing.

"What did you have in mind?" I replied, ready to offer several suggestions I had dreamed up since Saturday night.

"I was thinking first we'd have some fun and then some pleasure."

Her hands slipped off my sports coat, lingering on my arms as it slid to the floor. Then her fingers undid my tie.

She knotted the silk material around her neck. "Hmmm. This might come in handy later."

I silently groaned as she moved to close the door, her backside swaying. The lock engaged with a loud click, sealing in her wicked intentions. Her purse sat on the counter, and she rummaged through it until she found a vape pen.

"Madison," I said sternly. "You cannot get high during school hours."

Her laugh came deep from her belly, and I loved its genuineness. "Honey, that ship sailed long ago."

She flipped a wall switch, and an exhaust fan above her whirled to life. With a little jump, she pushed herself onto the counter and crossed her legs, her short skirt riding up and exposing more of her glorious thighs. Then she sucked on the pen, her gaze never leaving mine, and blew the vapor toward the ceiling.

She held it out to me. "Will you join me?"

I didn't hesitate. If this was the "fun" Madison offered, I couldn't wait for the "pleasure."

{ 38 }

ROSE

Monday, October 9

When Hank left his office and headed down the high school hall toward Ms. Taylor's room, I decided to forgo my lunch period and follow him. At breakfast, he had seemed more hyper than usual, and now his steps were one gear away from skipping. After all the unprofessional touching I had observed between him and my science teacher since the beginning of the semester, I figured he was up to no good.

He stopped before entering her room and quickly looked both ways. As the only other person in the hall, I darted into a nearby bathroom to avoid being seen. After counting to one hundred, I slipped out and continued to the science room but found it empty.

Puzzled but determined to confirm my stepdad's marital failings, I lingered in the doorway. As I pondered how else I could catch him cheating on Mom, a deep voice followed by a feminine laugh came from behind the closed door of the back room. My eyes narrowed with hatred as smutty images of Hank and Ms. Taylor filled my mind.

Without fully thinking it through, I strode to the nearest fire alarm and pulled it.

{ 39 }

HANK

Monday, October 9

"Oh, my God. There's a fire," I exclaimed, untangling Madison's arms from around my waist.

"Are you sure it's not a drill?" she asked wide-eyed. Her hands smoothed over her blouse and then tugged at her skirt.

"Yes, I'm sure. There's one scheduled for next week, but nothing for today."

As I reached for the doorknob, Madison grabbed my arm.

"You can't go out there. You're a mess."

"Right, thanks." I straightened my clothes and finger-combed my hair before flinging open the door.

I was halfway across the room when Madison called my name. She held up my coat and tie, and I gave her a grateful look.

"OK?" I asked breathlessly after shoving my arms into the coat and tucking the tie into my inside pocket. The weed we vaped had left me buzzed and disoriented, and I struggled to clear my mind.

She nodded but then stopped me yet again, pointing at my pants.

"Jesus." I tugged up my zipper and rushed from the room.

At the end of the hall, teachers directed the high school kids out of the lunchroom and to the nearest exit. Overcome with pride, I took a moment to appreciate the payoff from all the previous fire drills, which were often a source of complaint. Everyone was following the safety procedures to a T.

Everyone, that was, but my stepdaughter, who leaned against a locker several feet away with her arms crossed.

"Rose, what are you doing?" I asked. "You need to evacuate immediately."

I didn't wait for her to respond; instead, I pulled her along as I tried to get to the head of the crowd to lead the way.

Outside, I ran to each teacher, checking that all their students were accounted for. The Williams Bay Fire Department roared up a minute later with sirens blaring.

After a room-to-room search by the firefighters, the building was given the all-clear.

"We didn't find anything, Hank," the fire chief said with a shake of his head. "Do you think it was a prank?"

My shoulders slumped, disheartened that one of my students would do something so grievous. "If that is the case, then the punishment will be severe. You have my word on it."

He slapped me on the back as we shook hands, and I thanked him for his service before following everyone back into the school. The chatter level was high from both students and teachers, and I considered canceling the remainder of the day's classes, knowing that little would be accomplished over the next few hours. But the working parents wouldn't appreciate a call to pick up their kids early, so we would have to tough it out.

***

As the adrenalin that flooded my body during the false fire alarm dissipated, I rummaged through my office desk for something sweet to eat. Usually, I had a pack of M&M's or a Snickers bar, but I was out of luck today. While debating a food run to the mini-mart, I rested my chin in my palm and got a whiff of Madison's scent. The memory of her soft hair and skin made me grin like a lovesick boy. Man, she was something.

Walker knocked on my door, and I shifted my face to a more professional expression. "Hey, Ray." I smothered a giggle at the rhyme. "What can I do for you?"

"Can you take over Molly's Current Events class? She threw up and asked to lie down for a while. I would do it, but I want to write a report on the fire alarm incident for the school board while it's still fresh."

"Does she want to go home instead?" I asked. Molly was expecting her third child, and though she claimed it got easier with each pregnancy, I didn't want to seem callous.

"No. She said her morning sickness came late today and will pass. She has a parent-student meeting after school that she doesn't want to cancel."

"When is the class?"

"Now."

I hesitated. It was a bad idea, as Madison's drugs were still in my system, but my sluggish mind couldn't concoct an excuse. I nodded reluctantly. "Do you have anything to eat? Preferably sweet?"

He looked at me oddly—at least, I thought he did. I suspected my judgment might be off. "Let me check."

***

Sixth-period Current Events had a mixture of grades—and Rose, looking sullen and angry. I briefly wondered what had set her off. Still, teenagers were notoriously moody, so the question disappeared from my mind as fast as it had formed.

What worried me more was trying to be composed for the next forty-five minutes.

I sat at Molly's desk and read through the class list she had left out. I knew every one of the fifteen students before me and tried not to feel insulted that she would think I didn't. I shoved the offending paper to the side, leaned back in the chair, and laced my fingers over my stomach.

"So, what happened yesterday in the news?" I asked, expecting several answers to be shouted with enthusiasm. Instead, bored silence took over the room like an unwanted guest monopolizing the conversation. As I succumbed to its dullness, my eyes drooped with fatigue, and I regretted even more not escaping the school when I had a chance.

Someone coughed and then cleared their throat. My eyes popped open, and I saw a hand raised. I smiled at the student, grateful for her class participation.

"Yes, Tara, tell us something that happened yesterday."

She straightened in her seat when several heads turned her way. "Actually, I can't. But we have a quiz tomorrow covering the last two weeks of news. Could we study instead of having a discussion?"

Relief flooded through me, almost making me tear up. "That is an excellent idea. If you need to talk amongst yourselves, please do it quietly so as not to disturb your neighbor."

As soon as everyone bent over their notes, I put my head on the desk and fell asleep.

{ 40 }

ROSE

Tuesday, October 10

Ms. Taylor stopped me before I could escape her class, and now I fidgeted at her desk, waiting for the classroom to empty.

"What were you playing at?" she asked when we were alone.

Startled by her question, I didn't answer.

"Do you realize how much trouble you could get into? What you did is a felony, which means juvie or possibly prison."

How could she know I had pulled the fire alarm? Nobody was in the hall but me. And besides, no way was it a felony. Maybe a fine at best.

When I continued to stare dumbly at her, she shook her head impatiently. "I'm referring to the brownie you gave Dr. Clark before the pep rally. The brownie that was laced with weed. Ring any bells?"

My mind screamed, Deny, Deny, Deny. "I didn't lace a brownie and give it to Hank."

"Aren't you clever," she said with a snarky smile. "Correct. You didn't personally make the edible, but you bought it and gave it to Dr. Clark, and he had no idea it wasn't a regular brownie. That's despicable on more than one level. And a felony."

This woman, who flaunted herself at both boys and men and most likely was having an affair with my stepdad, called me "despicable." My face burned but from outrage rather than my usual embarrassment.

"Do you have any proof?" I demanded. "Because if I know Hank, which I do, the evidence is long gone."

"Correct again. I don't have any physical proof. I'm not sure what the police could even do at this time. But giving someone drugs without their knowledge is dangerous. Dr. Clark could have been seriously injured or taken ill. Was it a prank? Were you two fighting, and you were mad at him?"

"Even if I did what you said, it's none of your business." I sucked in a breath, suddenly realizing that it was her business. "You're Steve's drug dealer. He said, 'She has a background in science.' Looks like we're both guilty of illegal activities."

Her left eye twitched as panic cut into her confidence, but she recovered quickly. "We're talking about you, not me. I need you to promise you'll never do that again."

"Sure. And you promise to stay away from Hank."

"What? Hank—Dr. Clark is my boss. I can't 'stay away from him.' It's physically impossible."

"You know what I mean."

We glared at each other until the bell for eighth period rang.

"You're late," she said with a smug curve of her lips.

"Write me a note," I replied evenly, pretending to be unconcerned, though it would nearly kill me to be the last one to class.

She scribbled on a scrap of paper and handed it to me blank-faced.

I walked stiffly out of the room, content to leave it at a standoff. We would both lose if we talked to the authorities.

{ 41 }

WILLIAM SR.

Friday, October 13

I found Mary Kane waiting for me in my Village Hall office, and I apologized profusely, though she didn't have an appointment. The white-haired shrunken lady was a long-time resident well into her nineties who still drove herself about town, much to everyone's concern.

I gently took her offered hand before sitting behind my desk. "It's so good to see you again, Mrs. Kane. How are you?"

"Horrible, William." Her gnarled fingers opened a purse identical to one my mother had carried every Sunday to church and pulled out a letter with the village's logo in the top corner. "How do you expect me to pay more taxes? I'm on a fixed income."

I glanced at the paper she had laid between us, more for her benefit than mine. I already knew her gripe was with the newly assessed value of her house. Most of the residential property in the village had grown in value, which meant the owners' tax bills in December would be more than the previous year's.

She wasn't the first resident to complain about the recently concluded assessment, nor would she be the last. Usually, I would patiently explain the methods and sources used to determine the value of the constituent's property, highlighting how desirable our Williams Bay homes were. If that didn't pacify them, I would throw in some inflation figures and compare our property values and taxes to other villages. By the end of my lecture, ninety-five percent of the time, the person would grudgingly agree not to pursue the matter further.

But Mrs. Kane was old. She didn't care about financial statements or the future of the village. All she wanted was to die in the house she and her late husband bought over fifty years ago.

"Could you pay the same amount as last year?"

Her shoulders relaxed, but her face remained grim. "It would be better if the bill went down."

"You and I have been around long enough to know it never goes down. Work with me." I leaned forward, folded my hands, and gave her my warmest smile.

Her rheumy eyes narrowed, but after a moment, she conceded. "Yes, I can afford that."

"Wonderful because we'd hate to lose you as a neighbor." I tucked the letter under a paperweight of the American flag. "Now, you don't worry about this anymore. I'll have one of the girls adjust your bill."

She snapped her purse shut and struggled to stand. "You're a good man, William. Your father would be proud."

I fought the pain in my new hip to get around the desk to help her up and out the door. "Well, I try to follow Pop's example every day."

"That's the right way to live," she said with a firm nod.

I patted her on the back. "You take care now. Look out for deer when you're driving."

"And people," I murmured when she had reached the building's exit.

David came from the other end of the hall and called my name. I made an overblown display of checking my watch to show him I was busy.

"Please, William," he puffed as he hurried toward me. "Give me five minutes."

I nodded and sat back down behind my desk. David hesitated and then took the chair Mrs. Kane had vacated. He coughed into his fist, his go-to stall tactic, and I rolled my eyes. The man was so predictable.

"I was reviewing the police budget that the village board approved, and there seems to be an item missing."

"Oh?" My response hung between us, a soft challenge for him to speak his mind.

His face reddened, and I smiled at his discomfort.

"Yes, and let me, first of all, say thank you for the extra officer. It's going to be a big help during the tourist season."

"No need for thanks. I told you I'd try, and I did."

"And I appreciate it, but…" He dropped his head, and I waited impatiently, knowing what he would say next. "Everyone in the police department got a salary increase but me. Was that a mistake?"

I sighed and arranged my features to appear sympathetic. "I'm sorry, David. The board couldn't find the money for both an officer and your raise, so we had to choose which would serve the greater good. The obvious choice was the officer. And to be honest, we could barely fit that into the budget. Things are tight, and inflation has affected all of our expenses."

When he continued to stare at the floor instead of leaving, I stood and cleared my throat. "Rest assured, we appreciate all your hard work, and maybe next year, the village will be in a better financial position. Now, if you'll excuse me, I have some phone calls to make."

"Thanks for your time, William." He stopped at the door and found the backbone to look me in the eye. "I did all I could do. You know that, right?"

My lips twisted, recalling the personal and professional humiliation of meeting with the DA so he could question Liam. "But it wasn't enough, was it?"

"I'm so sorry." His distressed tone begged for absolution.

I let him squirm for a moment longer before releasing him. "It's in the past now."

{ 42 }

LIAM

Monday, October 16

After failing another anatomy quiz, this one on muscle groups, I accepted Madison's offer for tutoring. I had no problem remembering the shortened terms like pecs, abs, and glutes—I had known those since T-ball—but my brain refused to retain their fancy names. If the tutoring didn't help, I would fail the class and not graduate in spring. No pressure.

Madison moved between the whiteboard at the front of the room and an overhead projector, pointing out various muscles and explaining how their names often alluded to their shape or size. "For example, the rhomboid muscle looks like a rhombus with equal and parallel sides. The trapezius looks like a trapezoid, a four-sided figure with two parallel sides. Maximus means 'large,' as in gluteus maximus."

"That makes sense. Why didn't you say so in the first place?"

She stared at me, her mouth slightly open. "I did, Liam. You weren't paying attention."

"Yes, I was." Except for all the times I wasn't.

She shook her head. "No. I see you zoning out all of the time."

My eyes dropped to the notes I had taken, and I pretended to make a correction. "I got a lot on my mind," I said indifferently.

"I'm sure you do." She sat in her desk chair and swiveled toward me. "Have you ever been tested for ADHD?"

"I'm not hyper," I grunted. "I've been sitting still for the past half hour."

"That's not the only symptom. Even though your grades don't reflect it, I think you are intelligent. It may be that you have a problem focusing. If it is because of ADHD, your teachers must accommodate your condition, which could improve your life—at least at school."

"If I'm labeled ADHD and all the teachers know, then the whole village knows. There's no way my grandpa would allow that. Besides, he says all this mental health stuff is an excuse for laziness. Nobody had ADHD or depression when he was growing up."

"Yes, they did, but they called it other things."

"It doesn't matter either way. If you think a Clark is going to a cuckoo doctor, as Grandpa calls them, then you're wrong."

"Liam, you're a legal adult. You don't need anyone's permission to see a mental health professional." When I didn't say anything, she threw up her hands in defeat. "OK. Back to the muscle groups. Most of learning anatomy is memorization. You will have to put in the time if you want to pass my class. Have you ever tried flashcards?"

I snorted. "Yeah. In grade school."

"Believe it or not, they also come in handy in high school and college." She dug through the bottom drawer of her desk, then pulled out several stacks of worn cards secured with rubber bands. "Here. Study the muscle groups, and I'll give you another try at the quiz. Our next unit is on the nervous system. Start memorizing those cards now, and you'll pass the quiz the first time around."

"Thanks." I dropped the flashcards into my backpack along with my anatomy notebook and closed the zipper. "I have to get to practice, but…"

She walked with me to the door, and when I didn't continue, she asked, "But what?"

"Why are you helping me?" I said in a rush. "If it's because you feel sorry for me, don't. I'm fine."

"It's because that's what friends do. They help each other. And at the moment, you're my only friend in this village."

Then she kissed my cheek. Her lips were soft and only stayed a second, but it was enough to send a shockwave through my system.

"You're going to be late," she said, pushing me out the door and into the hallway.

I stopped short when I saw Tara filling a water bottle at a nearby fountain. She was dressed for volleyball practice in a cutoff tank and skimpy spandex briefs that showed off her killer body.

Her eyes narrowed as she considered Madison and me, an unspoken question behind them.

"Hey, Liam." She took a long drink, lifting her chest and shooting a not-so-subtle glare at our teacher. "Will I see you later?"

I looked back at Madison, who seemed interested in my response. "Maybe. I'll text you."

{ 43 }

ROSE

Tuesday, October 17

Entry from the Journal of Rose McCabe:

Though I didn't have the guts to ask Chris directly, Zoe and Isabel said we were a couple. He had changed seats in our Current Events class to sit next to me, and in the four minutes between periods, we talked at my locker a few times a day. Tonight, he was coming over after dinner to hang out at my house for the first time.

Having a boyfriend made my stomach feel queasy but in a good way. The only downside was it took me longer to get ready in the morning. Pre-Chris, hair, makeup, and clothes never mattered. Now, what color shirt I wore was a life-or-death decision.

***

I was drying the last of the dishes when the doorbell rang.

Mom turned from the refrigerator, a white wine bottle in her hand. "Are we expecting anyone?"

I ran for the front door, still holding a saucepan and dish towel, but Liam got there first.

"Hey, QB." Chris's voice reached me before I could save him.

"What do you want?" my stepbrother demanded.

"Me." I pushed between the alpha males to prevent any growling or snapping of jaws.

"Are you insane, Mouse?" Liam asked. "You're dating *him*?"

It might have gone smoother if I had mentioned my plans at dinner. But I had feared some degree of sarcasm from William Sr. and Liam and an overexuberant celebration from Hank and Mom. I didn't want either to happen, so I stayed silent.

"Hi, guys, what's going on?" Hank boomed from behind Liam.

Mom wiggled her way to the front of our "friendly" family. It only took her a split second to assess the situation. "Welcome! Come in, please. Rose, take his coat."

He flashed me an understanding smile as he slipped off his letterman jacket.

"Who's here?" William Sr. called from his recliner. I hadn't counted on him being around, as he usually watched television in his bedroom after dinner.

"A friend of the kids," Hank answered.

Then, Chris did the unthinkable. He walked into the living room and stuck out his hand to William Sr.

"Chris Anderson, sir. It's a pleasure to meet you."

My heart beat painfully several times before William Sr. grunted and shook his hand. He squinted at our group in the foyer and then at Chris. "And you are Liam's friend?"

"We're teammates, sir, but I'm here to see Rose," he replied, showing himself to be a first-rate diplomat.

Liam glared at his archenemy, and William Sr. looked shocked that someone besides my mother would be interested in spending time with me.

The old man sized up my boyfriend. "What sports do you play?"

"Football, basketball, and track."

"Track, huh? You've got the right build for that. Are you any good?"

"He's a junior, Dad, and the school's number three athlete," Hank interjected.

Thankfully, before the conversation deteriorated into individual stats, wins, and losses, Mom took control. "Rose, why don't you take your friend to the sun porch. Turn the fireplace on if it's too cold. Would you like any dessert, Chris? We have ice cream or peanut butter cookies, or both."

"No, thank you, Mrs. Clark. Maybe later." He smiled politely, showing the crooked tooth I loved.

Mom pushed Hank toward the stairs, and Liam stomped after them, leaving Chris and me staring at each other in the foyer.

I cleared my throat. "The porch is this way."

The small glass-enclosed room off the kitchen contained a television, an overstuffed love seat, a worn leather recliner, and a game table with four straight-backed chairs. A dozen dehydrated houseplants sat on the windowsills, waiting for Mom to declare them dead, which she refused to do. The space was designated for us to use when our friends were over, though Liam preferred his bedroom.

Chris dropped onto one side of the love seat and stretched his long legs across the coffee table in front of him. I flipped the switch for the fireplace and waited for the flames to poof to life. After a moment's hesitation, I joined him. He seemed totally at ease—I wasn't his first girlfriend—but I was a wreck after the ridiculous reception I had put him through.

"I'm sorry my family's so bizarre." I picked up the TV remote to give my hands something to do. "I'd like to say they aren't always that way, but they are."

He laughed off my apology. "I'm used to Liam giving me grief. Don't tell him this, but sometimes, I do things just to piss him off. And your grandpa is a legend, so it was cool to meet him."

"He's not my grandpa."

"No, not by blood, but—"

"Not by anything," I said pointedly. "The man hates my mom and me, and the feeling is mutual."

His head jerked back at my scorching bluntness. "Wow. Why?"

"I've overheard some fights. It's complicated." I liked Chris a lot, but I wasn't ready to share all my secrets.

He considered that for a moment, then asked, "Did he get along with Liam's mom?"

"I don't think so. Lily was an artist, and I can't see him appreciating her worldview. He doesn't even like it when my mom redecorates our house."

"My dad is in the Lion's Club with him, and he's always saying what a nice guy William Sr. is. He thinks it's great how multiple generations of Clarks have dedicated their lives to Williams Bay."

"I know people love William Sr., but he's a real ass to us, and I'm including Hank and Liam."

"That's so weird." His brow furrowed as he puzzled over our family dynamics. "It must make your home life rough."

"I stopped caring long ago, but I worry about my mom and Hank. When they fight, it's always about William Sr."

He took my hand and brushed his thumb over my skin. "I'm sorry. I had no idea."

"Yeah." I turned on the TV. "Anyway, do you want to watch a movie?"

{ 44 }

HANK

Tuesday, October 17

"What other drugs have you tried?" I asked Madison as we hid in the back room of her classroom. We had fallen into a pattern of vaping weed and then fooling around. How far the fooling around part went depended on our schedules. Often, we only had time to kiss, much to my dismay. Madison frequently had somewhere to be or something to do, and I had football practice.

"I did ecstasy a few times when I was clubbing with my girlfriends, but I like weed better."

The past week with Madison and her magical marijuana had made me feel young again. It was like reliving a part of my life that had been denied, and it awoke in me a greed for new thrills. After some research, I knew what I desired next, but it was hard to completely shed the straight and narrow ways Dad drilled into me.

Ignoring his unrelenting voice in my head, I asked in a casual tone, "If I paid for it, could you get some coke?"

She immediately crushed my fantasy with a frown.

"You don't want to go there," she said firmly. "I know people who messed up their lives when they started doing harder drugs. Stick with weed."

"Trying it once can't hurt me, can it?" I took her in my arms and pressed my body against hers. "My 'intellectual' curiosity was aroused when I read that certain activities are more intense on coke, and you're the perfect subject for my experiment."

I bent to nibble on her neck, and she pushed my head away. "Stop that. I don't need a love bite visible to the whole school."

"How about one that only we can see?" I ran my hands over her hips as if searching for the best spot.

"You are insatiable."

"Only with you. I can't get enough of you, Madison."

"Seems like you're addicted to me, Dr. Clark."

"Yes, and I won't even attempt to deny it."

"Then, that's even more of a reason you shouldn't try coke. Addictive personalities shouldn't do drugs. Period."

I kissed her earlobe. "Please? Just once."

"Why do you want to do it so badly?"

I backed away from her. "Because it sounds like fun. I don't expect you to understand because you seem like the kind of person who always does what they want. I haven't had that luxury. I want to be wild and damn the repercussions."

The silence grew between us as she debated giving in. "OK. I'll reach out to a few people. It's been a while, so I'm not sure of the price, but plan on at least a hundred dollars for a gram."

"Thank you so much," I said, pumping my fist in the air. "And how long will that last me?"

"If you aren't an addict, a couple of weeks. If you are one, a day."

"I'm not, so that sounds great." I kissed her hard on the lips. "I have some work to finish up before practice. See you tomorrow?"

"I'll be here." She folded her arms, and her chin dropped to her chest.

I smoothed a hand through my hair and straightened my shirt and tie. With one hand on the door handle, I said, "Thanks again, Madison. I appreciate it."

She gave a slight nod, but then her head snapped up. "I'm not, you know."

"Not what?" I asked, genuinely confused.

"I'm not the kind of person who always does what she wants. Not even close."

The seriousness on her face pricked a hole in my good mood, and I shivered as it deflated. "I'm sorry. I didn't mean to offend you."

She gathered her purse and coat, pushed me out of the way, and opened the door. "Goodbye, Hank. Lock up behind you."

"Madison?" I called after her but not too loud. If anyone were in the hallway, it would be awkward if they heard us. But there was no chance for further conversation as she kept walking, leaving me to ponder whatever mistake I had made.

{ 45 }

LIAM

Wednesday, October 18

During an open period in the library, I worked on a new drawing of Madison when I should have been reading about the Battle of Dunkirk. I figured I could stream the movie tonight and get the gist of it for tomorrow's history quiz. I hadn't had an art class since grade school when it was mandatory. Instead, I watched YouTube videos to learn different techniques. Some days, I thought I was almost good, but mostly, I thought I sucked.

No one knew I liked to draw, and I had to keep it that way. Dad and Nora would make too big of a deal about it, and Grandpa would insist I quit because it wasn't a manly enough activity. When Madison asked me what I wanted to study in college, I lied and said I didn't know. But I did. I would give anything to be an art major.

My real mom lived somewhere in France as an artist. Years ago, she sent me a postcard of the Eiffel Tower. On the back, she wrote that she'd buy me a plane ticket for my eighteenth birthday. She must have forgotten since I'm still here.

I was ten when she left. As she packed two big suitcases, Dad said over and over he was sorry, but she didn't forgive him for whatever he had done. I stood in the doorway of their bedroom, and she cried harder whenever she looked at me.

Soon after that, Dad invited Nora and Rose over for dinner. Nora was nice enough, but I missed my real mom. I asked Dad if I could visit her in the summer like the other kids with divorced parents. Grandpa overheard and vetoed the idea immediately.

I was finishing Madison's jawline when the school secretary appeared and headed toward my table. In one swoop, I closed the cover of my drawing pad and shoved it into my backpack.

Noticing my lack of homework and books, she said, "This may come as a surprise, but you need to pass your current classes to graduate."

"I was taking a break, Mrs. Parker," I said in my politest voice.

Her lips formed a harsh line as her eyes swept the room. They stopped on Sawyer several tables to the right of me. He was asleep with his head resting on a textbook, snores coming from his open mouth. Unlike me, the dude could sleep anywhere.

"Principal Walker needs to see you and Sawyer. Wake him up." She turned on her heel and disappeared between the reference and fiction stacks.

At the request, panic swept through me, flipping my stomach in its wake. Even though Grandpa acted like everything was settled in the death of the paddleboarder, people still posted comments about it on Facebook, insisting "a reckless boater" was at fault and needed to be charged. A few wondered if the witness who had reported the accident, meaning me, was actually to blame. Every day, I woke up thinking today was the day I would be arrested.

Would the police really come to the school? Maybe as a favor to Dad, even though I was legally an adult and didn't need a parent. But why would Walker ask for Sawyer? Would the police arrest him for lying?

My shaking hands made zipping up my backpack a struggle. I took a few deep breaths to steady myself before kicking Sawyer in the leg he had stretched into the aisle.

He sat up with a grunt. "What?"

"Walker wants to see us."

He took hold of his head and cracked his neck. Then, ignoring me, he shouldered his backpack and headed out of the library. I gave him the finger behind his back and followed at a distance.

Sawyer yawned loudly as we walked, the rubber soles of his hightops squeaking as he plodded along. Unlike me, he didn't seem worried about being summoned.

Mrs. Parker hadn't returned to her post at the front counter, which served as a barrier between the students and the school administration. So, we continued down a short hallway to the principal's office. We found Walker with his face inches from his computer screen, his mouth silently moving as he read whatever was displayed. With no police in sight, I let myself relax for the moment.

He waved us in. "Be with you in a minute, boys. Can one of you close the door?"

The room was small, and we awkwardly sidestepped around each other as Sawyer swung the door shut. Then, we dropped our stuff on the floor and settled in the chairs by Walker's desk.

He typed, deleted, typed, frowned, and nodded. Apparently satisfied, he clicked his mouse, and the printer in the corner spit out a sheet of paper. "Sorry to interrupt your day, but I wanted to talk to you about the Outstanding Student-Athlete Football scholarship."

We had our final game of the season this Friday night and the awards ceremony and banquet Saturday night. Besides the coveted scholarship, which went to a graduating senior, Dad would hand out a bunch of awards like Most Valuable Player and Most Improved Player. However, the winners were always kept a secret to amp up the surprise factor.

Walker seemed uncomfortable, his fingers straightening a row of pencils and pens on his desk before he spoke again. "As you are aware, for this award, the Athletic Boosters recommend a student-athlete to the athletic director, who then makes the final decision."

Sawyer's hands formed tight fists in his lap, and I could feel the tension coming off his body. The four-year scholarship was for twenty thousand dollars a year for tuition and housing at a Wisconsin college. The seniors were judged on athletic ability, community involvement, and personal character.

"It should come as no surprise that you two were the top contenders, and since you are best friends, I wanted to tell you in private who was chosen. I hope this honor won't damage your friendship, and you will be happy for the recipient."

Pain shot through my jaw and temples as I clenched my teeth while Walker talked. Someone forgot to tell him what the whole school already knew. Sawyer and I were no longer "best friends," and there was no way the loser would be happy for the winner.

Walker paused and looked past us, his eyes on the closed door instead of our faces. He took a deep breath as if summoning the strength and said briskly, "The scholarship will be awarded to Liam. Congratulations."

Sawyer's body spasmed violently when the principal said my name. "Are you kidding me? *He's* getting it?"

"I am sure you are disappointed," Walker began before Sawyer cut him off.

"He doesn't need the money. He's had a college fund since the day he was born!"

The principal shook his head. "It's not based on financial need."

"No, it's based on not pissing off his grandpa. God forbid the golden boy doesn't shine."

"Sawyer, language, please," Walker scolded but without much heat in his voice. "Liam is deserving of this honor."

"And I'm not?" Sawyer leaned forward, the veins in his neck popping out as his hands gripped the arms of his chair. "The only difference between us is his grandpa runs this town, and my parents are white trash."

"That's not true." Walker pointed his finger at my ex-friend. "Matt and Desiree are fine people."

When Sawyer let out a short, vicious laugh, the principal quickly changed tactics. "There are several local scholarships up for grabs. The Lions Club, the Rotary Club—"

"I don't have the grades for those, and you know it," Sawyer snapped. He grabbed his backpack and stood.

Walker rose as well, trying one more time to smooth things over. "You are eligible for the basketball and baseball scholarships, which aren't solely dependent on academics."

"Those aren't twenty thousand dollars a year for four years." He yanked the door open but paused to ask, "What if he doesn't go to college?"

"Then the football scholarship passes to you, but Liam applied to several state schools. He is bound to get accepted by one of them. I'm sorry, Sawyer, but I urge you to make an appointment with Mrs. Barry. The Guidance Department has numerous financial aid resources. It'll take some extra work on your part, but she'll help you apply for every scholarship and grant you are eligible for."

Sawyer scowled at me with pure hatred. When he slammed the office door behind him, I ducked and covered my head, expecting a shower of glass from the frosted window. I had never seen my ex-best friend so angry, and something like grief left me gasping for air.

Walker collapsed into his chair. "I knew that wouldn't go well, but better here than at the banquet."

The bell rang to switch classes.

"You should get going. And Liam?" Walker smiled wearily. "Congratulations."

***

In a zombie state of shock, I bumped along the hallway as everyone rushed to their next class. Four minutes was all we got, which wasn't enough time to change a tampon, according to my girlfriends. It also wasn't enough time to figure out how I would face Sawyer for the rest of the school year. I felt sorry for him, but it wasn't my fault. I didn't decide who won what, but he definitely would make me pay for it.

When I got to Madison's classroom, Sawyer sat at a lab table in the back of the room instead of the usual one we claimed. Several football players surrounded him, their heads bent, listening to whatever garbage he fed them.

Madison caught my eye and lifted her chin slightly at my teammates, a question on her face. I shrugged and dropped my backpack with a loud thud as I settled in my seat. It was a good thing the teacher was my tutor because I didn't listen to what she said for the rest of the lecture.

When the bell rang for lunch, I waited for everyone to leave, staring straight ahead, not moving a muscle.

"What happened?" Madison asked when we were alone.

"I got a big scholarship that Sawyer needed for college."

"Ah. The rich get richer."

"What?" I hadn't expected her to side with Sawyer, and my frustration erupted. "I had no control over the decision, yet I get the grief for it. I didn't ask to be born a Clark. I never wanted to be treated differently."

She sighed and walked to my lab table. "Life isn't fair, is it?"

I was about to rip on her unhelpful and seemingly endless supply of cliches when I noticed the sadness in her eyes. Worried, I asked. "Are you OK?"

"I'm fine, but you'd better go to lunch." She lifted my backpack, and the contents spilled onto the floor. "Ugh. Sorry, that was stupid of me."

"No harm done," I assured her as I quickly scooped up the textbooks and notebooks for my morning classes.

"What's this?" She picked up my drawing pad. "Do you have an art class?"

"No. It's nothing. Just some doodling." I tried to take the pad from her, but she moved out of my reach.

Terror stalled my fight or flight response, paralyzing me, as she slowly flipped through the pages until she reached my sketch of her.

"Liam, you're very gifted." She looked at me wide-eyed. "I didn't know you liked to draw."

"Nobody knows. Can I have it back, please?" I held out my hand, desperate to put away my secret.

"Why?"

"Why what?" I half-closed my backpack with a quick tug on the zipper and got to my feet.

"Why would you hide your talent?" She turned the page toward me and shook her head in disbelief.

I looked away, embarrassed by my crappy attempt at art. "You wouldn't understand."

"Is it me?" Her fingers traced the wild waves of hair across the paper.

"No," I said harshly, immediately regretting the sharpness of my tone when she flinched. "It's someone I made up."

She studied the sketch again, then gave back the drawing pad. "I can see that now. She's more beautiful than me."

Taking my free hand, she led me between the lab tables to the back room.

"Madison?" I said, confused by her actions. Moments earlier, she had told me to go to lunch.

She turned her head and held a finger to her lips. "Shhh."

Once inside the room, she locked the door and lightly pressed her hands to my cheeks. When her lips parted, I dropped my backpack and drawing pad on the floor and bent my head to meet them. As her kisses became more urgent, my hands decided it was time to explore her body, preferably without her clothes in the way. Before they could move under her blouse, she pulled away and laid her forehead against my chest.

"Thank you, Liam." Her chin tilted up, and she laughed. "Oops. I got lip gloss all over your mouth."

"Does it look good on me?" I asked, a bit dazed and a lot fired up.

"No, the shade is all wrong for your complexion." She bent down and picked up my drawing pad. "Can I keep the sketch of the woman who isn't me?"

"If you want, but you didn't have to…" I paused, unsure how to label the kiss between us. "I mean, you could have just asked."

"Where's the fun in that?" She wet a finger and rubbed it against my mouth. "There. I got rid of the evidence."

She carefully ripped out the sketch and tucked the pad into my backpack. Then, the sadness in her eyes returned.

"Time for you to go," she said with a half-hearted attempt at a smile.

My perfected "who gives a damn" attitude didn't hold up around Madison. She needed a friend, and for once, I wanted to help someone besides myself.

"I can stay if you want, or get some food and come back," I offered.

She shook her head. "Thanks, but I have assignments to correct." When I didn't move, she added, "Go. I'm fine."

"See you tomorrow?"

"I'll be here." But her expression and tone suggested she'd rather be anywhere else.

{ 46 }

ROSE

Monday, October 23

"I'm never going to understand this," complained Zoe. Her head dropped back in defeat. "It's so pointless. When will I ever use these theorems?"

Zoe and Isabel had come over to do homework, and we were snacking and studying in the dining room. After the first day of school, I realized that Zoe did not have a math mind and wouldn't pass geometry without help.

"What problem are you on?" Isabel asked.

She was in the other geometry class, and the two of us were doing everything we could to get Zoe a decent grade.

"Number five, but let's take a break. My brain hurts." She pushed aside her books and reached for a bag of chips. Then she asked me, "Have you and Chris done anything *interesting* lately?"

They both leaned toward me and waited for my answer. I knew what they wanted to hear but had no problem disappointing them. "Not really. We usually watch movies when he comes over."

Exchanging glances, the girls did their best friends' mind-reading thing.

"I don't believe you," Isabel said. "You're holding out on us."

"Maybe." I raised one eyebrow and sipped my soda.

They stared at me, willing me to crack, but when I didn't, Zoe changed the subject.

"Izzy, how's Sawyer?" she asked. "When I saw him today, he looked in a pretty pissy mood."

"I feel so bad for him. He didn't get the big football scholarship, and he really needed it." Isabel reddened. "I mean, no offense to Liam, but Sawyer's parents aren't in the best financial situation. They already said there's no money to give him for college. And they weren't too torn up about it. They don't have college degrees, so they don't think he has to have one."

"What does he want to study?" I asked.

"Sports medicine. He wants to be an athletic trainer, and you need at least a bachelor's degree. And some places require a master's, I guess."

"What colleges did he apply to?" Zoe asked between chips.

"All of the state ones, but it's too early to hear back from them. They have until March to tell him." Her fingers found her ponytail and combed it as she talked. "The whole thing really stinks. I had hoped Liam and Sawyer would kiss and make up, but now, I don't think that will ever happen."

Zoe shoved the bag of chips away with a grunt. "Probably not. It's too bad, considering how long they've been friends."

"Where does Liam want to go to college?" Isabel asked me.

"No idea. He barely acknowledges me, his dad, or my mom. The only person he doesn't dare to ignore is Williams Sr."

"Do you think he's still upset over the accident on the lake?" Zoe asked. "It was such a sad day. I mean, he basically saw a man die. That's not something you get over right away."

I longed for absolution from the guilt of going along with Liam's version of the paddleboarder's death. Perhaps if I confessed to my friends, I would find some peace.

I swallowed hard, lifted my head, and said, "It's more than that. We told the police we were passing by when the old man fell, but that's not the whole story. Our boat caused the wake that made him fall. Liam wasn't paying attention and had to swerve to avoid him."

Isabel inhaled sharply. "That's why Liam told us what to say before the police took our statements."

"And my family went along with his story, never doubting it, and I was too scared to speak up. Liam said if I told the police my version of what happened, it would ruin the family."

William Sr. suddenly appeared in the doorway of the dining room, and my heart froze between beats.

He jabbed a finger at Zoe and Isabel. "You two. Go home."

I checked the grandfather clock in the corner of the room. "Mom said dinner would be at six. That's not for another hour and a half."

His lips flattened, and his nostrils flared at my audacity to talk back. "Pack up. Now."

Zoe and Isabel didn't bother with the "pack up" part of the command. They grabbed their books and notebooks and bolted from the table.

"How dare you treat my friends like that," I said when I heard the front door close.

He barked out what could have been a laugh if he were human. "The little mouse has turned into a lion and found some courage. Too bad you lost your brain in the process. Do you even realize what you've done? By this time tomorrow, the whole village will know Liam's stepsister said he is responsible for a man's death. Where's your family loyalty?"

"Are you kidding me? I don't have any allegiance to you." My body trembled as I stacked my textbooks and pushed past him.

"Maybe it's time you and your freeloading mother move on."

I paused, considering my words. "That's the last prayer I say every night."

We glared at each other, rage flowing between us; then, I pounded up the stairs to my room.

{ 47 }

HANK

Thursday, October 26

I loved cocaine. I couldn't get enough of the finely crushed powder. My energy and confidence were sky-high, no pun intended. With coke, I was no longer the incompetent son of William Sr.; I was a superhero who could solve any problem sent my way. On the downside, though, the drug's effects quickly dissipated, leaving me empty. And because of the cost, I had to limit myself to snorting a few times a day.

Football season was over, and I didn't miss the daily after-school practices for the first time since I started coaching. My extracurricular activities with Madison were far more enjoyable than listening to thirty smelly adolescents complain about every little thing.

I locked my office door, settled at my desk, and pulled out the small baggie I bought from Madison on Tuesday. Well, technically, I still owed her for it. I frowned at the lack of content. There was barely any left. She would need to get me more.

I did my morning line, closed my eyes, and waited for the heart-pumping high. When it hit, I checked my nose for powder residue and then went to hunt down Madison.

{ 48 }

LIAM

Thursday, October 26

I was shooting baskets before classes started when Madison rushed into the gym.

"Liam! Liam!" She waved some papers at me, a huge smile on her face.

"Take off your shoes," I yelled as her spiked heels struck the polished court. I didn't need the janitor reaming us out for disrespecting his floor.

Stopping midstride, she hopped on one foot and then the other to slip them off. "I couldn't wait until anatomy class to show you. Look. Look at what you did."

She held the papers up to my face but was dancing around too much for me to read them. I cradled the ball and grabbed her wrist to still her. It was the test we took yesterday, and a large B+ in red ink was in the corner of the paper.

"I knew you could do it." She hugged the side of me that didn't have the ball, then glanced over her shoulder at the gym's double doors. "Sorry. I hope no one saw that."

"I think we're good, and thanks for all the tutoring. I guess it helped."

"Be proud of yourself, Liam. It took effort on your part to receive that grade." She folded the test and tucked it into the pocket of her cardigan. "Are you getting in some extra practice?"

"More like burning off energy. With football season over and basketball starting next Monday, I need to do something during this off-week."

"But you don't have ADHD," she teased.

"Whatever. Do you play?" I asked, bouncing the ball back and forth between my hands.

"I dabbled in a few sports in my younger days," she said, her tone indifferent, immediately making me suspicious.

"And this was one of them?"

"Would you like to find out?" She dropped her shoes and took off her cardigan. Then, without any warning, she hit the ball out of my hand and chased after it.

I grinned and let her take a shot. But then, she elbowed me hard in the ribs on the rebound.

"Oof, foul!" I yelled, pointing at her as I rubbed my side.

"Fouls are for babies." She threw the basketball at my chest. "Let's go."

After I made an easy layup, she dribbled to the three-point line, pivoted, and shot. The ball swished cleanly through the net.

Three fingers on her right hand punched the air. "In your face!"

"Are you kidding me?"

"You should see how I play in shoes."

I shook my head at her bare feet, and she wiggled her toes.

The warning bell for first period rang.

"I guess that's game," she said. "Better get to class, Mr. Clark, or someone might give you detention."

She picked up her sweater and heels and stared at me over her shoulder. I held her gaze, unable to do anything else.

{ 49 }

HANK

Thursday, October 26

I grabbed Madison by the arm as she left the gym and pulled her to a quiet corner away from a group of students who needed to head to first period. I thought of kindly disciplining them first, but what I had just seen took priority.

"What do you think you're doing?" I demanded.

She shook herself free. "Hank, what is wrong with you?" She peered into my face. "Oh, wow. You're high. What do *you* think you're doing? It's not even eight o'clock."

"Never mind that. Are you sleeping with Liam?" I whispered hotly, though I wanted to shout.

Her mouth dropped open, appalled at my accusation. "If we were alone, I would slap you."

"But I saw you—and him. You seemed pretty comfortable with each other's bodies." My coked-up brain took over, fabricating an X-rated movie between my son and his teacher. I shuddered as I imagined every touch and kiss.

"Are you even listening to yourself?" she asked, pointing at the gym doors. "We were playing an innocent game of basketball."

"Nothing is innocent with you, Madison," I scoffed.

Her face darkened. "You are unbelievable—and paranoid." She reached into the pocket of her sweater and pulled out some papers. "Liam got a B+ on his anatomy test, and I couldn't wait until class to tell him."

"And that involved you throwing yourself at him?"

"Do you mean when I hugged him? You saw that? How? Forget it. I don't want to know." She waved Liam's test between us. "I've been tutoring your son and was proud of him. So, yes, I hugged him, as unprofessional as that may have been. But, you should be thankful I'm helping him, considering everything he's up against."

"Sounds like you're pretty chummy with my son."

"Somebody has to be. If you bothered to talk to Liam, you'd see he'd benefit from some degree of therapy and possibly ADHD meds."

I laughed, and Madison's face froze in anger.

"I'm sorry," I said, "but I go through this with every first-year teacher. Suddenly, they can diagnose students because of what they learned in their Intro to Psychology college course. I'll tell you what I tell them. If you suspect a student requires evaluation, refer them to Mrs. Barry. Guidance counselors are better trained in this area than teachers. But don't send Liam. He is fine."

Without another word, she slipped on her heels, spun around, and marched away from me. Realizing I may have crossed a line, I went after her.

"I'm sorry," I whispered as we wove through the last of the stragglers in the hallway. "I was jealous. You looked like you were having so much fun with Liam, and well, you're practically the same age."

She stopped abruptly and faced me. "I. Don't. Sleep. With. Students."

"Of course you don't," I agreed with her. "Please, erase everything I said from your memory."

She let me stew for a few moments before continuing our walk. "OK, but you're wrong about your son. At the very least, it would be great if he had a trusted family member or older friend to talk to about his life and how he's feeling."

I realized I would have to give her what she wanted to get what I needed. "You're right. Let's discuss some possible solutions after classes today." I lowered my voice. "I'm running low on…you know what."

"You still need to pay me for last week's 'you know what,'" she reminded me.

"And I will," I assured her. "I'll go to the bank at lunchtime."

"OK, then give me a few days to get more."

I breathed out a sigh of relief. "Great. So, I'll see you around three-thirty?"

She hesitated, and I feared she was still mad at me, but then she nodded. "Remember my money, Hank."

As I watched her hips sway down the hall, I realized my high was fading. I fingered the small baggie in my pocket. I had a meeting with Ray at nine. Indulging would have to wait.

{ 50 }

ROSE

Thursday, October 26

My free periods in the library were more interesting now that Chris sat by my side. With our legs hooked together and his hand resting on my thigh, it was all I could do to concentrate on homework. I often glanced sideways to admire his blue eyes set off by impossibly long lashes or remember the feel of his chin stubble as we kissed. Sometimes, he rewarded me with a sexy smile that sent happy little tingles to my fingertips and toes.

It was during one of these moments that my world shifted.

"Do you want to come over tomorrow night?" he asked, his hand repositioning itself higher on my thigh. "It'll be one of my last free nights before basketball season starts."

My heart sank, hating to disappoint him. "I'm sorry. I already made plans with Zoe."

"Blow her off." He laid his head on my shoulder and gave me puppy dog eyes until I laughed.

"That's not nice. She's my best friend."

"What am I?" he asked with what I hoped was a fake, hurt expression.

"You're my boyfriend," I said hesitantly, my face heating up.

He reached for my hand and kissed my wrist before lacing our fingers together. "My parents will be gone for several hours. I'd really like to spend time with you when there aren't two hundred other people around."

"And, what, watch a movie?" It was a stupid question, but I needed some clarity on what he was suggesting.

He laughed. "Sure. We can Netflix and chill like they used to say."

"I'll ask Zoe if we can hang out on Saturday."

"Cool." He gave me another smile, but this time, it sent dread through my body.

I had expected this moment, but that didn't mean I wanted it to happen.

{ 51 }

HANK

Friday, October 27

It was Friday evening, and I had promised Nora I would be home for dinner. On the way, I stopped at the mini-mart and bought her several candy bars. Her attitude had been frigid lately, and I worried she suspected something.

When I walked in, she was mashing potatoes with a hand mixer. Though her indifferent nod was not the warmest greeting, I pressed a kiss on her cheek and emptied my shopping bag onto the counter.

"Sweets for my sweet," I said with a flourish.

She squinted at my gift, and her face turned sour. "Almond Joys? Mounds bars? Those are your favorites. Not mine. I hate coconut."

"Since when?" I asked, genuinely stumped.

"Since forever," she snapped.

"Oh, sorry. I guess I forgot. Maybe the kids will want them." I picked a cherry tomato from a salad on the breakfast bar and popped it into my mouth. "How long until dinner?"

"Less than five minutes. Can you let everyone know? The kids are upstairs, and William Sr. is in the living room."

My stomach sank. "Dad's here? I thought he was with the Lion's Club tonight."

"He doesn't share his calendar with me." She opened the oven and stuck a fork into a chicken breast. "Dinner's ready now."

"I'll round up the gang."

Dad was snoring in his chair, so I shook his shoulder gently. "Sir? Sir?"

He woke with a start and grimaced at me. "Dammit, Hank. What is it now?"

"Time to eat."

He sniffed the air. "What did that wife of yours make tonight to give me heartburn?"

"Chicken and mashed potatoes."

"Wonderful," Dad grunted. He reached for his cane and slowly stood. "I can hardly wait."

After he shuffled past me, I rushed upstairs, stuck my head in the kids' bedrooms, and then locked myself in the bathroom. So far, I hadn't done drugs in the house, but for once, I wanted to feel good around Dad, and a line of coke would help.

***

At dinner, Liam shoved forkfuls of his meal into his mouth, not slowing even for a sip of milk. In contrast, Dad took small bites of food and spat them out after chewing a few times. Rose sat as close to Nora as she could without being in her mother's lap. It was as if she didn't want to breathe the same air as the rest of us.

No one spoke, so I did. I told jokes that no one thought funny and stories that no one laughed at. When I knocked over Liam's water glass while gesturing a bit too wildly, Dad exploded.

"What the hell has gotten into you, Hank? You're acting like a teenage girl."

Nora's silverware hit her plate with a loud clang. With her lips pressed into a thin, hard line, she stacked her dishes and headed for the kitchen. Rose watched her leave the room, glanced at us with an uneasy expression, and did the same.

Liam paused his fork mid-air when he noticed the party was breaking up.

"May I be excused, sir?" he asked his grandpa instead of me.

He nodded. "Take my plate with you. There's nothing edible on it."

I waited alone at the table until the kids disappeared upstairs and Dad went to his bedroom. My high was fading, but I thought I could still put it to good use.

In the kitchen, Nora stood at the sink washing dishes. I went up behind her and began massaging her shoulders. "You feel so tense, baby. Let me work those knots out."

She flicked off my hands with soapy fingers, leaving wet splotches on her shirt.

Not to be defeated, I tried again. "It's been weeks, Nora. Let's make love," I whispered.

She whirled around, her hips knocking against my groin and making me groan. "What makes you think I'd be up for that?"

I leaned into her. "Don't you miss me? Because I've been craving you." I kissed her neck and gently bit her ear lobe. My hands slid over her body, hoping to arouse her. "You're so beautiful, and I'm so lucky you're my wife. Let me show you how much I love you."

Dumbfounded, she shook her head. "First of all, I've barely seen you since school started. Second of all, if you really, really, *really* loved me, you would get that horrible man out of our house."

"I'm sorry I haven't been around more, but I got behind on paperwork during football season. I'm almost caught up, so things should return to normal soon." Football had been a convenient excuse, and I would need to find another one if I continued to spend time with Madison.

I sensed her giving in, but I hadn't addressed all of her complaints. "If you want our relationship to improve, get rid of your father."

"Consider it done." It was the coke talking because I didn't have the guts to tell him to leave.

I pulled her toward the walk-in pantry, and her body stiffened. "In there? Don't be silly. Everyone is home, and they'll hear us."

"No, they won't. Dad has the TV blasting, and the kids always have their earbuds in. I can be quiet if you can," I teased and tugged at her again. "Please? It'll be exciting—and a little dangerous. Something to spice things up."

I knew it was the wrong thing to say the second the words left my mouth.

She gasped, her lips forming an O in disbelief. "I didn't realize our sex life was boring you. Is that what's been going on lately? I'm dull?"

"That's not what I meant. I only thought it would be fun to do something different."

"In the pantry. Next to the canned goods and chips." With arms akimbo, she tilted her head. "How romantic."

"OK. Then let's go upstairs. Please, Nora? I need you. Now."

She stared at me and then set her jaw. "Not until William Sr. moves out."

"What? Are you serious?"

"Yes. You said you would tell him, so go tell him. Right now. He can leave in the morning."

Even with coked-up courage, the thought of confronting Dad made me nauseous.

"I…I…" My brain failed to find another excuse or lie to tell her.

"Mom?" Rose appeared, startling us both. With cold eyes, she flicked a look of disgust my way, and I wondered how much she had heard. "I'm going over to Zoe's. Is that OK?"

"Of course, honey. That sounds like *fun*. Doesn't it, Hank?" Nora snatched her purse from the counter in a violent motion. "I'll drive you."

"That's OK," Rose replied. "I can walk. It's not far."

"No, I need some fresh air anyway. Are you ready now?"

"Yes."

I sank against the breakfast bar in defeat and watched them go, the last traces of my high deserting me as well.

{ 52 }

WILLIAM SR.

Tuesday, October 31

I dropped into my recliner and closed my eyes. Alone in the house, the only noise came from my heavy breathing. With one hand over my heart, I tried to slow its beats but soon gave up.

I burped, and acid bubbled up my throat. Jeanie at the Igloo warned me about the chili I ordered for lunch, and damn it, she was right. I slowly ground two Tums with my teeth, the only thing working on my body today. My eyelids drooped, and I didn't resist. I'd rest until my stomach settled and then return to work.

The ringing of my cell jarred me awake, and for a moment, I didn't know where I was. My fingers fumbled with my pants pocket, and I cussed in frustration as I freed the phone. Its display read "Chief of Police."

"David, what can I do for you?" I asked in a civil voice despite being annoyed.

"I'm sorry to disturb you, William. Did I catch you at lunch?"

"No, no. I'm at home. I spilled some chili on my shirt and needed to change it before going back to Village Hall."

The line went quiet, and I thought the call had disconnected, but then David cleared his throat. "I wanted you to hear it from me first." Another wave of dead air traveled between us. "The DA filed charges against Liam."

"What? That's absurd. I thought this was all settled."

"I did, too. But a witness contacted me, and the DA finds him credible."

"Who was it? Another half-blind person on shore? The DA is wasting taxpayer money over this."

"No, this person was on the boat, William. You will have a hard time discrediting the story."

"Why? Who is it?"

"It's Sawyer Reed. He said Liam had several beers and was distracted. He didn't see the paddleboarder until Sawyer pointed him out. Liam had to swerve sharply to avoid a collision. Since Sawyer's account now corroborates the other witnesses, the DA has concluded that Liam's reckless driving was the cause of the wave that knocked the elderly man into the water."

My breath hitched, and a stab of pain radiated through my chest. I never liked that ungrateful brat. Years ago, I told Hank he'd get Liam into trouble, and I was right.

"And did the boy say why he has suddenly changed his story?"

"He said the guilt was eating him up."

"What are the charges?" I demanded.

"Criminally negligent homicide."

"No." I shook my head. "No. My grandson will not go to prison, David."

"Listen. I'm waiting on the paperwork, so hire a lawyer and bring Liam in. It will be less traumatic for him than being picked up in a squad car."

"This is beyond absurd," I fumed. "If the DA thinks I'll stand down while he commits this injustice, he's a bigger buffoon than you."

I disconnected the call and threw the phone across the room. It bounced against the wall and landed several feet away. My mind whirled through the mental index I kept of every government official and their misdeeds. There had to be someone who could make this go away, someone who would lose too much if they didn't.

Deciding on a few that I could put the fear of God into, I struggled out of my recliner to retrieve my cell. But as soon as I was upright, pain raced down my left arm. I dropped my cane and doubled over, gasping and clutching my body. The room blurred as the worst case of heartburn spread across my chest. I sank to all fours and forced breath into my lungs.

I rested for a moment to recover, and when I didn't, panic set in. I tried to crawl toward my phone like a baby, but my mutinous limbs refused to hold me up. Flat on my belly, I stretched out a foot for my cane behind me but couldn't reach it. Focused on the phone again, I dug my elbows into the thick carpet and pulled my body forward an inch. Another spasm left me whimpering.

It was no use.

I was no use.

And Liam needed me.

{ 53 }

ROSE

Tuesday, October 31

I swore out loud as I approached the house. Mom's van was gone, per a volunteer meeting on the family calendar, but William Sr.'s car was in the driveway. I was supposed to be in gym class, playing basketball with the other girls in my grade. Being short and uncoordinated, no one ever passed me the ball. Instead, I ran up and down the court the whole time, flailing my arms and feeling stupid.

Most days, I would stomach the humiliation to keep my GPA up. But today, I woke with cramps that refused to subside, even after multiple doses of Midol. I couldn't face the world anymore, so I headed home.

I opened the door and listened to the house. All was quiet. Maybe William Sr. was in the backyard. He sometimes pruned the flowers and bushes so he could rag on Mom for not caring for the garden. I wasn't avoiding him because I was skipping school. He had no clue what I did with my life beyond eating at the supper table every night, so he wouldn't even register my rebellion. I was sneaking in because I didn't want to give him a chance to throw more insults at me as if I were a dartboard.

Deciding it was safe to enter, I set my backpack on the foyer's wood floor with a soft thump, then kicked off my shoes and hung up my coat. A low moan from the living room replied to the noise from my movement.

Curious, I peeked into the room and saw William Sr. sprawled on his stomach, his head turned away from me and facing the couch. One arm was extended at an awkward angle, and his hand stretched toward his cell phone, several feet from his fingertips.

Mom would pitch a fit when she found out he fell and broke another bone. But then again, if Hank insisted William Sr. had to continue living with us, maybe that would be her last straw.

I went upstairs to my bedroom, feeling hopeful that the Clarks were on their way out.

{ 54 }

HANK

Tuesday, October 31

Madison's playful mood, which I loved, was turned off when I went to her classroom after school. Without a smile or a hello, she rose from her desk and walked to the back room.

"Did you have a bad day?" I asked as I closed and locked the door to our hideaway.

"No."

I waited for her to say more, but instead, she got out her vape pen and took a hit. Since trying coke, I didn't bother with weed. At first, Madison would do a line with me, but now she passed, and I missed her participation. Mainly because the only time we had had full-blown sex, she was high on coke. It was intensely insane, and I wanted to relive that moment.

"Were you able to buy some coke?" I asked, unsuccessfully keeping the worry out of my voice.

She nodded. "But I won't do it again until you pay me back everything you owe me. I don't have much extra cash, you know. I live paycheck to paycheck."

"Of course, I'm sorry." I pulled out my wallet and counted the bills I had. "Here's a hundred. I can give you more by Friday."

She took the money and dropped it into her purse. "I need three fifty for this," she said, pulling a small plastic bag from a metal lock box.

"That's more than last time," I protested.

Her expression was less than sympathetic. "The drug market is volatile. Take it or leave it."

I snatched it out of her hand. "Cross my heart; you'll have what I owe you at the end of the week."

I quickly dumped some of the powder onto the counter and pushed it into a line with a credit card. "Should I make you one?" I asked hopefully.

"No."

There was that attitude again. If only she would loosen up, we could have fun like we used to. Maybe she had PMS. Nora turned into a witch once a month.

I snorted the coke, rubbed my nose, and waited for the glorious rush of fearlessness to take over. When I looked at Madison, she seemed—concerned. Man, she was a killjoy.

"Do you want to make love?" I asked. "It's been a while."

"Make love?" She let out a cold laugh. "You mean have sex."

"No, I don't. I care for you, Madison. Don't you care for me?"

"Hank." She stopped and pressed her lips together, and I hoped she'd finish her thought before the high hit me. I didn't particularly like where our conversation was going. "I think you need to slow down on the coke."

"I'm just trying to have fun," I whined, feeling cranky. "My life is pretty stressful."

"There are other ways to relax."

"Oh, do you have anything in mind? Otherwise, I can offer a few suggestions." I started undoing my belt.

"I think you should leave."

She headed for the door, but I grabbed her arm. "I'm sorry. That was crude. Let's start over."

She stared at my hand until I released her. "I have papers to grade."

When I heard the scrape of her desk chair against the floor, I knew she wasn't coming back.

I slipped the baggie of coke into my wallet and checked the time. It was too early to go home, so I would have to return to my office. At least my high would help me plow through the stack of paperwork that was due.

I drifted slowly toward the classroom door in case Madison changed her mind, but she didn't even look my way.

{ 55 }

LIAM

Tuesday, October 31

Grandpa was dead; honestly, I never believed it could happen. He was such a stubborn prick I figured he'd tell Death to take a hike when it came for him.

After a policewoman retrieved Dad from his office and me from basketball practice, we drove home in silence. Dad reminded me of a robot with his stiff face and jerky movements, though his hands shook whenever he tried to use them.

Now, the chief of police, the policewoman, and two EMTs stood in the foyer, waiting for the coroner. Despite their radios turned low, I flinched every time they squawked. On the front porch, three old men that Grandpa hung out with and a few neighbors showed their support but kept their distance.

Nora held Dad on the couch, Grandpa's covered body at their feet. Dad was a mess, unable to respond when asked even a simple question. The policewoman had found a box of tissues, and he clutched several in his hand to wipe his nose and cheeks. Nora seemed calm, offering coffee to anyone who came in.

And me? Was I sad? Angry? Relieved?

When I was little, my friends would talk about their grandparents, and I'd make up stories to match theirs. My grandpa was the best, I'd say. He read books to me, and we went fishing and had tickle wars. I laughed so hard once that I couldn't breathe. But it was all lies. He'd never been loveable.

Even so, he was the core of our family; without him, I guess I felt—hollow.

He had seemed fine this morning. Maybe a bit quieter than usual, but well enough to rag on me about my latest math test grade.

"You need to study harder," he had said. "Discipline. It's like a dirty word to your generation." Then he slapped the back of my head, and I spat out my apple juice.

I joined Rose at the breakfast bar in the kitchen, leaving a chair between us. She had been in her bedroom when Nora found Grandpa. Her mom gave him CPR, but it was too late. The EMTs figured he had a heart attack.

"You didn't hear anything?" I asked Rose for the third time. She wore an oversized sweatshirt with the hood up and her legs tucked under it. I imagined it swallowing her like a python eating a rodent.

"No," she replied, her tone flat and her eyes vacant as she stared at nothing.

I grunted, and at the same time, my phone pinged. I tipped it to read the notification. Word had spread, and the RIPs were pouring in.

"I killed him! I killed him!" Dad's agitated voice came from the other room.

Low murmurs followed, but he countered with, "On the first day of school, I found him here on the couch in the middle of the afternoon. I knew something was wrong even though he denied it. He was never sick, and naps were for the weak."

I left my catatonic stepsister and moved to the edge of the living room to hear better.

"Hank, these things can happen suddenly," the police chief said. "We talked on the phone earlier, and it must have been right before he—" The chief stopped, unable to say the "D" word. "My point is he seemed fine. Feisty as ever."

"He sounded good? Then why was he home?" Dad asked.

"He said he spilled chili on his shirt and needed to change it."

Dad shook his head. "He's wearing the same white shirt from this morning."

Nora patted his thigh. "Maybe he hadn't had a chance to change yet."

"When you did CPR, did you see a stain on his shirt?" he asked her.

"I…I don't think so. Why does it matter, Hank? You need to stop torturing yourself."

"What did you talk about?" Dad asked the chief, pivoting back to the phone call.

The chief's face turned red, and he shifted uncomfortably. "We can discuss that later."

Dad stared at his father's body for several long seconds. "No, tell me now. You were his friend and probably the last person to talk to him. Were you joking around? Did he laugh?"

I doubted it. Grandpa rarely laughed, though he did act differently with the village residents than with us, turning on the charm when it suited him.

"Please, Hank," the chief pleaded. "Now isn't the time."

Dad stood and held a hand up when Nora reached to pull him back onto the couch. "Yes, it is. I deserve to know how he spent his last moments alive."

The chief sighed, hooked his thumbs in his utility belt, and pulled himself a little taller. "I informed him another witness to the paddleboarder's death had come forward. Based on what the witness said and the fact that the person was in the boat with Liam, the DA filed felony charges. I urged him to hire a lawyer and bring the boy in."

A high-pitched ringing filled my head, and I slid down the wall, landing on my butt.

"And how did my father react to that news, David?" Dad asked in a low, quivering voice.

It was really a rhetorical question. We all knew Grandpa had lost it.

The chief's gaze dropped, unable to bear Dad's grief. "He was angry. Furious."

"He shouted?"

"Yes."

"His blood pressure rose?"

"Probably."

"I see."

"Hank, I'm sorry, but I was only—"

I interrupted them. "So, I killed him."

Everyone turned, noticing me for the first time.

Nora stepped over Grandpa and knelt in front of me. "No, Liam. No. That isn't true. Don't think that for a moment."

"What else should I think? Chief Wick told him I was going to prison, and his heart couldn't handle me destroying his reputation."

"Son, from day one, I told your grandfather I doubted it would go that far," the chief said. "I was sure the DA would offer a plea deal. The felony charges were to satisfy the public and the victim's family, who were saying the police were either incompetent or showing favoritism."

"Doubted?" I repeated. "But you couldn't guarantee him that."

"Well, no." His shoulders rose, and his mouth opened and closed a few times without sound. "The DA and a judge would make the final decisions."

"Who was the witness?" I demanded.

Instead of a straight-up answer from the chief, silence filled the room, pressing on my chest until I couldn't breathe.

"Nevermind. I think I know who," I said, the realization bringing me to my feet.

"Who?" Dad asked. "Damn it, Chief, tell us who."

The chief answered him, but I was out the front door and plowing through the people on the porch. One lady yelped as my shoulder hit hers, but I didn't care. I sprinted away from the house, the cold air chapping my wet cheeks and the thudding of my shoes against the sidewalk in my ears.

***

A cramp in my side shot pain across my midsection. I tried to run through it but finally slowed to a walk. As I recovered my breath, the stitch eased, and I stopped to wipe the tears from my face with my shirt.

When I left the house, I had no destination in mind; I only needed to put distance between myself and everyone else. But my body automatically took me to the high school.

Basketball practice must have been over, as only a few cars remained in the parking lot. One of them was Sawyer's, a rusted-out Ford pickup truck.

Gritting my teeth, I ran toward my ex-best friend's junker. When I got closer, I saw he was making out with Isabel in the front seat. I didn't care. Maybe it was time for her to find out what an asshole her boyfriend was.

I yanked open the driver's door, pulled Sawyer out by the back of his shirt, and threw him on the ground. His face registered surprise, then confusion before settling on fear.

Isabel scrambled out of the truck and screamed, "Liam! What is wrong with you?"

"Yeah, what's your problem, dude?" Sawyer asked.

The question lit me up, and I remembered why I hated him. Possessed by anger and guilt, I kicked him in the ribs and then kicked him again. It was a low move on my part, but he deserved it.

He curled up in pain and yelled my name. I went to punt him one more time, but Isabel jumped on my back. Her nails raked my cheeks, and one finger found my eye socket. Grunting, I grabbed her wrists to pull her hands away from my face before she could do any more damage. Through my one working eye, I saw Sawyer crawling away and someone running toward us.

"What…the hell…is going on?" panted the head coach of our basketball team.

The coach was built like a barrel. He rarely did more than stroll the sidelines during games and practices, shouting vague instructions and leaving the real work to his two assistant coaches. Ten years ago, the basketball team was stacked with super athletic guys and won the state tournament despite his coaching incompetence. He took the credit, and even though every team since never made it past the first round, he still had his job.

Isabel slid off my back, and I felt my face for blood. None of us answered him.

"Listen, Liam." He inhaled deeply several times, and his breathing found its natural rhythm. "Dr. Clark told me what happened while you were getting your gear together. I'm sorry for your loss. Maybe it has something to do with your actions here." He waved a hand between the three of us. "But, you need your friends now for support. I'm going to let you talk it out. No more fighting, you hear me?"

The coach waited until we all nodded. "Good. Sawyer, I'll see you tomorrow. Liam, take as much time off as you need."

He looked back a few times as he walked to his car to confirm we were behaving ourselves.

Sawyer slowly stood, arms wrapped around his middle. "What's Coach talking about?"

"My grandpa's dead." My anger rose again as I said the words out loud.

"What? Wow. Like just now?" Sawyer asked.

"Yeah. They think he had a heart attack. At first, I blamed myself, but then I realized you are the one responsible for his death."

He seemed stunned by the accusation but quickly deflected. "You must be high. Why would it be my fault?"

"Right before he died, the police chief told him the DA filed felony charges against me because of another witness coming forward. Someone who was on the boat."

Sawyer's eyes shifted to Isabel and then back to me. "And you think I'm the witness?"

I nodded. "Remember in Walker's office when we found out I got the football scholarship? You asked what would happen if I didn't attend a Wisconsin college. I thought it was a stupid question because you knew that was where I would end up. So, you had to figure out a way to stop me from going. If I'm in prison, the scholarship will be passed to you. Tell me you didn't go to the police and change your story."

We stared at each other, me daring him to speak and him debating what to say.

His lips twisted into a sneer. "I can't. I decided I had to tell the truth."

My body jerked at his confession as if he had hit me. I hadn't been one hundred percent sure it was him. In fact, Rose was my second guess.

The high-pitched ringing in my ears returned. I clasped my hands behind my head, my elbows squeezing together and blocking the world out. With Grandpa gone, who was going to save my life? The answer echoed in my head. No one.

I dropped my arms and whispered, "You were my best friend."

"Yeah?" He lifted his chin defiantly. "And look where it got me."

{ 56 }

HANK

Friday, November 3

"You have to help me."

It was the lunch period, and Madison was in her classroom eating while reading a book. She was smartly dressed as usual in a tight-fitting dress while I was a mess, not even sure my socks matched. The surprise on her face, which quickly turned to alarm, confirmed my fears.

She put down her book and focused on me. "What is going on?"

Unable to keep still, I moved in circles from her desk to the whiteboard and then to the first row of lab tables. "I feel like I'm going crazy since my dad died. I can't concentrate on anything. I don't have an appetite. I barely sleep at night."

"That all sounds like physical reactions from grief, Hank. Cut yourself some slack. It's only been three days."

I pulled at my hair, further rumpling my appearance. "I want the noise in my head to stop. Part of me is sad that he's gone—I loved him. Don't get me wrong. But part of me feels…free."

"Family is complicated. William Sr. was an unusual man."

"Everyone in town admired him and his dad before him." I stopped my pacing and held out my hands. "The village board wants me to run for president!"

"Why are you surprised? Isn't that how things are done around here? You're next in line."

"But I'm not my dad," I said, shaking my head. "And I never will be."

"No, Hank, but you could be better."

"That's not possible." I sank into the chair by her desk.

"What can I do to help?"

I grabbed her hand and kissed it, inhaling the hypnotic scent at her wrist. "Do you have anything to get me through his funeral?"

"I don't think that's a good idea," she said firmly.

Ignoring her refusal, I pressed on, desperate for relief. "Not weed. It would be terrible if I had a laughing jag in the middle of the service. And I don't think I want coke. You've seen how hyper it makes me. What else can you get?"

"Hank, you can do this sober. Lean on your family. Liam's grieving, too. He needs you now more than ever." She took back her hand. "Besides, your tab is pretty high. I don't want to be insensitive to your loss, but you promised to pay me today."

I turned away, unable to meet her eyes. "I know I owe you a lot. But even though I'm strapped for cash right now, my dad's financial affairs were in good order. Soon, I'll be flush."

"Hmmm." She picked up her fork and stirred the salad she had been eating before I interrupted. "I guess I can hold out a little longer. Go home to your family, Hank."

Her dismissive tone sent my stomach spinning with worry. But how could I blame her? Who would want an inconsolable lunatic at their side? I had to man up or lose the only fun thing in my life.

"OK, I will, and thanks for listening and setting me straight."

She smiled slightly, then took a bite of her salad.

I stopped at the door. "See you later?"

My voice came out both hopeful and needy. Madison didn't look up, but her fingers waved at me. I would take what I could get.

{ 57 }

ROSE

Wednesday, November 8

On a crisp fall afternoon, the leaders and residents of Williams Bay gathered to bury the meanest man I had ever met. Piles of dried-up leaves lined the funeral route, signaling the end of my favorite season. Still, the sun provided a welcomed fifty degrees of warmth, leaving the mourners comfortable in their coats.

William Sr. ruled the village for two decades, and the crowd surrounding his gravesite at the Union Cemetery was twenty rings deep, a testament to the respect and admiration he had hoarded over the years. Hank and Mom had picked out a mid-priced casket with a walnut stain and brass trim. It stood above a hole, ready to be lowered by the groundskeepers after the service. Fake strips of grass covered the mound of fill-in dirt nearby.

I thought cremation would have been better since I hoped William Sr. was headed to Hell.

Earlier at the wake, his closest friends told stories that showed a warmth and charm he never shared with his family. If it weren't for the numerous photos of the dead man displayed throughout the funeral parlor's main room, I would have thought they were talking about someone else.

William Sr. never entered a church unless invited to a baptism or wedding by a prominent village resident or to attend their funeral. He may have believed in God—he used His name in vain often enough—but I would bet he thought himself equal or, more likely, above God's rank. So, I thought it funny that Hank had asked a minister to preside at the burial. Maybe he was worried about the final impression his dad would leave on his constituents if there wasn't at least one prayer said.

The minister opened with a short reading from the Bible and then read William Sr.'s obituary, which listed his many services to the community. He finished his portion of the ceremony by reciting a poem. "The author is unknown, but please take the following words to heart as we say farewell to our friend William:

A life well lived is a precious gift
Of hope and strength and grace,
From someone who has made our world
A brighter, better place
It's filled with moments, sweet and sad
With smiles and sometimes tears,
With friendships formed and good times shared
And laughter through the years.
A life well lived is a legacy
Of joy and pride and pleasure,
A living, lasting memory
Our grateful hearts will treasure

He bowed his head, allowing a moment of reflection punctured by sniffles and coughs from the mourners. When a respectable amount of time had passed, he said, "Dr. Clark, would you like to say a few words about your father?"

Hank had been drinking spiked orange juice all morning and carried a flask in his coat pocket. My stepfather rose unsteadily and moved toward the minister. On the way, one foot caught on the uneven ground. He grabbed wildly at the casket, which stopped his fall, but not his leg, which slid into the hole below. A collective gasp escaped the crowd, and Liam and the minister rushed to his side to pull him upright.

He shook them off and brushed unsuccessfully at the dirt on his pants and shoe. After a few more swaying steps, he turned to address the mourners. With closed eyes and chin tucked into his neck, he rocked on his heels. Then his head popped up, and he proclaimed loudly, "My father was a great man."

The crowd sighed and murmured. Someone even threw out an "Amen" from several rows behind me.

Hank's chin dropped again as if weighted down. "But he could be a tough son of a—" He caught himself and finished with "gun."

"He loved this village, just like his father did before him, and his grandfather did, and so forth." His hand circled in the air as his voice faded away. "The Clarks dedicated their lives to making this the best place to live, and my father met every goal he set but one."

He covered his mouth with his fist, his face disfigured with despair. When he could speak again, he repeated, "My father was a great man. But I'm not his equal, and he hated me for that."

My stepfather's confession shocked the crowd into an awkward silence. To top off his performance, he fell across William Sr.'s casket, and the sound of his wailing rose above the cawing of the crows in the bare trees.

I almost felt sorry for him. Almost.

{ 58 }

LIAM

Wednesday, November 8

Rose and I helped Dad into the funeral home's limo while Nora finished accepting condolences from Grandpa's friends. The gravediggers stood off in the distance, one of them drawing heavily on a cigarette, waiting for everyone to leave.

Madison found me as I paced the roadway that ran through the cemetery. "I'm sorry for your loss." She gave me a quick hug, conscious of the people still at the gravesite. "How's your dad?"

"He's a mess," I answered angrily. "We had to pour him into the car. I'm pretty sure he's been drunk since the day Grandpa died."

"Grief is hard," she said with too much sympathy for the loser. "Sometimes, people pick coping mechanisms that aren't for the best. Give him some time."

"I don't have time." Then, realizing how awful it sounded to only think of myself at Grandpa's grave, I shook my head. "Sorry. I'm being a selfish, privileged, rich boy. I guess the internet trolls are right about me."

She checked if anyone was near us before asking in a low voice, "How are you doing? I heard the police charged you."

I pawed at the gravel roadway with my dress shoe, scuffing the leather tips. "I'm tired of people staring at me. And then there's this." I lifted my pants leg to show her my GPS ankle monitor.

"What did your lawyer say about the charges?"

"He thinks he can plead them down. I guess Grandpa thought this might happen and had already talked to him back in September."

She nodded. "Avoiding a trial would be good."

"Yeah. Nora and I are meeting with him tomorrow. She's been great. I'd be screwed without her since Dad is useless."

We watched the thinning crowd around Nora, who was doing everything Dad should be doing right now.

"You know, every morning since the accident, I've woken up and thought, 'Is this the day I'm finally arrested?' And I assumed I'd feel differently than I do."

"How so?" she asked.

"I mean, I'm scared. Really scared. But I feel…lighter. I'm relieved it will be over soon." I let out a bitter laugh. "All I wanted that day was to have some fun before everyone took over my life. A few laughs and a few beers. Nothing else. And I've tried to convince myself the paddleboarder's death wasn't my fault. He should have known better than to be in the middle of the bay. But he was, and I wasn't paying attention. I was too worried about getting yelled at by Grandpa for spilling beer on his boat. They're both dead because of me."

She stepped closer to me, her eyes holding mine with their intensity. "Liam, you are not to blame for your grandfather's death. A lot has to happen, sometimes for years, before a person's heart gives out."

"But he didn't need me to add the stress of being charged with criminally negligent homicide." I shoved my hands in my coat pockets and clenched them to keep from screaming. "I can't believe I'm barely eighteen, and I've already blown up my life. I'd give anything to re-do that day on the boat."

"I've done some things in my life that I wish I hadn't," she said softly. "Everyone has. None of us are perfect."

"Oh, you've killed people?" I immediately regretted my smart mouth when she stumbled back a step as if my words had hit her. "I'm sorry. I know you're only trying to help me."

"If you don't go to prison, consider it a second chance at life. Maybe do something that will make a difference," she offered.

"Like stay in Williams Bay and keep the Clark legacy going?"

"Only if you want to. You don't have to do what your Grandpa planned for you. You no longer have to be the selfish, privileged, rich boy. Do something that makes you proud."

A few teachers passed by, smiling sympathetically. I acknowledged them with a nod, then waited until they were out of earshot. "Will any college accept me now? Can the school take away my scholarship? Because that's why my ex-best friend went to the police."

She checked if anyone was watching us before touching my cheek with her gloved fingers. "Take it one day at a time. If you need to talk, I'm here." She pointed with her chin at Nora several feet away. "I think your stepmom is ready to go, and I'd better head out, too."

"Thanks, Madison." As she walked away, I wondered why she was so nice to me because I certainly didn't deserve it.

Nora took a final look at Grandpa's grave, and I was surprised when her shoulders shook briefly. But when she turned, her face was dry and serene.

{ 59 }

ROSE

Wednesday, November 8

I sat in the limo with a bawling Hank and slowly shredded William Sr.'s funeral program. Occasionally, my stepfather stopped long enough to sip from his flask, giving me a needed break from his hysterics. In the distance, I watched Mom graciously accepting condolences from our neighbors and friends. She was amazing to watch and perhaps missed out on a career as an actress.

Could I have saved William Sr.? I swear I didn't know he was having a heart attack. I honestly thought he had fallen and deserved some payback pain for how he treated Mom and me. If I had known it was more serious, I would have done something immediately. When I went upstairs to my bedroom, I had every intention of calling for help in fifteen or twenty minutes.

But Mom came home and found him before that. Her CPR didn't revive him, so even if I had dialed 9-1-1, he still could have died. At least, that was what I told myself.

I checked my phone for a text from Chris, even though it hadn't pinged. He had been distant since I chose Zoe over his invitation to "Netflix and chill" a few weeks ago. I wanted to fix things between us but didn't know how. Actually, I did, but I didn't want to go there yet.

Liam stood far away from the remaining mourners as he talked to Ms. Taylor. That fateful Saturday had finally caught up with him, and I was impressed by how well he soldiered his arrest. With William Sr. gone, his chances of getting away without punishment were slim. I had expected him to be shouting his innocence for all to hear. Instead, he appeared resigned to face his fate.

As Liam and Ms. Taylor's conversation continued, I realized it was more than a routine condolence. Though their faces weren't clear, their body language showed a familiarity beyond student-teacher. More than once, they leaned toward each other, then broke apart. The conversation seemed heated but then cooled. She left after touching his cheek. Interesting.

I settled into the limo's comfy leather seats and closed my eyes.

Two Clarks down, one to go.

{ 60 }

HANK

Thursday, November 9

I snuck out of the house while my family slept and went to the high school before anyone would be there. Dad's funeral yesterday was the worst day of my life, and alcohol wasn't dulling the pain. There was no guarantee I'd find a solution in Madison's back room, but I had to try.

After retrieving a set of master keys from my office, I headed to the science room. My footsteps echoed in the vacant halls, and I shivered at the eerie silence. I didn't like being here without the chaos of a few hundred voices.

I left the lights off in the classroom and crept forward half-blind, avoiding the lab tables that stood between me and what I hoped would erase my sense of failure as a son and a

Clark. Coke-induced confidence didn't last long, but I would take any amount of respite at this point.

It took several attempts to unlock the door with my shaking hand, and the unpleasant sound of metal scraping metal added to my agitation. Once inside, I closed the door and turned on the light. Madison kept her goodies in a steel lockbox, but the times we had been together, the box had already been on the counter. I scanned the room and debated where the best hiding place would be. No particular spot stood out, so I opened each cabinet and rummaged through the contents. Then I moved on to the half-a-dozen drawers, even the ones that were too small.

Nothing. Not a damn thing. But it had to be here. I grasped handfuls of my hair and pulled. Think, Hank, think.

The only places left to look were the cardboard boxes on top of the cabinets. An image of Madison stretching on her tiptoes to reach one of them popped to mind. I grabbed the nearest carton, ripped it open, and dumped it out. Three tries later, the metal lockbox clattered to the floor.

"Yes," I whispered in relief.

Something slid back and forth when I shook it, and my hopes rose. I examined the lock. It seemed inferior enough. Maybe I could pick it, though I lacked skills in that area. But they did it on TV all the time. How hard could it be?

I straightened a paperclip from one of Madison's desk drawers and jammed it into the lock. Then, I wiggled it, waiting for a satisfying click to signal success. Instead, it snapped in two.

Stunned, I stared at the broken metal my fingers held, the matching half stuck firmly in the lock. I shook my head. Of course, that happened. Nothing ever went my way. In a fit of rage, I smashed the lockbox against the counter several times, which only resulted in a large scar across the Formica that would be hard to explain.

I started to cry—not a few manly tears, but all-out, choking sobs—and I fell to the floor. Holding the lockbox to my chest, I wept until I couldn't breathe. I stopped long enough to clear my nose before launching into round two of hysterics.

Finally, I quieted and forced my mind to consider my options. I could bawl some more while waiting for Madison to get in, but she had made it plain that I was on my own when dealing with my grief.

My stomach grumbled to remind me I had skipped breakfast. Probably the best thing I could do would be to put the lockbox back where I found it and eat something. If Madison confronted me, I would deny everything.

Squinting through my remaining tears at the jammed lock, I fingered the sharp end of the paperclip. Then, the obvious occurred to me. Mr. D's shop class, officially known as industrial arts, had tools. There had to be something I could use there.

***

My left pinky itched as I entered the dark classroom. During my freshman year, I had sliced the tip off with a circular saw while making a birdhouse. Dad was so embarrassed that he didn't fight me when I refused to take any more of Mr. D's classes.

I flipped on the lights, not caring at this point if I drew unwanted attention to my mission. Across the room, tools hung on a pegboard that covered the wall. I didn't know how to use most of them, but I could swing a hammer well enough. I picked the biggest one, set the lockbox on a nearby work table, and let loose.

Ten blows later, I stopped to check my progress. The box had caved around the lock, and the lid had separated from the base several centimeters, leaving a slit. I hammered some more, then forced a wooden wedge in the opening and struck that to widen the gap.

Panting from the effort, I untucked my sweaty shirt and flapped the tail, the cool air drying my skin. Then, I turned on my phone's flashlight and peered into the box. Whatever was sliding back and forth didn't look like drugs. But what else would Madison hide?

Confident that success was within my reach, I renewed my efforts until the lid bent enough to shake out the box's valuables.

Photos slid across the table. I picked up one, and my curiosity quickly changed to fear. It was me. And Madison. In her back room. Being unprofessional. My fingers rifled through a dozen shots of us vaping, kissing, undressing, and *more*. But how?

"Hank, can I help you with something?"

Mr. D, the grizzled shop teacher who had held a dirty rag to my bleeding pinky thirty-two years ago, stood in the doorway with a justifiably puzzled expression. I only set foot in his classroom on the first day of each school term, so entering it in November was unprecedented.

I swept up the photos and the mangled lockbox and hugged them to my chest.

"No. Thank you, but no. I lost the key to this box, but I got it open." I smiled, but it felt unnatural, too wide and stiff. "Sorry about using your stuff, but it was an emergency."

One of his calloused fingers scratched his ever-present stubble as his eyes tried to reconcile my explanation and disheveled appearance. After a moment, he accepted my apology with a nod.

"At least you didn't lose any digits this time, but you could have opened the box without pounding the crap out of it. A drill through the lock would have done the trick."

"Ha, I'm such a numskull. Next time, I'll be sure to ask your advice." I attempted to smile again to show him I was reasonably sane but faltered after a few seconds. "Have a great day, Mr. D."

***

The halls were still empty as I ran to my office, closed the door, and locked it. Sitting at my desk, I scrutinized the photos, the dread building in my stomach with each scandalous depiction. There could be no refuting the man was me, and it was clear my career and marriage would be over if anyone saw these. I reached for the wastebasket and dry-heaved until a mouthful of bile came up.

My head ached as I tried to make sense of my discovery. Why would Madison take photos of us? Did she plan to blackmail me? Was it to ensure I paid her back for the drugs?

But maybe the whole thing was innocent, and she liked to keep souvenirs of her trysts. I didn't consider myself kinky by any means, but occasionally I watched a soft porn movie. Perhaps she did, too.

Then, another alarming thought popped into my whirling brain. It didn't matter that I had these photos. Madison had the digital files. I would have to make her delete them or be forever at her mercy.

A knock sounded on my office door, and I yelped at the interruption. My fingers felt like fat sausages as I wrestled with collecting the photos.

"Hank?" Ray called out. "Are you in there?"

"Yeah, just a sec." I shoved the incriminating photos into the inner pocket of my sports coat, where their weight mocked me. Then, I opened the door a crack and stuck my head out.

The shock on his face quickly turned to concern. "Go home, Hank. We'll manage without you."

That was the last thing I wanted to do. I needed to talk to Madison, but Ray's troubled expression told me it would be a hard sell.

"Seriously. You look terrible," he said.

I nodded. "OK, I will, but I need to do something first."

He grabbed my arm as I moved past him. "No. Now. I don't think the kids should see you looking like this."

I sighed, suddenly exhausted. Confronting Madison would have to wait.

{ 61 }

LIAM

Thursday, November 9

Grandpa's funeral yesterday gave me some closure, but the rest of my life continued to be a disaster. Dad drank from the moment we got home until he passed out after supper. I couldn't sleep and must have looked like hell because Nora suggested I skip school, but I needed the distraction. And also a friend.

I found Madison kneeling in the back room of her classroom. Cupboard doors and drawers were wide open, and papers and boxes littered the floor.

"Wow, what happened here?" I asked.

She stood and added the papers in her hand to a pile on the counter. "Well, either someone hates me, or they were looking for something."

"Like what?" I asked. "A test?"

"I don't keep hard copies of tests, but maybe they didn't know that."

"Is anything missing?"

"So far, it doesn't look like it. There's nothing valuable in here except for the microscopes, and that box wasn't touched."

"Did you tell my dad about this? He'll probably want to call the police."

She mumbled something under her breath but then said louder, "I'll make sure he hears about it."

I examined the doorknob. "How did they get in? I see a few scratches, but the lock doesn't look damaged."

"I don't think I left it open, but maybe."

"It should lock automatically. Like for safety. Ask my dad to change it."

Suddenly, she covered her face with her hands and let out a frustrated groan.

"Hey, it's OK," I said, surprised by her actions. "Don't let the moron who did this get to you. We can clean up the mess in no time."

When her hands fell away, her eyes shined with tears. "No, you need to get to class. The first-period bell is going to ring in a few minutes." She grabbed a tissue and wiped her nose. "But thank you."

"I can be late." I stowed my backpack in the nearest corner. "You shouldn't have to deal with this by yourself."

She made a noise that might have been a laugh or a cry. "You're such a sweetheart. Here you are worried about me when you have your own troubles."

My troubles. The reason I had sought Madison out in the first place. To ease our miseries, I wrapped my arms around her, expecting to be pushed away, but her fingers fisted my T-shirt and held tight. I wasn't used to caring about someone more than myself, but once the strangeness passed, I liked it. Which scared me, to be honest.

The bell sounded, breaking us apart with its jarring tone.

"You're late," she said with a resigned twist of her lips. "I'll write you a note."

{ 62 }

HANK

Friday, November 10

With my car heater running full blast to combat the November morning chill, I stared at the banking app on my phone, willing it to tell me better news, but numbers don't lie. After I paid the retainer for Liam's lawyer, my account barely had enough for the mortgage. Luckily, the judge released Liam on his own recognizance; otherwise, my boy would be sitting in jail until I had access to Dad's estate. The old coot never discussed his finances, but he never spent money unless he had to. I suspected he had piles of cash hoarded away, and I needed it for groceries and utilities—and Madison.

My life was a moral septic tank filled with illegal drugs, sporadic infidelity, and damning photos. My vices got the best of me, and now I was up to my waist in feces.

I popped three aspirins in my mouth and drank deeply from my travel mug, which contained orange juice and vodka—another sign of my decline. Yes, I had my after-dinner drinks, but I never sat in a car at seven in the morning drinking a screwdriver.

I switched to my texts and reread Madison's last message.

```
WHERE R U? We need
to talk ASAP. And
don't forget my $.
My credit card
payment is due.
```

The timestamp was from yesterday at 7:38 a.m. She must have found the mess I had left in her back room, and I was glad I had gone home for the day. She seemed angry, and I couldn't blame her, but so was I. Yes, we had to "talk ASAP." I needed to know her intentions regarding the photos she took, but first, I had to resolve my money problem.

Across the street, the lights went on in Frank's Barbershop, and through the large window pane, I saw the owner moving about. A moment later, he flipped the Closed sign and unlocked the door. It was the oldest business in the village, and Frank was one of the wealthiest residents. Sometimes, I wondered how he made his fortune—his rates were bargain basement—but he was a generous athletic booster and possibly a stopgap solution.

The bell above the door rang as I pushed it open, and Frank spun around, not expecting a customer so soon. He was a short man in his early seventies with precisely combed silver hair. As his official barber uniform, he wore a red and white checkered shirt and a navy blue apron, all starched and ironed.

Entering his shop was like time-traveling to the 1960s, complete with a penny gumball machine, a water cooler, and a shoeshine stand. Even the magazines shelved neatly in racks were decades old. Two swiveling barber chairs decked out in mahogany leather and shiny chrome faced a mirror that took up most of one wall. The counter under the mirror displayed everything Frank needed, from towels and combs to razors and scissors.

"Didn't mean to sneak up on you, Frank," I said too loudly with a half smile that felt wrong, considering what I was about to do.

He waved away my apology. "I'm sorry for your loss, Hank. William Sr. was a good friend who never missed his weekly haircut. I talked to Nora at the burial, but you were…"

Thankfully, he stopped. I didn't want to hear how anyone would describe my behavior at the cemetery.

"What can I do for you?" His eyes narrowed, almost disappearing, as he appraised my wavy hairstyle.

I nervously ran my fingers over my scalp, hoping he wouldn't suggest a buzzcut.

"As you know, my father loved the village and dedicated his life to it," I said quickly to divert his attention. "I want to create a memorial in his honor. Maybe something football-related since his high school team won the state tournament twice. He was terribly proud of that."

And he never failed to mention it every football season that I coached.

Frank pursed his lips and moved to a color photo on the wall of his senior year football team. Like Dad's, they were state champs. "William Sr. was an excellent three-sport athlete. It seems like your boy inherited some of his talent."

"I guess it skipped a generation," I said with a fake laugh. "But you're right. Liam is the school's top athlete without a doubt."

"You came in to ask for money?" Frank was blunt but not mean. I appreciated that about him.

Unable to lie while looking at his face, I focused on the black and white linoleum floor. "Yes, I was hoping for some community support. I would solicit the Athletic Boosters, but I don't want to take any funds away from the kids."

He reached into the pocket of his pressed khakis and pulled out a wad of bills. He peeled off several and held them out. "Maybe add my name to the basketball game programs. Remind people I'm still alive and cutting hair."

"Of course." I nodded vigorously and snatched the money before I changed my mind. "That's a great idea. And I truly appreciate your generosity." I stood for a moment in the middle of the barbershop, feeling like a criminal. "Well, I'd better get to the school. I don't want to miss greeting the kids. It's my favorite part of the day."

I pumped Frank's hand and thanked him again.

"You and your family take care," he called after me as I fled the shop, and his kind words punched me in the gut.

Out on the street, I looked over my shoulder and through the window, but Frank had disappeared. I opened my fist and quickly counted the crumpled bills as I walked. Five hundred dollars. It was almost what I owed Madison. I inhaled deeply, trying to steady my racing nerves.

"Hi, Hank."

The high-pitched scream I let out proved I was near my breaking point, and things had to change. Rose stood by my car, her typically expressionless face now wary.

"Are you OK?" she asked slowly as if a normal tempo might send me running through the streets.

My mouth refused to form words, so I did what I always did when faced with an uncomfortable situation. I laughed. Manically.

"I'm fine," I assured her in a shaky voice. A drop of sweat slid from my brow despite the frosty temperature, and I swiped at it with my sleeve. "You startled me, that's all. Didn't you leave with Liam?"

She took a sip from a to-go cup from the café across from the barbershop. "I had a late night studying and needed extra caffeine today."

"Ahhh. And your mother's coffee is anything but strong."

She grimaced, wrinkling her nose. "Exactly."

I scanned the street. "Where's Liam?"

"He didn't want to wait for me."

I sighed. My son had never been considerate to his stepsister, and I didn't possess the parenting skills to change him.

"I'll talk to him," I said halfheartedly, then pointed at my car with my chin. "Hop in. We should make it before first period starts."

She buckled her seatbelt and asked, "Were you getting a haircut?"

"What?"

"At Frank's. Don't you usually go to Mom's salon?"

"I…I was picking up a donation."

"Looks like a lot."

"I'm sorry?"

"In your hand. Are those one-hundred-dollar bills?"

"Yes." I shoved the money into my pocket and tried to ignore the bulge they made.

She nodded, and I thought that would be the end, but Rose was the smart one in the family. "Isn't it the Athletic Boosters' job to collect donations?"

"This is for William Sr. I want to create a memorial for him." The more I repeated the lie, the easier it got.

Her lip curled in disgust, but I didn't blame her. My father hadn't shown her an ounce of kindness in five years. She tapped her phone open, apparently done with our conversation.

I pushed at my pants pocket to flatten the lump from Frank's money. There were a few more business owners I could hit up for a donation during the noon hour. Maybe once I was square with Madison, she would delete the photo files. Then, I would stop these crazy shenanigans. No more sex. No more drugs. I would be the devoted husband and father my family deserved.

{ 63 }

ROSE

Friday, November 10

"Rose, Rose McCabe!" Mrs. Parker waved at me from the doorway of the high school office.

I hesitated, debating whether I could pretend I didn't hear her calling out to me. Pizza had been served at lunch, which meant longer lines than usual. I was running late and had to go to my locker before class. But you didn't want to get on Mrs. Parker's bad side, so I weaved through my classmates until I reached her.

"Yes, Mrs. Parker?" I asked, bouncing on my heels.

"Do you know where your dad is?"

Automatically, my brain replaced "dad" with "stepdad," but I didn't correct her. Nobody grasped how significant the difference was to me.

"I haven't seen him for over an hour," she continued, "and he has a meeting with a parent in five minutes." Her usual pinched expression deepened as her fingers fiddled with her watch as if she could slow its ticking. "Did he go home? I would understand if he did, but he should have told someone."

"Sorry. I have no idea. Did you try calling his cell?"

"Of course I did," she snapped with a withering glare. "It went straight to voicemail."

There was no one left in the halls except us now, and my anxiety went up several notches. I had to give her something, or the conversation would drag on.

"Maybe he's out collecting more money for his dad's memorial," I offered.

"A memorial? What is Dr. Clark planning?"

I shrugged. "He didn't say, but that's why we were late this morning."

"If he needs more donations, I'm sure we could have a school fundraiser. William Sr. was a very important alum. I'll discuss it with Principal Walker."

The bell rang, and I pointed to the air. "Sounds good. I have to go."

Mrs. Parker dismissed me with a nod and turned her hawk-like nose to the school's front doors, awaiting Hank's return.

{ 64 }

HANK

Friday, November 10

"Why, Madison? Why?" I threw the proof of my transgressions onto the counter of the back room, the place that used to be a sanctuary from my dull life but was now a den of lies.

I had decided to go on the offense and focus on her treachery, skipping over how I found the photos. But she had her own battle plan ready.

"How dare you come in here mad at me. You trashed this room." She waved her arms at the cupboards, drawers, and boxes I had rifled through. "It took me over two hours to clean up your mess—time I should have used on my billion daily teacher tasks. Tell me you weren't trying to steal drugs from me."

"I…I…needed something to get me through the day, and I had every intention of paying you for it." I puffed out my chest and lifted my chin. "In case you forgot, my father died, and I'm grieving. *You* made it clear I was on my own."

Her eyes widened. "This was my fault? I drove you to act like a madman?"

"I asked you for help, and you said no."

"You wanted to be high at your father's funeral," she shot back. "That would not have been a good idea."

"It didn't matter, did it? Instead, I got drunk and made a fool of myself."

She gazed heavenward, her face reflecting the pain of her thoughts or maybe my presence. I couldn't tell.

After several moments, she said, "Hank, I'm not going to sell you any more coke. Ever. I'm sorry if I started you on this road, but I think you have a drug problem that needs to be addressed."

Her words offended me, and I immediately denied her declaration. "I don't need your drugs. I can stop anytime I want to."

"Spoken like an addict," she said softly.

I sunk to the floor, exhausted. Somehow, I needed to get the upper hand or, at least, convince Madison I had it. "Those photos can't hurt me. I'm a Clark. I can survive an infidelity scandal. All I have to say is my marriage was over, but we hadn't gotten a divorce because of the kids. Everyone will believe me, and it will be true once Nora finds out."

Her ample bosom rose and fell as she sighed, her backside against the counter and her beautiful legs crossed at the ankles. Even after her betrayal, she was hard to resist.

"No one will care," I said, hoping to sound nonchalant.

She went to her purse and pulled out an envelope. A dozen more photos spilled onto the counter as she shook it.

"I printed these last night. I had hoped I wouldn't need to use them, but…" She held one up with her thumb and forefinger. "This one is my favorite."

She flipped it around, and my brain stuttered, unable to make sense of the image. But then it became clear, and I saw me snorting coke off of a textbook.

My hand flew to my mouth, and I gasped in horror. My life, as I knew it, was officially over.

"You're evil," I whispered.

Her flat laugh chilled my blood. "I didn't force you to do anything you didn't want to do."

"I thought you liked me. Why would you take pictures of me—of us? And you sold me the drugs in those photos. Don't you realize you will get into trouble as well?"

"Maybe. But I doubt it. I'm young, pretty, and vulnerable. It won't take much to twist this into an authority figure abusing his power over a subordinate. Ever heard of

#MeToo?" She tilted her head and mockingly batted her eyelashes at me. "We'll both be fine if you keep your mouth shut and pony up what you owe me."

"And I have some of it." I stood and dug in my pocket. "Here's five hundred. And as soon as I deposit a few checks and they clear, I can give you the rest."

She counted the bills as if I would cheat her before tucking them into her wallet.

"Will you delete the photo files now?" I hated how my voice trembled, revealing how weak I really was.

She shook her head. "No. I'll be keeping those in a safe place."

"You want more money? Once Dad's estate is settled, I'm sure we can work something out."

"No, I only want what you owe me." She gathered up the photos and waved them in my face. "I'll be holding on to the files for job security. If you or the school board even thinks about firing me—for whatever reason—you'd better remember I have them."

"Is that what this is all about?" I exclaimed, relief flooding my body. Things weren't as bad as I thought. *Madison* wasn't as bad as I thought. It was all a big misunderstanding easily cleared up. "We could have talked about your fears like two grown adults. You didn't have to resort to blackmail."

"Yes, I did." She slapped the photos onto my chest, and my hands quickly covered hers. "Because this is over."

"You don't mean that," I said, clutching her fingers like a lifeline. "If I promise to have your back with the school board and you delete the files, we can forget this happened. Why would you want our fun to end?"

She ripped her hand away, and the photos fell to the floor. "You're embarrassing yourself, Hank. Just accept it's over between us."

"No, I know you enjoyed being with me. And I need you now more than ever. My life is falling apart. My dad is dead, my son is probably going to prison thanks to his best friend, and my wife won't sleep with me."

In desperation, I stepped on the proof of my misbehavior and pushed her against the counter. My hands circled her waist, and when she didn't reciprocate, I tried kissing her neck.

"Please, Madison, please?" I begged.

{ 65 }

LIAM

Friday, November 10

"Hey, Mouse, have you seen my dad?" I asked. Classes were over, and basketball practice wouldn't start for another hour. So, the high school was mostly deserted except for a few teachers and nerds like my stepsister.

Rose juggled the book she was putting away in her perfectly organized locker. I didn't know why she bothered keeping it so neat. It wasn't like there was a Most Anal Student award up for grabs.

She didn't turn around, but she did answer me. "He went into Ms. Taylor's room about ten minutes ago."

My stomach rolled, though I was probably being paranoid. If Madison were in any kind of trouble, Principal

Walker would handle it. Dad was most likely killing time, avoiding whatever his real job was.

The classroom door was open, and I expected to see Madison at her desk, respectfully listening to one of Dad's boring stories that was supposed to teach something. But there were only empty lab tables, a clean whiteboard, and an overflowing wastebasket.

In the air, I smelled her musty perfume mixed with the leftover sour odor of high schoolers, and my groin reacted like one of Pavlov's dogs. The steady tick of the wall clock filled the afterschool silence, and I turned to leave, but then a rustle, a thump, and a moan came from behind the door of the back room.

"Please, Madison, please?" A deep, male voice begged.

I had been with enough girls in the back of my car to recognize horny pleading when I heard it. And though Madison and I weren't in a normal boyfriend/girlfriend relationship, it didn't stop rage and jealousy from hijacking my body. Not thinking about the consequences, I charged between the lab tables and yanked open the door. Dad had Madison up against the counter, his face buried in her neck.

They both screamed, and I answered with a roar. "How could you? I…I…How could you?"

I doubled over, one hand on my chest as I fought for air. Then I sprinted from the room.

I passed Rose, and a second later, Dad shouted from the end of the hallway, "Liam! Stop! Please! Liam!"

But I didn't. I never wanted to see him again.

{ 66 }

HANK

Friday, November 10

What have I done? What must my son think of me?

In front of the school's office, feeling helpless and ashamed, I covered my face with my hands—which smelled of another woman's body—and the tears started to fall.

"Hank? I heard shouting. Are you all right? Is Liam?" Ray asked after coming out of his office to investigate.

Slowly, my arms dropped to my sides, and I exhaled. "No, I'm not. And Liam definitely isn't."

"Come with me." He took my elbow and guided me past Mrs. Parker to the chair I sat in after the pep rally debacle. I was such a screwup.

"Do you want something to drink?" Without waiting for my answer, he opened a desk drawer and took out a flask and a coffee mug. He poured about an inch of liquid into the cup and handed it to me. "I knew you weren't doing as well as you said. Grief can come in waves and hit you when you least expect it."

I hung my head. Ray thought we were distraught over William Sr.'s death. If only he knew the truth.

"Mrs. Parker said you're collecting donations for a memorial for your dad. That's a great idea, and I bet it will help your family heal." He pulled out his wallet from his back pocket and thumbed through the contents before removing several bills. "I can only spare fifty today, but I would be happy to contribute more on Monday."

I stared at the money he had placed on my side of his desk, unable to move a muscle.

"Take it. Please. And Mrs. Parker said she'd spearhead a school fundraiser. Your dad did so much good for Williams Bay, and we'd like to help honor him. Have you hit up the village board yet?"

I downed the liquor in the coffee mug in one gulp and wiped my lips with the back of my hand. "No, it's still early days. I haven't even properly discussed the idea with Nora and the kids."

He nodded. "Let me know what we can do. We're your family, too, and we'll support you in any way we can."

My stomach rejected the shot of alcohol, forcing me to swallow the regurgitated liquid or throw up in Ray's garbage can. My fist flew to my mouth as the mixture of digestive acid and liquor burned my insides for the second time.

"Thank you," I managed to say. "I think I should go home now."

I stood but had to grab the edge of the desk as my legs refused to hold up my weight.

Ray popped up and hurried to my side. "Let me drive you, Hank."

"No." I inhaled deeply and slowly turned away from him. "I need to be alone."

{ 67 }

LIAM

Friday, November 10

I hated that the lakefront I used to love now reminded me of when my life first went to hell. Ever since the paddleboarder died, one bomb after another blew up my life. Melodramatic, yes. But that was how it felt.

Anger pulsed through my veins as I strode past the boat launch and the beach. I ignored the dog walkers and the ducks. All I saw was Dad with his hands all over Madison. I didn't listen to the water lapping against the shore or the seagulls screaming. Instead, I heard his pathetic pleas.

The clicking of heels on the concrete path broke through, and I knew who was behind me. I picked up my speed. I had nothing to say to her.

"Liam," Madison called in a frantic voice. "Let me explain."

What could she possibly say to justify what I had seen?

The clicking stopped, and I figured she had given up, but then she grabbed my arm with one hand. Her shoes dangled from the other.

"Please." Mascara and tears streaked her face. "Give me five minutes."

It was so unfair when girls cried. I collapsed onto a nearby bench and folded my arms like a spoiled child. She sat beside me and wiped her cheeks with her fingers, her breath coming in short gasps.

"Thank you," she said once she had recovered. "Please believe me when I say I didn't start the school year planning to have an affair with your dad. At first, we only flirted, but then I needed some job security."

"You've lost me," I gritted out.

"As a new teacher, I would be one of the first to be laid off if there were budget cuts. And these days, there are always budget cuts." She inhaled deeply and said in a rush, "I also sell weed to your classmates."

My head exploded from yet another bomb. "You're a drug dealer? How can you do that? Teachers are supposed to care about their students."

"Which is exactly why I do it," she said defensively. "Teenagers will score drugs with or without my help, either from their parent's medicine cabinet or the meth head in the next town over. My college roommate is a partner in a dispensary in Illinois. She sells me regulated weed at a discount, and I turn it around at a modest markup. My customers get safer products, and I have money for my student loans. It's a win-win situation. And anyway, because of buying restrictions, I don't sell a high volume of product. I'm not running a drug cartel."

"So, if my dad found out about the weed or needed to fire teachers, you would what—blackmail him about having sex with you?"

"That and the drugs he did."

I laughed bitterly. "I don't believe you. My dad is totally uptight about rules. Yeah, he likes his whiskey, but he would never do anything illegal."

"I'm not lying to you, and I have the pictures to prove it. Your dad is a coke hound. I tried limiting our…sessions to weed, but he wanted more thrills. Maybe he's having a midlife crisis. Like you, he rarely has a choice in how to live his life."

I scrubbed my head with my fingertips, willing my brain to comprehend everything she claimed. "OK. Let me summarize your lecture, Ms. Taylor," I said, lacing the words with every ounce of sarcasm that I could. "You tricked my dad into having an affair and doing drugs so that you could blackmail him and have job security."

Her eyes flashed. "There was no tricking. If the rumors are true, I wasn't the first mistress your dad had. He's no different than all the other men I have met since I turned twelve and hooked my first push-up bra. They look at me and see only one thing—someone to screw.

"When your dad interviewed me for this job, it didn't matter that I had graduated from college in the top ten percent. He stared at my chest the whole time. So, yeah. I took advantage of that because, you see, I didn't grow up in a big house with family meals and yearly vacations. I grew up dirt poor in a city where the only stat higher than the unemployment rate was the alcoholism rate. Getting a degree was my way out of that pit. I can barely pay my regular bills, let alone my student loans, on the salary of a first-year teacher. I do what I have to do to survive. I always have."

I stared at the boats on the water as I considered her story. How many times had I seen Dad cozy up to a woman and I passed it off as him being goofy?

"At the Homecoming dance, I saw you and Dad in the parking lot. I wondered what you were doing."

"That was the first night he got high with me. It escalated fast after that." She laid a hand on my arm. "Please believe me. I never thought he'd get so out of control."

I knew I was privileged to live in an upper-middle-class village. I had never wanted for any basic need, so who was I to judge what she did?

"Where do I fit in?" I asked, not sure if I could handle an honest answer. "Were you pretending to be nice to me?"

"No, not at all. I like you. I really do." Her green eyes, filled with tears, held my gaze. "But, Liam, there's more. I think he is addicted to coke. I've cut him off, but he needs help."

"Like an intervention?"

"That would be a good start. If he can't stop by himself, your family should consider a rehab facility."

"Are you high right now? A Clark going to rehab? Grandpa would come back from the dead to keep that from happening."

"Believe me. It's better than the alternative."

I stared at the lake, trying to process everything she had thrown at me.

"Liam," she said softly, "you need to help him now before he destroys his life."

{ 68 }

HANK

Saturday, November 11

"Hank? Are you getting out of bed today?" Nora asked.

The comforter over my head muffled her voice, but the irritation came through loud and clear. I pretended not to hear her. My head felt heavy, and my eyes itched from dryness. I tried to peel them open, but it was too painful. Water. Every fiber of my dehydrated body begged for water.

I couldn't go home after Liam caught me with Madison yesterday, so I did the next best thing: I got plastered. The individual actions of each minute of last night were a dim blur and unrecoverable from my alcohol-soaked brain. Still, I remembered visiting the two drinking establishments in town. Was I responsible enough to leave my car at one of the taverns? Yes, or I would have already heard about it from Nora if I hadn't.

She shook my shoulder. "Answer me. It's almost noon."

I made a small opening in my cocoon. The fresh air was a nice change from the stale smells emitting from my pores. I ran my tongue over my cracked lips and croaked, "I'm sick."

"Of course you are. You were so drunk last night that Rose and I had to help you up the stairs. Why didn't you call or text me? I was worried when you weren't home for dinner."

"Please, stop." A wave of nausea spun the bed, and I fought the urge to vomit whatever poison was in my stomach.

"Stop what?"

"Talking," I gasped, hugging a pillow tighter to my chest.

"I can't believe you." Her irritation had grown to anger. "Yes, you're allowed to grieve for William Sr., but you need to pull yourself together. You're setting a terrible example for Rose and Liam."

Liam's name struck me like a dagger in the heart. "Did he see me last night?"

"No. He was in his room, but he might have heard you. You stumbled several times in the hallway."

I let out a long sigh. "Give me a minute."

"Whatever. Rose and I are going to run errands."

She yanked the door shut on her way out, and the resulting sound was as effective as if she had smacked me in the forehead. A sob escaped my lips as a burst of pain radiated through my skull. When it subsided, I sat up slowly and eyed our bathroom. If I could make it there without dying, unlimited glasses of water and a hot shower would be my reward.

An hour later, I crept out of my bedroom, stopped in the hallway, and listened to the house. All was quiet, and Liam's door was closed, but that didn't mean he wasn't home. He could be in there, and if he saw me, I would have to explain my shameful actions. I eased past his door and tip-toed to the kitchen.

The coffee pot held a few ounces of pale, cold liquid. I poured it into a cup—but not the one with #1 Dad printed on its side, which I usually used—and brought it to my lips. Bile filled my mouth a second later, and I ran to the sink. Even with a desperate need for caffeine, my body rejected Nora's version of coffee. I settled for dry toast and a soda.

I felt mildly better and sat at the breakfast counter to ponder how to proceed with my disaster-packed life.

My marriage was on life-support. Nora's eyes, which once reflected love, now flashed with disdain.

Madison controlled the future of my professional and personal life. One wrong move from me, and the whole town would know about those photos. She also ended our trysts, taking away the one fun thing in my life.

With Dad gone, I was expected to step into his place as village leader, but I had lied to upstanding residents as I gathered the money I owed to Madison. I was a disgrace and not fit for office.

Sawyer, a kid Nora and I practically raised, turned his back on us and ruined Liam's life. My boy wouldn't survive prison with his good looks. That realization had me running to the sink again, but my stomach settled after several feeble gags.

I asked my brain to find a solution to at least one of these crises, but it was like listening to a foreign language. A few words were recognizable, but the rest was jibberish.

My phone hadn't buzzed all day. I was foolish to expect it, but I had hoped Madison would text me. Maybe she would change her mind about us with some time and distance.

Above me, a door opened and closed. I froze, fearfully eyeing the hallway and stairs beyond the kitchen. When Liam didn't appear, my body went limp in relief. The sound of water rushing through the pipes came from the far wall, then a door opening and closing again. It was only a bathroom break, but the adrenaline rush had sparked my brain. I had a plan.

{ 69 }

ROSE

Saturday, November 11

Entry from the Journal of Rose McCabe:

I'm going to talk to Mom again about Hank. After last night, she had to realize she'd be better off without him.

***

"What are you going to do about Hank?" I asked Mom as she pulled into a parking space at the grocery. "Are you going to leave him?"

"Because he came home drunk?" She laughed, though I didn't find anything amusing in what I asked. "No, honey. He's grieving. I can forgive him for a lapse in good judgment."

"But he's been acting weird for a long time now. I never told you about the pep rally and the homecoming dance. I think he was wasted then, too."

"I know all about that. The ladies in the Lioness Club made sure of it." She scowled at the memory. "When I asked Hank, he said he reacted badly to some medicine."

"And you believed him?"

"Of course I did. He's my husband." She dismissed my doubt with a pat on my thigh. "You'll understand when you're older."

I understood now, and I wasn't going to let it go. My stepfather didn't deserve my mother, and I needed her to realize it.

"Football season is over, but he still isn't home much. Where is he? What's he doing?" I asked.

"Honestly, Rose, you sound like a police detective. He's behind in his school paperwork and has deadlines to meet."

"Mom, I…I see him with Ms. Taylor all of the time. Have you seen what she looks like?"

Her face remained impassive as she stared out the front windshield, but her chest's sharp rise and fall told the true story. Finally, she said, "Ms. Taylor is a first-year teacher. I'm sure Hank is mentoring her. It's part of his job description."

"You don't have to put up with another man who treats you like dirt," I insisted, willing her to open her eyes and face reality.

"OK, that's enough." She shut off the engine and reached between us for her purse in the backseat. As she searched it for the shopping list, she added in an unsteady voice, "Hank is your stepfather and a very good one. I've made bad choices before, but Hank isn't one of them."

She got out of the car, and I slowly followed. I hated that my words hurt her, but I wanted her to protect herself. Whether Mom was ready to accept it or not, we needed Hank out of our lives.

{ 70 }

LIAM

Saturday, November 11

I had the house to myself and was scrounging for something to eat when Madison texted me.

```
Have you talked to
your dad yet?

                                        No. He got drunk
                                        last night. He was
                                        in the kitchen a
                                        while ago, but I
                                        think he left.

You need to talk to
him.

                                        I don't know what
                                        to say.
```

Start with how you feel.

I don't know how I feel.

Really?

OK, I'm pissed. I've lost all respect for him. I always thought he was kind of a dufus but in a funny way. My Grandpa was always a jerk to him, but Dad seemed to have it together at school. But he didn't. And he cheated on Nora. She didn't deserve that.

I'm sorry about Nora. I'm sorry about everything.

You didn't make him do any of this. He could have said no.

You need to confront him about the drugs.

Are you sure he has a problem? Maybe he was blowing off steam, and it's all out of his system now.

He's texted me thirty times since last night. He alternates between asking me to keep seeing him and begging me to get him some coke. I finally blocked him.

OK. I get it.

{71}

HANK

Saturday, November 11

If Madison wouldn't sell me more drugs, I'd buy them from someone else. She couldn't be the only dealer in the county. A few lines of coke would give me the concentration I needed to figure out how to fix the mess I was in. Then, I would be done with it. I would prove to Madison that I wasn't an addict, and she would take me back.

But first, I required more money. Up to now, taking school funds had been off-limits, but these were desperate times. Ray kept some petty cash for student emergencies in a locked file cabinet in the office, but I had a key. So, a short detour was in order before I started my quest for a drug dealer.

The village of Williams Bay sits within a ten-minute reach of four towns. After stopping at the school, I headed for the one nicknamed "Little Chicago." I figured I'd have a better chance of finding a dealer or someone willing to part with their private stash there. Either way, I was determined to buy what I needed—and by "needed," I meant in a non-addict way, thank you very much.

The summer tourist season had been over for a few months, but it was the weekend, so the downtown streets of Lake Geneva were full of cars and people. I circled several blocks until I found a parking space and then walked to the Lakeside Saloon, a busy drinking establishment.

Since I was worried someone might recognize me, I had switched my usual Williams Bay High School jacket for a Cubs baseball sweatshirt and hat. I even added mirror sunglasses, but those had to come off after I bumped into the hostess station in the semi-dark room.

The place was hopping, with every bar stool and table occupied. TVs lined the walls and displayed various sporting events. A few servers circulated the room with trays loaded with drinks, and the smell of fried, greasy food saturated the air along with loud classic rock from a corner jukebox.

Relying on my drug knowledge from movies, I decided to wait in the hallway where the bathrooms were. I watched people go in and out and could tell that most of them were too drunk to drive, but I wasn't sure if they were also high.

Then, a twenty-something man came out of the men's room wiping his nose. Bingo.

Before he could rejoin his friends, I stepped in front of him.

"Excuse me?" he said, clearly peeved by my blocking his path.

I held up my hands in apology. "Sorry, I just wanted to ask you something."

"You're not my type."

"No, that's not it."

"OK, so, what do you want?"

I rubbed a finger under my nose and sniffed, hoping he'd know what I meant.

He looked perplexed. "Do you need a tissue?"

I leaned in and whispered, "I want to buy some coke. Do you have any?"

"What? Why would you think that? Are you a cop? Because I'm in law school, and this is entrapment."

"No, no, no. I'm just a guy. You were wiping off your nose. I thought you might help me out."

"Dude, I have a cold."

"Oh, so that's a 'no'?"

He answered with a glare.

"I'm sorry to bother you. No hard feelings, right?"

"The Cubs suck," he said with a sneer at my sweatshirt.

I nodded in agreement as he walked away.

A stool opened up at the bar. I ordered a whiskey sour and downed it in one gulp. After two more drinks, I tried my sniffing routine on the heavily tattooed bartender. He gave me a pile of cocktail napkins.

To avoid another misunderstanding, I decided to hang out in the men's room. I hoped I'd see or hear something to confirm a person was snorting up. At first, I pretended to wash my hands while monitoring the bar's patrons. But I felt like a pervert after a few suspicious stares, so I moved into a stall.

More than an hour of foul smells later, I found a man willing to part with some of his powder. Feeling triumphant, I headed to my car.

{ 72 }

ROSE

Saturday, November 11

The house was quiet when I got home from having dinner with Zoe. Before William Sr. died, a TV would be blaring from some room, usually his, and Mom and Hank would be hanging out in the kitchen or living room. Despite what Mom said earlier today, she seemed to be avoiding him. And Liam shunned everyone, only abandoning his room to leave the house.

I poured a glass of water and leaned against the counter. My phone dinged, and I stared at a text from Zoe.

```
OMG, I just heard.
What an ass. Are
you OK?
```

```
                        Heard what?
```

```
Isabel texted me
that Gabby texted
her that Chris
broke up with you.
She saw him with
Tara.
```

I read her reply three times before it sunk in, and even then, it made no sense. I slid to the floor and put my head between my knees. When I could breathe again, I sent my "boyfriend" a message.

```
                      Why are people
                      saying you broke up
                      with me?
```

```
Wow, my bad. But,
yeah, I was going to
tell you tomorrow.
```

```
                      I don't understand.
                      I thought you liked
                      me.
```

```
You're great, but
IDK, I want to see
other girls.
```

```
                      Like Tara?
```

```
Yeah, maybe. Guess
she's over Liam.
```

The tears came pouring out, and I was too blind to reply, not that I had anything else to say. I wasn't going to beg him to be with me.

Zoe texted me again, but I ignored her. A mixture of shame and grief smothered me, leaving me weak and trembling. This pain was why I should have kept to myself. If I hadn't been friends with Zoe and Isabel, I wouldn't have gone to Sawyer's party. I wouldn't have talked to Chris. We wouldn't have danced at Homecoming, and we wouldn't have dated—and broken up. If I had stayed a loner, he couldn't have hurt me.

Then, I remembered an offhand remark from my ex-boyfriend that made me seethe.

"Sometimes, I do things just to piss him off," Chris had said about Liam our first night on the sun porch.

Was I one of those things? Liam had pitched a fit when he found out we were dating. Was our whole relationship a lie to get a rise out of my stepbrother?

No. That couldn't be right. Chris would deserve an Oscar if the past month was all an act. The reason had to be something else. Like…me not sleeping with him. God, guys were so fricking shallow.

I hauled myself off the floor, needing the comfort of my bed. Halfway up the stairs, I heard an animal-like cry from the dining room and froze. The hallway above me was dark, and I considered making a run for the safety of my bedroom and calling the police. But then Hank's voice came from the room.

I crept along the wall and peeked into the doorway. My stepfather sat at the table with the room lit by two ivory tapers in brass holders, which was a mortal sin. Call it a quirk of Mom's, but there were dozens of candles throughout the house, and we weren't allowed to burn any of them.

His face looked drawn and a bit deranged in the flickering light. With a shaking hand, he poured whiskey into one of the crystal glasses reserved for special occasions. Before taking a long gulp, he mumbled something and shook his head.

My grief over Chris had quickly morphed into anger. I turned away, done with all men, especially those with the last name of Clark. They were losers, not worthy of my—or Mom's—love.

But he had seen me.

"Rose! My favorite daughter!" he slurred, wiping wildly at his nose with his sleeve. "Take a seat. Join me. I'm having a nightcap." The words shot out of his mouth like rapid fire.

I moved to the table but didn't sit, and he didn't notice.

"Are you OK?" I asked automatically, though I didn't care if he wasn't.

He ran his hands over his head and sighed. His eyes were bloodshot, and his pupils so big there was nothing left of the Clark's trademark blue irises. He momentarily focused on my face before his gaze skipped around the room, stopping at random objects.

"I don't know what to do. I've been sitting here thinking for hours"—he rubbed his temples—"but nothing. There's no solutions."

"Where's Mom?"

He tried to shrug, but it came off like an odd shimmy dance move. "Upstairs? She took a sleeping pill."

"And Liam?"

"Liam," he croaked. "My boy. My boy's going to prison."

Hank suddenly stood and leaned in my direction. His face was even scarier up close. "Rose, you're smart. What can I do?"

"About Liam? I don't know. What would William Sr. do?"

He thrust a finger at me. "Of course. I'm thinking like myself when I should be channeling Dad. He always knew what to do." Tears shimmered in his eyes. "But I'm not as crafty as he was."

He plopped down into his chair, chugged the rest of his drink, and wiped his mouth with the back of his hand. He hadn't shaved, and the skin rubbing across his stubble sounded like sandpaper.

"He'd call in favors to keep Liam out of prison," I offered in a flat voice. "Don't you think?"

It wasn't rocket science how William Sr. operated.

Hank nodded but then shook his head. "I don't have powerful friends like he did."

I realized Hank was presenting me with another opportunity to show everyone his true nature. For Mom's sake, I had to run with it.

"You have something better." When he looked baffled, I spelled it out for him. "You have a relationship with the star witness."

"Sawyer?" He stuck his jaw out and moved it from side to side, making him look even more unstable. Under the table, one of his legs bounced, hitting the underside with random thumps.

"Yes. Go to Sawyer. I heard he went to the police because Liam got the football scholarship. Promise Sawyer whatever he wants if he'll take back his statement."

His face scrunched up. "But would the police let him do that?"

"He can say he was mad at Liam and lied to hurt him. Kids do stupid things all of the time. They'll believe him."

"Maybe." He stared at the bottom of his glass, grinding his teeth before looking at me again. "It might work."

"You've been like a father to him, Hank. He owes you."

His face lit up, and he was finally on board. "You're right. I've always taken care of him. It's the least he can do."

He jumped up and patted his pockets. The second time around, he felt what he was searching for and smiled with relief.

"Go to bed, Rose. I got this."

{ 73 }

HANK

Saturday, November 11

I waited until Rose's bedroom door shut before I divided almost all of my remaining coke into two lines and quickly snorted them. The only immediate flaw I found in her suggestion to talk to Sawyer was the timing. It was Saturday night. There was a good chance he would be out with his friends.

I paced the dining room, planning what I would say. Love and loyalty had to be emphasized. Sawyer's home life left much to be desired, which was why Nora and I always welcomed him with open arms. I would remind him of everything we had done for him—and could do for him in the future. He'd be grateful, perhaps repentant, and then he would do what I asked, and Liam would be saved.

What if he refused? No. He would see it was the right thing to do and agree to it. But what if he didn't?

I stopped in front of the china cabinet. Inside the bottom drawer was a possible incentive. No, I wouldn't need it. It would be beyond crazy to resort to such means, so I walked away.

But then I came back. My fingers felt along the top of the hutch until they found a slim piece of metal. I squeezed the key, leaving a deep impression across my palm. It might be good to have it, just in case.

***

While I drank and snorted in my dining room, Mother Nature had unleashed a rare and vicious November thunderstorm. My car's wipers swished furiously to clear the windshield as the rain fell in torrents around me. Through cracks of lightning brightening the night sky, I caught glimpses of water and debris coursing through the drainage ditches lining the road. Flooding would be imminent, and I imagined my father working the phones, getting all the resources into place. He lived for these moments where he could save the village from destruction.

Fighting the elements, I drove to Sawyer's like I was ninety. As I crept along the village's main street, my heart raced, and sweat coated my upper body, leaving my flannel shirt damp and stuck to my skin. I eyed the liquor bottle in the passenger seat and debated which would give me more fortitude for my mission—my last line of coke or a swig of whiskey.

By the time I reached the farmhouse and parked in the driveway, I had decided to do both. As I held the bag of powder above the armrest at my side and began to shake it, lightning and thunder exploded across the heavens. My hand jerked, scattering my "courage" across my lap, the front seats, and every unreachable car crevice. Dumbfounded, I froze, and then I became a vacuum, inhaling and licking up all the specks I could find. High-strung laughter at my blunder bubbled out of me. When it stopped, I brought the liquor bottle to my lips and took a long drink and then another for good measure.

I flipped down the vanity mirror, and a man on the edge of madness with wild eyes stared back. My son's future and the Clark family legacy depended on whether a lunatic could convince a seventeen-year-old boy to lie.

It wasn't right. I needed to go home and think of another way to keep Liam out of prison. But then the coke flooded my system like the rainwater in the drainage ditches. Feeling invincible, I slammed the visor into place and reached for the glove box.

***

The storm soaked my clothes as I ran from the car to the house, but at least my sweat stains were no longer visible. I stood dripping under the porch light and rang the doorbell, my body moving to an uncontrollable, jittery beat. A second before the door opened, I quickly finger-combed my hair and inhaled deeply. The same breath whooshed out of me when I saw Sawyer.

"Dr. Clark?" His expression turned from puzzled to worried. "Why are you out in this storm? Is something wrong?"

I wiped the water from my face with my wet sleeve. "Are your parents home?"

"No, they're gone for the weekend, but they'll be back tomorrow afternoon if you need them."

I nodded. "No, I'm here to see you. I thought we could talk—man-to-man."

He closed the door so only his body filled the opening, and his eyes narrowed. "Are you OK? You sound…funny."

I balled my fists to rein in the hysteria crawling up my throat. Now was not the time to lose it. I needed to be calm, confident, and, above all, caring. Sawyer's teachers didn't give him much credit in the smarts department, but I knew better. You had to be cunning to survive in a family like his. If I weren't convincing, he'd see right through me.

"I've had a few drinks," I admitted, seeing no reason to be dishonest. "Can I come in? I'd really like to talk to you. And maybe dry off?"

He glanced over his shoulder. "I'm kind of busy. Isabel is over."

I edged forward. "It'll only take a minute. Please."

All of Sawyer's years playing sports had trained him to obey a coach. Though his body sagged with reluctance, he stepped back, pulling the door wide. "We can go into the kitchen."

He leaned against the counter by the sink, which held a mound of dirty dishes, while I moved about the room. A potpourri of smells permeated the air, the most dominant being stale alcohol, cigarette smoke, and spoiled garbage. My heart cracked for the boy who grew up in the house, and I almost abandoned my mission, but my family came first.

"What do you want to talk about, Dr. Clark," he finally prompted me. His gaze went to the doorway and the room beyond where I assumed Isabel waited.

I tapped the kitchen table with one finger as words whirled in my head, but none of them stopped to form the coherent and convincing sentence, let alone the paragraph, that I needed. Stalling, I grabbed a handful of paper napkins and blotted my neck. Across the room, Sawyer shifted impatiently.

"I've known you since you were five years old," I began. "Your first T-ball game? You and Liam were determined to be the best players, your little legs chugging around the bases. It was adorable. The coaches made sure every kid scored once, so the game ended in a tie. You guys were so mad you didn't win."

He crossed his arms. "That was a long time ago."

I nodded. "You've grown into an upstanding young man. Hell, I'm proud to say we contributed to your development with the sleepovers, sports tournaments, and family dinners we shared. And what about all those Sunday night homework sessions? I always found the time to help you. You've been a second son to me and a brother to Liam."

A dissenting noise came from deep in his throat.

"No, it's true," I said, aware of the desperation in my voice. "We loved having you at our home. You were always welcome."

His mouth opened as if he would object again, but instead, he set his jaw and remained silent.

I wasn't reaching him.

"Why do you want Liam to go to jail?" I exclaimed. "He's your best friend."

"He used to be my best friend," he corrected. "We haven't been friends since his birthday. I don't give a rat's ass what happens to him."

"But why?" I spread my arms wide. "Why now?"

"You wouldn't understand."

"Try me. Please, Sawyer. Tell me how we can make this right."

"But that's the whole problem," he said with disgust. "You're a Clark, so you assume your name can either fix things or make them disappear. No matter how much a member of the royal Clark family screws up—and apparently, that includes killing an old man—they don't get into trouble. I'm so sick of it."

I sank into a kitchen chair, and the gun in the back of my pants pressed against my spine, reminding me of my last resort.

"What if Liam doesn't attend college, and the scholarship passes to you?" I asked. "Would you retract the statement you made to the police? You could tell them you were mad at Liam and lied."

His head snapped back with surprise. "Why would I do that? An upstanding young man wouldn't lie. Anyway, I have the scholarship now."

"Only if Liam goes to jail, which isn't a given." I pointed a finger at him. "You just said we Clarks can get away with murder."

"Huh." His eyebrows pinched together, and his head dropped to the side. "But you must be worried, or you wouldn't have come here."

"I…I'm trying to make a bad situation better—because I love both of you."

"Yeah, right." He leaned over the sink and spat before returning his hostile eyes to me.

"Sawyer, I do." My distraught voice brought Isabel from the living room.

"Is everything OK?" she asked from the doorway, biting her lip, hesitant to enter the tension-filled room.

Sawyer nodded. "Dr. Clark was just leaving."

I stood too quickly, and black spots dimmed my vision. I grabbed the table's edge and blinked them away.

"I can't leave until you agree to help Liam." Tears spilled down my cheeks. "Please understand. He's my boy. I have to save him."

"No," he replied defiantly. "I won't lie to the police."

"Then, I'm sorry to do this," I sobbed. "I really did love you, Sawyer."

I reached behind my back, and my fingers wrapped around the hard metal of the gun. I pulled it out and pointed it with a trembling hand.

A high-pitched scream followed by a thundering boom filled the room, and then blackness.

{ 74 }

LIAM

Sunday, November 12

My phone pinged for the thousandth time since last night. It didn't take long for everyone to find out what Dad did, and they were all up for some trash-talking. Everyone, that was, except Madison.

```
Have you talked to
your dad?

                     No

Where is he?

                     They kept him
                     overnight at
                     Lakeland Hospital.
```

Where are you?

At the hospital

To see your dad?

Yes. No. I don't know. I want to see Sawyer.

My phone went dark, and it seemed she wouldn't respond. Did that mean she thought it was a good idea or a bad idea? When it pinged again, I figured it was another moron gloating over my multiple humiliations, but I was wrong.

OK. Text me later if you want to talk. I could make dinner or get takeout.

I sent Madison a thumbs-up and then took a deep breath.

{ 75 }

HANK

Sunday, November 12

Fear of where I might be kept me from opening my eyes when I woke. The sheet covering my body felt thin and scratchy as it brushed my skin, so I knew I hadn't made it home to my bed. Nora was a linen snob, always insisting on the highest thread count we could afford.

I tried to raise my hand to block the bright light seeping around the edges of my eyelids, but something hard dug into my wrist, and metal clanged against metal. I groaned, realizing that wherever I was, the handcuff at my wrist wouldn't allow me to leave.

Muffled voices and steady beeps gave me my final clues, and the memory of a police officer next to me in an ambulance floated to the top of my floundering brain. Resigned, I sighed and blinked at my new reality.

Liam stood at the foot of the hospital bed, every ounce of his body simmering with fury.

"How could you?" he asked through gritted teeth. "Why would you try to kill Sawyer?"

I squeezed my eyes shut, caught off guard by the one person I would do anything to save—including murdering a child I had helped raise.

"What the hell were you thinking?" He gripped the foot railing and shook the bed, sending bursts of pain through my head. "Talk to me," he shouted. "Tell me something that will make sense of last night."

I swallowed what moisture I could find in my mouth, but it did nothing to soothe my raw throat, leaving me mute.

He spun away and paced the room. "Maybe we can share a prison cell. At the very least, we should get a discount on legal fees."

With my free hand, I reached for the water glass on the tray beside me and drank greedily. "Liam," I breathed.

"No." He pointed a finger at me. "Only talk if you can justify what you did."

"I love you."

His incredulous stare hurt my heart.

"That's not a good enough reason," he said. "What about hooking up with Madison? Did you do that because you love

Nora? And the drugs? The *coke*? Did you do that because you love *yourself*?"

I winced at his recap of my sins. "You know about the drugs?"

"Madison told me *everything*," he said, the last word dripping with venom.

"I can explain." However, it was evident that any defense I could offer would fall short.

He yanked the plastic chair meant for visiting loved ones away from the bedside and flopped into it. "I dare you to try."

I focused on the pebbled white ceiling as stray tears ran down my cheeks and pooled around my neck. "I wanted to feel good for once."

When that admission elicited zero reaction from my son, I tried again. "You must understand what I mean. The pressure Grandpa put on us? The protecting of the Clark legacy above all else? The need to be perfect?"

He shifted in his chair but didn't meet my eye.

"Nothing I did ever made him happy, and I needed the escape coke gave me, even if it only lasted a short time."

He rested a foot on the opposite knee, and his fingers tangled with his shoelace. "What about me and the boat accident." His eyes flicked to my face. "Did that also make you do these dumbass things?"

"The thought of you in prison ripped me from the inside out. I was losing my mind with worry and didn't know how to save you."

"Christ," he huffed. "I'm responsible for two murders and an attempted murder."

"Liam, please." I leaned toward him, willing him to believe me. "Don't blame yourself for your grandpa's death or what I tried to do to Sawyer. None of that is on you. I didn't have to do what I did. I am the only one at fault for my actions these past three months."

"The police won't tell me what happened at Sawyer's. Did you shoot him on purpose? Like it wasn't an accident?"

I rubbed my eyes with the heel of my palm, wishing I could erase the few memories I had of last night. "It's all a blur. I was high and drunk and desperate." I touched the back of my head, where it curved to meet my neck. "I think Isabel hit me with something. One minute, I was pleading with Sawyer to recant his new statement to the police, and then I was pointing the gun, and then a burst of pain came out of nowhere. I must have blacked out because the next thing I remember was the ambulance ride."

"That's why you went there? To ask him to change back his story?"

I flapped my hand, and the handcuff rattled against the bedrail again. "It was Rose's idea."

"Huh." He puzzled over that for a few silent moments. "So, maybe the gun went off accidentally when you fell?"

"I don't know. I'd like to think I didn't purposely pull the trigger, but I honestly don't know."

He made a disgusted noise deep in his throat.

"How's Nora?" I asked, painfully aware that my wife wasn't by my side.

"She's a wreck, but Rose is taking care of her."

"That's good," I sighed. "She's a smart kid."

"What happens now?" Liam asked quietly.

"I don't know. The police will transfer me to the county jail, I suppose. After that...I guess we'll have to wait and see. I vaguely remember asking for a lawyer."

"Our lives are going to be a shitstorm. You realize that, don't you?" he said harshly, his rage flaring. "My lawyer was meeting with the DA this week to talk about reducing the charges. What if that doesn't happen now?"

"Don't worry. I will admit to anything and everything if it keeps you out of prison." My strength was fading, but there was one more thing to discuss. "Liam, I need you to do something for me."

His face clouded. "What?"

"Tell Madison I will do my best to keep her name out of this. I won't tell the police about our affair or her selling me drugs. Nora doesn't deserve the humiliation, and anyway, I got last night's coke from some stranger. That's all anyone needs to know."

"I gotta go," he said without agreeing to deliver my message.

He shot to his feet and stuffed his hands in his coat pockets, but his departure was halted by the sudden appearance of the police chief. My time was up.

"Liam," David said solemnly with a nod.

"Chief Wick." He glanced at me. "Are you taking Dad away now?"

The chief cleared his throat with a cough. "Yes, the attending doctor has signed off on his release."

"Good." His shoulders bowed toward his chest, and he sidestepped around David.

I never heard a single word spoken with such hatred, and it shattered my already aching heart. But I only had myself to blame.

"I love you, son," I said, hoping to dissolve some of his fury.

His head snapped around, his eyes slit with anger. He looked as if he wanted to reply but pressed his lips together instead. And then he was out the door, and I was left alone to face my punishment.

{ 76 }

LIAM

Sunday, November 12

I felt like my insides had been pulverized after I left Dad, but I needed to see my ex-best friend.

Outside his hospital room, I hesitated at the closed door. What do you say to the guy your dad tried to kill? Maybe he'd kick me out as soon as I walked in. He had every right. I mean, I would if things were reversed.

What a fricking mess. What was Dad even thinking? I guess he wasn't, and that was the problem. Madison thought he was an addict, and he admitted to being high and drunk. The police were surprised his heart was beating when they got to Sawyer's house.

I rested my hand on the door and willed myself to push it open, but I couldn't move a muscle.

Jesus, Liam. You're such a wuss. Suck it up.

I took a deep breath and walked into the room without knocking. Isabel sat in a chair at Sawyer's bedside. Their eyes widened when they saw it was me. She jumped up and put a protective hand on his arm as if I might try to finish Dad's botched job.

Tubes ran from his chest, nose, and arms, and his shoulder was bandaged. I focused my gaze there, unable to meet his eyes.

I cleared my throat. "Looks like your basketball season is over."

He grunted. "Guess you'll get to start."

"I already was."

"Not the way you were playing in practice. Rumor has it that Coach was going to sit your ass."

"Bullshit. You don't bench your best player."

"In your dreams."

I let the silence hang between us for several moments before finally shifting my gaze to his face. I expected some degree of hatred or resentment, but there was only weariness.

"I'm sorry, dude." I pinched the bridge of my nose and hung my head. "I should have realized how you felt all these years."

"Yeah, well, you Clarks aren't the brightest."

I laughed a bit at that, mainly because it was true. "Are your parents here?"

"They're taking a smoke break. Guess I've inconvenienced them," he said gruffly.

He shifted in bed, and when he winced from the movement, Isabel was all over him. "Can I do anything? Should I call the nurse?"

He shook his head and smiled at her. "I'm OK."

But she wasn't. She shot me a glare over her shoulder that could have burned a hole through my chest, which I deserved.

"I'd better go." More needed to be said, but I couldn't face Sawyer's parents yet.

I was almost out the door when Sawyer called out. I stopped but didn't turn around.

"You aren't your dad, Liam," he said. "And you aren't your grandpa either."

I squeezed my eyes shut to hold in the tears. "And you aren't your parents."

"Thank God."

"See you later?" I asked. When we were best friends, it wouldn't have been a question.

"Not if I see you first."

The words cut me, but then he laughed. It was a start.

{ 77 }

ROSE

Sunday, November 12

I found Mom wrapped in a heavy blanket on the sun porch, staring into an unlit fireplace. Her eyes were red and puffy, and snot ran from her nose. As I took a wine bottle from her hand, a deep sob shook her body, and a pile of photos fell from her lap and onto the floor.

I picked a handful up and gasped when I saw what they documented. I had known from the beginning Hank wasn't worthy of Mom's love, and his actions last night at Sawyer's proved it. But now Mom had hard evidence that even her gullibility couldn't ignore. I flipped through a few more, my contempt growing, before gathering them all up and tossing them on the nearby end table.

"Did you eat anything?" I asked. "Can I heat up some leftovers for you?"

Her empty eyes told me she had checked out from reality—probably with help from a pharmaceutical—and wouldn't answer. She tipped over on the couch with a shuddering sigh and curled up like a child.

"Let's get you in bed." She didn't protest, so I helped her upstairs, undressed her, and tucked her in. "We'll figure everything out in the morning. OK?"

She gave a final heartwrenching moan before passing out.

***

"Hi." Zoe stood under the porch light, holding a plastic grocery bag. "I thought you might need some girl time." She raised the bag and jiggled it. "I brought ice cream."

I blinked back tears, floored by the universal gesture of friendship. "Are you sure you want to be associated with my family?"

"Stepfamily," she shot back with a gentle smile.

"Ice cream would be great." I moved to the side to let her in.

"Are you alone?" she asked, kicking off her shoes.

I took her coat and hung it on a peg by the door. "My mom's asleep. And, well, Hank's at the hospital or the police station. I don't know which."

"And Liam?"

"I haven't seen him since he left for the hospital this afternoon to see Sawyer. Is there a greeting card that says, 'Sorry my dad shot you. Get well soon.'?" When Zoe didn't laugh, I quickly apologized. "My coping mechanism is to say stupid things."

She nodded sympathetically. "How are you doing?"

"I'm worried about my mom. She's a total wreck." The tears were back, and I wiped at them furiously.

She gave me a crushing bear hug that made everything worse as I remembered my initial feelings toward her.

"Let me know what I can do to help," she said, releasing me.

"Well, ice cream is definitely a good start," I replied with a watery chuckle.

"Then let's do some damage before it melts."

{ 78 }

ROSE

Friday, November 17

Entry from the Journal of Rose McCabe:

William Sr. was dead.

Hank was in jail, awaiting numerous court dates.

And Liam agreed to plead no contest to a misdemeanor. The DA will ask for probation and community service. If Liam doesn't screw up again, his record will be cleared in two years.

Mom, Liam, and I had a family meeting after dinner. Thanks to a hefty inheritance from William Sr., we don't have to make any immediate major life decisions. I guess he was good for something in the end.

Liam said he wants to finish the school year in Williams Bay. He surprised us with the news that he applied to several art schools, some near, some far away. Who knew my stepbrother was more than a jock?

Mom asked if I wanted to continue living here. I don't have an answer yet. Starting over at a new school terrifies me, and I think I would miss Zoe and Isabel. Mom said the gossip would eventually die down if I wanted to stay. I'm not sure if I believe her.

I'm still having trouble sleeping at night. I wonder if I should also be punished for my part in the events that tarnished the Clark family's golden reputation. When I realized Mom wouldn't do anything about Hank's cheating ways, I only wanted to show her and everyone else in the village what a loser he was. And it wasn't hard to do, being the nerdy invisible child who sees more than she should.

No one but Ms. Taylor suspected I was up to no good. I wouldn't go so far as to thank her for helping me on my quest, but her drug dealing was an unexpected bonus. Hank's behavior became increasingly erratic as his affair with her went on. I eventually figured out Hank was getting more than sex from the woman. Add on his blatant lie about needing money for a memorial for William Sr., and you have the signs of an addiction.

I didn't plan on Liam discovering his father with Ms. Taylor. But when I saw Hank go into her room, I guessed he was on the prowl. It was dumb luck that Liam came along looking for Hank. I knew Liam would be jealous because Ms. Taylor had her claws in him, too, so I was more than happy to point him in the right direction.

I had to wonder, on the spectrum of degrees of murder (or attempted murder), did I fall closer to Liam or Hank? If I had called an ambulance for William Sr., maybe he would still be alive, but the world was better off without that bully. My initial inaction wasn't premeditated. It was more that I seized an opportunity, unlike Hank.

I admit I had a part in setting his crime in motion, but Hank had to find a key, unlock a gun box, and drive to Sawyer's house. He had plenty of time to rethink his decision, and I never suggested he kill *Sawyer. That was all him. At the most, I hoped the police would pull him over for drunk driving, thus adding another embarrassing incident to the list of Hank's moral lapses.*

And Liam? He was young and stupid. The paddleboarder's death was a tragic result of my stepbrother wanting to have fun but not being responsible. Hank and William Sr. are partially to blame since they raised him.

To be clear, though, I didn't mean for Sawyer to get hurt despite my dislike for him. I only wanted to expose Hank and save Mom. But you couldn't wage a war without collateral damage. My real dad's death taught me that.

The End

Additional Books by Elizabeth McKenna

The Great Jewel Robbery – A Front Page Mystery – Book 1

(Cozy Mystery)

Chicago Tribune reporters Emma and Grace have been best friends since college despite coming from different worlds. When Grace is assigned to cover an annual charity ball and auction being held at a lakeside mansion and her boyfriend bails on her, she brings Emma as her plus one. The night is going smoothly until Emma finds the host's brother unconscious in the study. Though at first it is thought he was tipsy and stumbled, it soon becomes clear more is afoot, as the wall safe is empty and a three-million-dollar diamond necklace is missing. With visions of becoming ace investigative journalists, Emma and Grace set out to solve the mystery, much to the chagrin of the handsome local detective.

Murder up to Bat – A Front Page Mystery – Book 2

(Cozy Mystery)

After falling in love with the quiet lake life and a certain police detective, former Chicago Tribune reporter Emma Moore trades interviewing jocks for chasing champion cows at the county fair. As a small-town newspaper reporter, she covers local topics both big and small, but when her friend Luke is arrested for the murder of the head coach of his club softball team, she'll need to hone her investigative skills to clear his name. Emma calls up best friend Grace for help, and together the women go up against cutthroat parents willing to kill for a chance to get their daughters onto a premier college sports team.

The game is tied with bases loaded, and murder is up to bat. Can Emma and her friends bring the heat and win the game?

Killer Resolutions

(Mystery)

Friends gather for a festive New Year's Eve weekend in a remote lodge in northern Wisconsin. When a blizzard traps them with a murderer, who will be left to kiss at midnight?

Five years ago, a tragedy shattered the friendship between Dani, her older brother, and their college pals. When her brother invites the old gang for a weekend of outdoor winter fun at a remote lodge, she sees it as a chance to reconnect and heal. But when her friends are murdered one by one, Dani must determine whom she can trust before she becomes the next victim.

First Crush, Last Love

(Contemporary Romance)

In high school, Lee Archer was Jessie Baxter's first and only crush, but the popular athlete never wanted to be more than just friends. Ten years later, after a failed marriage and with her journalism career on shaky ground, Jessie's come home for her high school reunion—and Lee still has the power to make her knees weak and her pulse pound.

Lee's teenage years were filled with more trauma and drama than anyone guessed. Though his damaged past has made him a successful police detective, it's hurt every relationship he's tried. But seeing Jessie again might just change his commitment-phobic mind.

Jessie's psycho ex-husband had her convinced no one would ever love her, but Lee is ready to step out of the friend zone and into her heart. Can she learn to trust again before she loses her chance to turn her first crush into her last love?

Elizabeth McKenna's novel will have you remembering the angst of high school, the grief of a failed relationship, and the joy of finding true love at last.

Venice in the Moonlight

(Historical Romance)

Considered useless by his cold-hearted father, Nico Foscari, eldest son of one of the founding families in Venice, hides his pain behind gambling, drinking, and womanizing.

After her husband's untimely demise, Marietta Gatti returns to her hometown of Venice in hopes of starting a new life and finding the happiness that was missing in her forced marriage.

When Fate throws them together, friendship begins to grow into love until Marietta learns a Foscari family secret that may have cost her father his life. Now, she must choose between vengeance, forgiveness, and love.

Elizabeth McKenna's novel takes you back to eighteenth-century Carnival, where lovers meet discreetly, and masks make everyone equal.